Naados and His Kin: The Beginning is the most creative story I've ever read. Even though I knew the story line and what would happen next, I still couldn't put the manuscript down. Now that's a good book! In keeping with the finest literary traditions of *Watership Down, Bambi, and The Lion King,* a hero emerges from the animal kingdom and touches the reader. The pages bristle with surprises, with conflict and terrifying consequences, with an amazing understanding of Bible facts. From Creation to a post-flood culture, *Naados and His Kin* tells the old, old story through new eyes and in new ways.

—Jack Williams
Director of Communications
Free Will Baptist Bible College
Nashville, Tennessee

NAADOS

AND HIS KIN

EDDIE PAYNE

Eddie Payne (signature)

NAADOS
AND HIS KIN

the beginning

TATE PUBLISHING & *Enterprises*

Published by Tate Publishing & Enterprises, LLC
127 E. Trade Center Terrace | Mustang, Oklahoma 73064 USA
1.888.361.9473 | www.tatepublishing.com

Tate Publishing is committed to excellence in the publishing industry. The company reflects the philosophy established by the founders, based on Psalm 68:11,
"The Lord gave the word and great was the company of those who published it."

Book design copyright © 2010 by Tate Publishing, LLC. All rights reserved.
Cover design by Leah LeFlore
Interior design by Nathan Harmony

Published in the United States of America

ISBN: 978-1-61663-157-4
1. Fiction: Christian: General
2. Fiction: Fairy Tales, Folk Tales, Legends & Mythology
10.04.15

DEDICATION

To my wife, Sandra; our daughters, Laura and Debbie; and our seven wonderful grandchildren, Whitney, Cason, Cara, Stuart, Corbin, Lydia, and Isabella.

Acknowledgments

I extend my heartfelt thanks to my dear friend Jack Williams. In 2005 I asked him to examine the manuscript for *Naados and His Kin*. He kindly agreed, dropped ongoing projects, and responded to my cry for help. Jack took the half-finished work on a Friday afternoon. True to form, this tireless professional writer and editor called me the following Monday morning. "Got a minute?" he queried. "Sure. Your office or mine?" I asked. With, "I'll be there in two minutes," he finished the call.

Hurrying in, he thrust the sheaf of papers into my hand and waited. I quickly scanned the pages, stopped, looked up to him, and asked, "Where is the red?" I had asked him to be brutally honest in evaluating the manuscript. "No red," he said. "You know there should be," I retorted. Jack laughed and replied, "Not now. Write, and write quickly. Finish this manuscript. This story needs telling."

After nearly thirty years of uncertainty, Jack gave me the push forward that I wanted but was afraid to believe possible. "On one condition," I said. "Will you edit as I write?"

His yes provoked me to take long-overdue comp time from my ministry position. I wrote Friday and Saturday. Jack took the work on Monday and edited before Tuesday morning. Jack, you are a true friend and encourager.

Thanks also to the great numbers of friends who knew of the project. Over a period of nearly thirty years, they nudged me forward, leading up to that day in 2005.

My deep gratitude and thanks to my family, especially Sandra, Laura, and Debbie, who continued to believe in me even when my progress was painfully slow. I'm especially thankful for the occasional, "How's it going with the book?" from my parents. At ages ninety-six and ninety, they are young in spirit and hope to see the project completed.

I offer a special thank you to Tate Publishing. You gave my work serious consideration and kindly accepted it for publication. All my contacts with the wonderful professionals at Tate have been positive and encouraging. I look forward to a long, mutually beneficial working relationship with Tate.

And to you my dear Lord Jesus, nothing is possible apart from you. For the last fifty-eight years, you have been my dearest friend, teacher, guide, and redeemer. May you be glorified as lost sheep find you and your followers snuggle closer to ponder your grace, love, and mercy. It is my desire that *The Beginning ~ Naados and His Kin* help many know and love you more completely.

Table of Contents

FOREWORD

By Jack Williams

Every once in a while, a manuscript crosses my desk that lights up the night sky. That's what happened in the spring of 2005 when my longtime friend, Eddie Payne, asked me to read and comment on a biblical historical novel he had written titled *Naados and His Kin*. Before I finished chapter one, I *knew* that it needed to be in print. The gripping, almost overwhelming story drew me into its swirling pages and refused to let me go. Even though I knew the storyline and what would happen next, I still couldn't put the manuscript down. Now that's a good book!

Moses squeezed the first two thousand years of human history into 299 verses (Genesis 1–11), painting with broad strokes the sweeping accounts of creation, the fall, and the flood, which means he left many intriguing questions unanswered. And that's where Eddie Payne steps in with unforgettable characters and crisp dialogue, weaving a cyclopedic understanding of biblical details into a well-known plot that roars to a stunning conclusion and sets the stage for future volumes.

In keeping with the finest literary traditions of *Watership Down*, *Bambi*, and *The Lion King*, a hero emerges from the animal kingdom and touches the reader. The pages bristle with surprises, with conflict and terrifying consequences, with an amazing understanding of biblical facts. From creation to a post-flood culture, *Naados and His Kin* tells the old, old story through new eyes and in new ways.

It's fiction, fantasy, and facts blended like you've never seen it done before. It's a children's book written for adults, a theology lesson explained in the language of a Walmart greeter, a philosophy and history course taught by a journalist who pulls back the curtain of time and invites the reader to stroll through the garden of Eden. *The Beginning: Naados and His Kin* is the most creative story I've ever read. I can't wait for the next book in this series.

—Jack Williams
Director of Communications
Free Will Baptist Bible College
Nashville, Tennessee
June 2009

Glossary

Ancient language of creation: The capacity of all creatures to communicate with one another and with Likeness's kin.

Beaufang: Generic term for serpents; used to identify first serpent's role in the bending of Likeness and Image; name of the first serpent.

Becoming: Created, coming into existence.

Behemoth: Generic name for dinosaurs.

Bent: Term to describe the moral inclinations of the offspring of Likeness and Image.

Bending: The act of disobedience by Likeness and Image in their turning away from Giver; the continued act of disobedience by Likeness-Image kin.

Central Grove: Center of towns and cities of Likeness-Image kin who follow Giver; town square.

Cleansing: The taking away of all air breathing life in a worldwide flood.

Covering: Skin of animals; also used as covering or clothing for Likeness's kin.

Escape vessel: See vessel.

Deliverance vessel: See vessel.

Fire flyer: Rocket, rockets.

Fire sticks: Gun, guns.

Giver: The creator; God.

Guardian, guardians: Heavenly beings charged with keeping humanity out of Home Valley after the bending.

Home Valley: Paradise, Eden, the first home for humans.

Image: First female human; mother of mankind; mata, mate of Likeness.

Knowing tree: A tree in Mystery Grove capable of giving the knowledge of both good and evil.

Life tree: A tree in Mystery Grove capable of giving endless life.

Light orb: A device giving artificial light.

Light sticks: Handheld device to produce artificial light.

Likeness: First human created; also used to speak of the offspring of the first human, as in Likeness's kin; mata, mate of Image.

Likeness's up-down compartment: Elevator in the deliverance vessel.

Lhaloo: First mata of Naados.

Lohaa: Second mata of Naados.

Lubah: Third mata of Naados.

Mata: Mate; used to designate life partners of both Likeness's kin and Noumaso.

Mystery Grove: The place in home valley where the creation of Likeness and Image occurred; the location of the knowing tree and the life tree.

Naados: Generic term for a species of Nouma; animal; a specific, individual Nouma who eats from the life tree and as a result has endless life.

Night sky orb: The moon.

Nouma: Generic term for a species of animal or for an individual animal; used primarily singular but sometimes plural.

Noumaso: Generic term for all of animal life except Likeness's kin; sometimes used interchangeably with Nouma.

River house: Term designating boats or small ships used on rivers.

Sky orb: The sun.

Spirit of Beaufang; Satan, the enemy of all Giver's creation.

Sting, the sting: Cessation of physical life; death.

Vessel: Term used to designate the large ship by which life was preserved on earth during the cleansing; also called the escape and deliverance vessel.

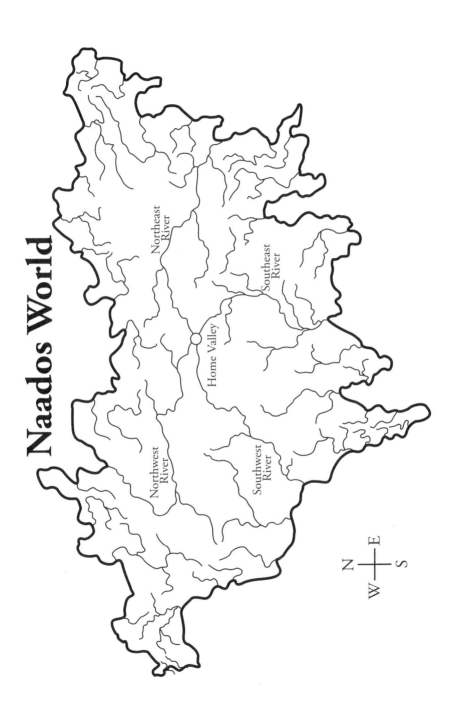

Naados World

Northeast River

Southeast River

Home Valley

Northwest River

Southwest River

N
W — E
S

Northeast
River

Southeast
River

Guardian Outpost
○

Mystery
Grove

Four
River
Lake

Northwest
River

Southwest
River

N
W ——┼—— E
S

Naados World

Home Valley

PROLOGUE

I am Naados. My life has spanned 2,017 of what
Likeness calls years. The usual ebb and flow of days
and seasons has ended as some of us begin a frightening journey into the unknown. Goodbye is never easy.
The pain of this parting has overwhelming implications. We are going away from the only home we have
ever known. The future is distressing and uncertain.

Why I, Naados, was chosen will become evident in
the telling of my story. I am one of seven of my Nouma
chosen to board the vessel. I weep. Life is a beautiful
experience, even with the sting. Most of our kind is

unaware of the chaos to come. I grieve for my young Nouma friends because there is no hope for any of them.

Compelled by a deep and profound sadness but bowing to Giver's instructions, I leave you my story, the story of my Nouma. I remember the joy of the unveiling. I remember the unutterable sorrow of the first sting. So now I leave this memory for those who may follow.

PART ONE

EXPLORING THE
NEW WORLD

WHEN NAADOS AWOKE

How can I describe the delicious, scintillating light that greeted my eyes when I awoke that first morning? My sense of well-being was so acute that it was almost physically painful. I was the first of my Nouma to become. Many days would pass before I learned that others of my Nouma were being seeded over Giver's new world just as I and other Noumaso were *becoming* in this special valley. I would find them in my discovery journeys.

The azure blue of the sky soared protectively overhead. Light and shadow and blazing colors dazzled my consciousness. My newly made eyes opened wide with wondering. *He is, so I am*, resonated my being. The thought escaped as long, melodic laughter through my lips. Utter peace, contentment, and awareness flooded my sleek new body.

I saw her a short distance away. As if watching a reflection of myself, I sensed, I knew that she was my mata, fresh from the hand of Giver, as was I. Perfect serenity flooded my senses as I breathed the cool, sweet air of paradise and praised the great giver of life.

All across the tree-ringed valley, others were becoming. They were different from me, completely original, yet with the same divine beauty that I possessed. From one end of the vast valley to the other, voices lifted praise toward the shining sky. Light and beauty surrounded us, filling the atmosphere with love.

Giver moved among us as the essence of love. We responded to his presence with worshipful praise in the universal tongue of creation. The moment was forever, and forever was in the moment he spoke.

I saw incredible forms materializing in every direction—always, it seemed, in pairs. I felt a satisfying oneness with all other newly made life. Then, from within or without (I did not know), a gentle voice drew me, my mata, and the other creatures toward a small hill in the center of the valley. We all moved at a steady but leisurely pace toward the appointed place. Then the gathering was complete. Facing inward from every direction stood the family. Anticipation surged as we awaited the unknown reason for our gathering.

Giver revealed himself in the clear central space as a hush spread across the vast valley. Darting birds suddenly fell silent before his presence. Soft breezes whispered through the leaves of thousands of trees articulating the awe of the multitude.

Giver seemed to hover above the dusty covering of the valley floor, lifting, sifting, swirling, and forming until out of the indescribable light and glory another form appeared. Leaning forward, Giver blew into its face. Excitement tingled my entire being. Others were similarly affected as we moved, one after another, and bowed before Likeness, the one so newly become. Again, from the throats of the gathered Noumaso came the cry of adoring praise.

He is, he wills, we are. To Giver alone be glory and praise.

From above the melodic expressions of praise came a voice as vast as the expanding heavens, musical as the waters rushing through the valley's expanse, loud as reverberating thunders; Giver spoke to the assembled Noumaso.

As I am
He is become
He my image bears
Bow I down
To raise him up
He my glory shares
Formed of dust
Yet made to reign
Matchless beauty his domain
Lord of earth
All to subdue
Hail him sovereign over you.

Giver spoke again and directed his instructions to Likeness.

Tend this garden
It is yours
Freely take the bounty
Eat from all but knowing tree
This order I repeat
Lest come the sting and lay you low
Your glory to defeat

After Giver finished speaking, with no thought of why, I desired more than all else to submit to Likeness as I had to Giver. Nameless creatures bowed before their newfound sovereign, so recently formed from the dust. Majestic bearing crowned Likeness as he reflected Giver's glory.

An elemental urge compelled me to join the many moving forward toward our lord. As if to pledge fidelity forever, the Nouma passed, each stopping before his glowing countenance, dazzled by the splendor.

As I neared the hill, I realized the reason for the silent inner urging. Likeness placed his hand on the head of each creature passing by and spoke into each adoring face. As my turn came, I suddenly understood that I had known all along the meaning of this moment. I was called along with my mata. Likeness spoke.

Giver made you for his praise
Boundless joy to fill your days
Monarch of the forest glen
Naados called by Nouma kin

I had known my own name, but to hear it from Likeness's lips brought boundless joy. So I, Naados, learned from Likeness my family name and heard wonderful secret truths for my Nouma only, wisdom to be passed on to my offspring and to their offspring forever. I found out at a later time that Likeness kin would know me as a red deer stag.

Likeness, so recently become, gave to each creature, large and small, his absolute attention. Giver had charged him to name all living things. Perfect harmony and joy abounded as each heard the others' names and functions in the family of Noumaso.

I paused to munch a juicy mouthful of grass. Leisurely stretching my glossy body on the valley floor, I pondered the view before me. The valley extended farther than the eye could see. Roaring streams cascaded from rocky heights of neighboring hills and mountains. Rivers ploughed the valley plains. The air glistened with the misty, transparent quality of sparkling light diffused from above. The creatures who passed under Likeness's hand soon found places to satisfy their hunger and thirst. With intelligent interest, they waited and watched as the remainder of their brothers met with Likeness.

Strange, I thought. *None of the fellow beings scattered across the hillside about him seem to resemble Likeness.* Nearly half of the vast company had already received their names from Likeness.

Looking toward Lhaloo, my mata, I felt contentment beyond comprehension. I was not alone. I was a two-one creature, complete with my own likeness. I noticed the same sentiment expressed by a pair of elands conversing nearby.

Peace, contentment, and joy marked us all. How does one describe the feeling that Giver is, we are, and all is well?

Still, I wondered why Likeness was alone. A pair of spindly-limbed monkeys halted before Likeness. I thought, *he is upright as they are, but evidently not of their Nouma.* As Likeness spoke in their ears, they began a series of acrobatics only their kind can perform evident joy of being in their hearts.

When at last the final pair of creatures had passed by Likeness, a great hush fell over the valley. Likeness sat on a flat stone. Surveying the beautiful world over which he had recently been appointed sovereign, he seemed to ponder the vastness of his domain.

High on a mountain ledge, bighorn sheep stood sentinel. Nearby, other four-footed Noumaso silently regarded the new world unfolding below. Flocks of the feathered Noumaso darted above the valley in waves of blue and yellow and purple while eagles rode high thermals into the beautiful sky. Fish splashed in the brooks and rivers as the trumpeting of Djhubu the elephant signaled down the mountain side that all was well.

I gazed silently, as was becoming my habit. Then, just as before, from deep within, a thought surfaced to my consciousness. Giver must have placed it there, for I mused, *It is not good for Likeness to be alone. All Noumaso are two.*

Likeness sat deep in thought, head in hands. Only occasional brief sounds disturbed the silence. My breath caught in my throat as I saw the glowing form of Giver descending to the valley floor. Pausing before Likeness, Giver's voice broke like rippling thunder across our valley home.

Two by two came Noumaso
To live upon this land
Only Likeness dwells alone
From his Maker's hand

Then a stunning spectacle unfolded before the curious eyes of the thousands of Noumaso assembled in the valley. Giver gently touched Likeness on the head. He yawned, gazed around slowly, and then stretched himself full length on the flat stone. His deep breathing indicated sound, satisfying sleep.

Giver hovered over Likeness in protective, creative splendor. Swirling color like spiraling light galaxies surrounded the stone altar as Giver opened Likeness's side. From the small opening, he took one rib bone. I stared openmouthed as another form was becoming. Behind the dazzling veil of light, Giver shaped the new creature. Finishing the task, Giver blew upon the new being as he had upon Likeness. Closing the opening in Likeness's side, Giver gently raised him and spoke him awake.

With an even larger yawn than before, Likeness stretched himself. Turning, he saw not only Giver but another exquisite form beside him. Likeness appeared not to believe his eyes. He made as if to speak but was quieted by a nod from Giver. It was apparent that the new creature resembled Likeness but was not identical to him.

Likeness knew intuitively, as had we all, that this was his mata. His heart beat rapidly, and his face flushed as full realization seized him. He too was not to be alone. He too would share the joy of the Noumaso with his own kind.

Giver, standing silently by, let all those thoughts pass through the amazed awareness of Likeness. Then his voice once more rang across the valley.

Hear, Oh heavens
Earth give ear
Noumaso, both far and near
In your presence now stands she
Mother of humanity
Mother Likeness springs, today
From her mata's side
Out from her all life shall flow
In her care abide
Two are one, and in my plan
Ever shall remain
Go forth now in joyful praise
Possess your vast domain

As if in benediction on the Likeness couple, Giver covered them in his shining presence of light. From their thankful hearts, adoration bubbled up and overflowed their lips. Likeness and Image, his mata, hand in hand, surveyed their valley kingdom.

Giver's shining presence rose quickly skyward as the sun slipped behind the westward mountains. We were completing our incredibly eventful first day of being. Soft shadows reached out and enfolded me and all creation in velvet arms. Likeness, his mata, and all the Noumaso prepared to spend our first night in the valley.

Naados's Canticle of Praise

Faint glimmers of red and gold broke through the leafy canopy of my sleeping place. Leaves moved by the soft breezes turned the forest floor into an explosion of whirling light and color. I awoke as a beam of sunlight flickered on my eyelids and then sighed with contentment as I realized that it signaled another day in our new world.

The night had been filled with pleasant sounds as members of the family discovered their voices and functions. I rested but had awakened often to hear unfamiliar night sounds. None had been frightening. It was a learning experience as I strained to identify voices from the darkness.

Lhaloo lay close beside me, her steady breathing indicating peaceful rest. I walked several paces from my resting place as a blue songbird settled in a nearby tree and began a morning serenade to Giver and to whomever else might be listening. I enjoyed the melody my feathered friend produced. Then, from within, a canticle of praise came from my own thankful heart and overflowed through my lips. I moved away from where Lhaloo rested to offer up my morning thoughts to Giver.

Beauty flows from your good hand
Covering rivers, hill, and land
Joyful peace floods all creation
Raising hearts anticipation
You are present everywhere
On mountain peak and valley fair
Life and hope you give to all
In gratitude to you I call.
Giver, you alone deserve
Glorious praise without reserve
Unchanging, you alone remain
I honor you in your domain.
Make this new day a day of glory
As we live your perfect story
Born of dust, I bow to you
To your plan I will be true

With overflowing heart, I walked to the nearby brook and drank of the cool water. The entire valley stirred as members of the family offered their morning canticles to Giver. Songs from thousands of feathered creatures and voices of Noumaso of every kind formed a symphony of exaltation.

Instructions in Mystery Grove

Members of the family moved slowly around the valley, taking in the beauties of their home. Expressions of wonder and amazement arose. Lhaloo and I joined the excited throng going from place to place. The variety of growing things was astounding. Trees filled with luscious fruit were everywhere. Aromatic smells, coupled with the lush foliage, made one's senses explode with satisfaction.

We all quickly discovered which growing things satisfied our particular taste and enjoyment. Luscious grasses of every variety tantalized our inquisitive taste buds. I found a special herb that sent shivers down my entire body. I ate my fill and urged Lhaloo to share it with me.

Likeness observed the discoveries of his subjects in the valley. He and Image had begun their day as the first golden rays of the sky orb flashed a wake-up call to the mountain peaks. Contentment was evident in the graceful moves of his body and the expressions on his face as he studied the valley before him.

I saw a movement in the sky as Giver appeared over the valley. He descended to the alcove in the trees where the Likeness couple surveyed the pastoral scene before them. The meeting was exhilarating to watch. Giver wrapped the Likeness family in light. The entwined forms then moved in a joyous flowing dance as laughter erupted and resounded down the gentle slope to the valley floor. It was evident to me that Giver and the Likeness couple shared an intimate and deepening friendship. I watched and pondered the meaning of it all. I would soon come to consider this normal behavior between Giver and the Likeness family.

Giver moved around the valley with Likeness and Image. His deep and melodious voice instructed Likeness about his duties as reigning monarch. Giver gave special consideration and much time to two trees that grew in the middle of a small grove in the valley. He continued speaking, but much of what he said was a mystery to me.

This world is all made just for you
To govern and rule over
Care for the plants and all that grows

From fruit trees to green clover
Freely eat of fruit and seed
The plants are all your food now
With your subjects share these things
From lion cub to brown cow
There is one fruit you may not eat
Found midway in the garden
Alluring though it seems to be
Transgression has no pardon
A test is yours and know for sure
This is a weighty matter
The knowing of both good and bad
Your perfect world will shatter
Should you choose to disobey
And try forbidden treasure
This luscious fruit of such desire
Will steal your earthly pleasure
You do not yet know of the sting
Her time has not been born
Obey my voice and heed my word
A shroud need not be worn
Choose life instead of vain desire
Its pleasure is unending
Heed not the plea of Enemy
Nor to his will be bending

Likeness nodded in understanding and acceptance of the terms as Giver explained. The trio soon moved out and across the valley. Stopping from time to time, they talked about different aspects of Likeness's responsibilities as lord over this vast domain.

I was left with many more questions than answers. I

paused under a small tree to munch a mouthful of grass, and pondered what I had just heard. Lhaloo joined me, and we stood silently as I gazed at the two trees in the small grove.

As evening sounds welcomed the coming time of rest, my attention was drawn to the place where golden sky orb had appeared this morning. A brightly glowing object knifed across the evening sky. Millions of glittering pieces swirled and trailed in its wake. It was difficult to tell how distant the noiseless object was. It fell silently somewhere toward the farthest end of the valley. I had not seen anything like it and wondered if I could find the place it landed. I determined to make a special trip to see what had occurred.

Exploring
the Valley

Time passed quickly in the valley as day followed day in harmonious sequence. What had been strange and new was now familiar and comfortable. Life was full, exciting. New discoveries were made every day by members of the Noumaso. Deep, cool caverns scattered along the mountain slopes were explored. Varieties of plants were springing out of the rich earth. Foods were found that were even more delicious than those already enjoyed.

I began roaming far from the small central grove of

trees now called Mystery Grove by the Noumaso. I explored the distant reaches of the valley, crossing and recrossing the streams and rivers. Heights intrigued me because of the splendid views from the high places. I was curious about the four rivers that branched off from the huge water source in the valley. They moved in different directions from our home. I determined to explore each one and discover their destinations.

My sure and steady feet carried me easily to every part of this beautiful world. From time to time, I was too far from Mystery Grove to return with the darkness. On those nights, I slept lightly and listened to the sounds of whatever Nouma lived in the area. I searched for any sign of an impact by the fiery glow from the sky.

One day, I crossed some peaks and descended into the next valley. It was even larger than our home, and I made an astonishing discovery. At least a five-sleep cycle walk from Home Valley, I topped a small rise near a steep, tree-covered incline. There, in a large, semi-circular area, was evidence of an unusual occurrence. Every growing thing looked as if the sky orb had dried them dark brown and left them without life. I sniffed to inspect the area, and my nostrils were struck with a sharp, pungent odor that caused me to gasp for breath and become momentarily disoriented. In the next instant, a sensation caused the hair to stand on end all over my body. I turned and ran as quickly as possible to escape the distressing, dark sensations. I determined not to return to this new valley alone. I could not forget my shocking find.

My return to home valley was cautious. I stopped often and looked back on my trail with a strange sensation that I was not alone.

What's wrong
with Beaufang?

The females of the Noumaso were all swollen with life waiting to be born. Giver had said to fill up their world with offspring. The Noumaso were obedient, and Lhaloo was no exception. Her bulging flanks promised new members of our Nouma before many days. I could only stare in wonder at the transformation taking place. I had yet to understand the concept but was sure it was perfect since Giver had ordered it.

Likeness and his mata, Image, had not yet traveled great distances from the valley home. They were busy with oversight duties in the valley kingdom. Likeness cleared an area not far from Mystery Grove where he and Image passed their nights. Ringed by flowering trees and shrubs, the grasses growing there were softer than rabbit fur. Food gathering was easy since many varieties grew within a short walk.

Giver came every day and visited the Likeness couple. He walked and talked with Likeness and Image among the trees and fields. Giver provided them with new understanding and insight about their home and their duties as caretakers. Members of the Nouma family anywhere near listened in on the conversations. Most of what they discussed was easily understood, yet there were many mysteries for me. I often left bewildered by the depth of the talk between Giver and Likeness.

Image was happy in her home. She wanted to learn everything possible about her beautiful world. She especially enjoyed visiting with members of the Noumaso. I also noticed her, on several occasions, sitting silently near Mystery Grove, gazing intently at the two central trees. She often looked around as though someone were peering over her shoulder. When satisfied that no one was there, she moved away to other duties.

Life was complete harmony and peace in our valley. I often looked heavenward and poured out praise to Giver for his perfect creation. My greatest desire was to be obedient to him. No other thought occupied so much of my time.

Perhaps this nearness I felt to Giver made my next experience so strange and new. Until that time, all the family had lived in perfect harmony. We shared food and water sources. It was normal for us to pass the night in close proximity with Nouma different from ourselves. We were, after all, members of the same family. As such, we had mutual interests and needs. Animosity or hostility of any sort was unknown.

One day, I greeted Beaufang, a reptilian member of the family. As we passed, I had a strange tingling sensation as if a cool current of air had passed over my body and left me chilled. I noticed a vague, misty translucence wrapped around Beaufang as if another presence, in some way resembling Giver but shadowy and sinister, enveloped the serpent.

I felt compelled to follow as Beaufang hurried toward Mystery Grove. Beaufang was an extremely beautiful creature. He moved quickly in his upright position toward the grove where the Likeness family lived. He was certainly no stranger there. Although Beaufang was a great favorite of Image, all members of the Noumaso were welcome. It was rare to have no visitors while the golden sky orb shined. Until now, I had given no serious thought to the fact that all members of the family could communicate. I did not understand how, but I knew that I could understand Likeness and Image as well as all the other Noumaso.

Beaufang approached Image with the flattering speech he was noted for and was welcomed as usual. I cropped and munched a mouthful of grass while moving closer to listen in on their conversation. The concepts of *private* and *secret* were introduced to our world at a later time.

Beaufang asked, "Is it true that Giver told you not to eat fruit from this part of the garden?"

Image seemed shocked by the question. "Of course not," she answered. "He has only said we must not eat from the knowing tree in Mystery Grove. We are not even to touch it."

"Why not?" said Beaufang.

"I'm not sure I understand it all," said Image. "It involves something Giver called the sting, and it is very bad."

I stopped grazing and strained my ears to hear every word. "Why, that isn't true," whispered Beaufang.

I could not believe my ears. Beaufang had questioned the truthfulness of Giver.

Beaufang hissed. "Giver knows when you eat that fruit you will become just like him. You will understand everything. Would I, your friend, lie to you? Doesn't that fruit look good? I would say that it is probably the tastiest in the garden!"

Image looked confused. She had evidently never considered that kind of thought. She looked closely at the tree and admitted to Beaufang that the fruit appeared beautiful and desirable. She also admitted that the thought of being as wise as Giver was appealing.

"Go on," urged Beaufang. "What do you have to lose?"

My heart was pounding so hard that I thought it would burst. I tried to cry out but could hardly breathe and was unable to make a sound. Inside, I was screaming, *No! No! Don't disobey Giver*. I started to run forward to stop Image and then hesitated for an instant. In that lost second, Image reached for the fruit. I regained my composure and bounded from my listening place toward the center of the grove.

Beaufang heard me coming and quickly turned his

head to face me. With eyes opened wide, Beaufang sent a strong burst of hate that stopped me in my tracks. I staggered and then fell to the ground. That was all the time Image needed to pick the fruit and take a big bite.

Still struggling to regain my footing, I could not understand how Image could be doing this. Giver had not given me the ability of choice that he had given the Likeness couple. My instinctive response is to joyfully obey all I understood Giver to desire. This action by Image was beyond my comprehension. I shivered as if a great darkness had suddenly covered the sky orb.

As I struggled to my feet, I saw Likeness standing nearby. He had been listening from behind the trees. I again lunged in their direction but was too far away to prevent Image from holding the fruit to Likeness's mouth. He too took a bite, chewed, and swallowed the fruit. Beaufang was bent double, trembling all over. I realized he was shaking with laughter.

Innocence fell from Image like a pristine covering slipping from her beautiful shoulders. The radiant glory that had encircled her flickered and dimmed. I saw another side of Image for the first time. What I saw troubled me greatly. The Likeness couple lost the transparent glow surrounding them and took on the hue of the dust under their feet.

The air about them turned heavy and oppressive. Singing birds fell silent. Gentle breezes faded to stillness. Members of the family observing the drama stopped and stared in confusion. I backed, unsteadily, a few feet from the grove. Unsettling emotions stirred part of my consciousness I never knew existed.

Likeness and Image appeared confused and then very troubled. They stared at one another. Beaufang almost fell over in delight. The couple suddenly ran for the cover of some low bushes in the grove and then stopped and looked around. Something I would later come to recognize as shame marred their still-beautiful faces and eyes. Each grabbed large leaves and attempted to cover their bodies. I had no comprehension of why they were acting so strangely.

Beaufang moved away from the trees and passed within a few feet of me. A twisted smirk replaced his normally pleasant countenance. He stared at me and laughed. A new smell reached my nostrils, triggering a memory as Beaufang passed. Later, after the first sting, I understood that it was the distressing odor from the far valley where the fire from the heavens destroyed trees and herbs. It was mingled with the nauseating smell of hate.

I turned and ran to find Lhaloo. My beautiful, peaceful world had been turned upside down. Shaken to the depths of my being, I felt hot droplets of water coursing down my long cheeks. I was to experience this many times in the days ahead as the Likeness couple continued their headlong rush into their chosen destiny.

BEAUFANG'S BOAST

News of what happened in Mystery Grove reached
Lhaloo before I could find her. She was pacing
quickly around the small grove that served as our
sleeping place, her heavy sides heaving. Anxiety
marked the questions she asked about the encounter between Image and Beaufang. I was still stunned
by the events and admitted my confusion over the
meaning of what I had witnessed. I was not alone.
The entire valley buzzed with animated conversation. I could hear loud exclamations of confused
disbelief from every direction. With comforting

words to Lhaloo, I rushed off to see the effects of the bending on other Noumaso in the valley.

Confusion prevailed everywhere I went. No one understood how it could have happened. All Noumaso shared my lack of ability to understand Likeness couple's gift of free choice so did not grasp the full meaning. Obedience to the will of Giver was all we understood or desired.

I decided to seek out Beaufang and try to reason with him. I was still unable to understand what had gotten into the serpent. Beaufang had always been such a fine member of the Nouma community. His dry humor and crafty way with words were always welcome. I headed toward the rocky edge of the valley where members of the reptilian Noumaso chose to sleep. I wanted to find Beaufang and ask why he falsely accused Giver of unfairness to Likeness and Image. I arrived as Beaufang, mumbling to himself and walking unsteadily, slipped into a great opening in the rock wall.

Beaufang was a picture of contrasts as he returned to his sleeping place in the shadow of a great overhanging rock. The translucence that surrounded him during the encounter with Image and Likeness faded slightly, and he cried, "What have I done? No! No!" Then, as the translucence regained control, he again became the malevolent, crafty creature who instigated disobedience in the household of Likeness. Beaufang seemed locked in a deep struggle with himself. Slowly, but ever so surely, the translucent presence won over the old Beaufang. He grew stronger and more confident as the presence enveloped and overwhelmed him. Then he lifted his voice and cried aloud.

"At last, Giver, I have defeated you. In your dominion,

my plan was thwarted. I, who deserve praise and adoration for my matchless beauty and wisdom, could not be like you in that shining place. Why could you not see that I had a right to share your adulation and worship? Did I not serve you well in that high kingdom?

"Now I have regained what I lost when you threw me out of the high city and down to this newborn world. I have shown Likeness your weakness and snatched him out of your hand. He is mine. I will become the mighty ruler over his entire race. By my hand, they will conquer this world. They will build me a great kingdom. My name will be known and feared from the coming up to the going down of the golden sky orb. Everywhere, Likeness's sons and daughters go, I will go with them. Their lives are in my hands.

"I will be the great destroyer of your dreams for them. I will steal all that you designed to do for them and remake it in my own image. My world will be powerful. I will raise up rulers to follow my will. By my iron hand and power, I will make new creatures of Likeness's seed. They will be free from your restrictions and will joyfully do my bidding. I will give them every pleasure they desire. I will fill their hearts with joy and bloodlust.

"The Noumaso will tremble at the sound of their voices. The great creatures of the earth will fall before their might and power. They will fell the mighty trees of the forests and build cities to call by their own name. They will make a mighty name for themselves as they reach up to touch your dwelling. I will cause them to climb up and drag you down. Your name will be dishonored in the dust. They will go out in my pride and share my great renown.

"I have won. What was yours is now mine. I will gain all you made for yourself and hold it up before you every day. Did you think you could cast me out of your domain without penalty? I will be the ruler of the air above this planet and the master of all of Likeness's seed below. No place will be found for you. I have won.

"Sing for me the sweet song of victory. Gather round me all my hosts. Dance with joy to the defeat of Giver. He would but could not hold the feeble creatures he made. Write songs to my honor. Compose verse to my great deed. I will deceive and rule the sons of Likeness. Great is my name. Great is my might. Honor me one and all."

I became ill in the presence of such prideful evil. With my ears ringing and my mind reeling, I rushed away from the darkening grotto.

This would prove to be a night like no other. Members of the Noumaso were running aimlessly in confusion. Normally, soft voices were loudly telling and being told of the events at Mystery Grove.

I passed by Mystery Grove and found Likeness and Image still there. Each was covered by large leaves fastened together with woven blades of grass. I wept when I saw their darkened, tear-stained faces. The lord of the valley and his mata sat, huddled together, weeping and trembling.

Perhaps it had been the unusual nature of the day, or maybe it was just time. In any event, when I arrived home, Lhaloo was not alone. Nestled beside her were two miniature replicas of the two of us. I stared in wonder. Lhaloo had become the first of the large Nouma to bring forth life in the valley. The twins were eagerly feeding on the abundant food from a proud, smiling giver of life.

I puzzled over the day's events. Great tragedy and disappointment were tempered by this greatest of joys. *So this is what life is all about*, I mused.

SETTLING THE ACCOUNT

I awakened to the gentle noises and cries of new life facing an unknown world. Lhaloo and the twins were busily involved meeting the most urgent and pressing need of those newly become. I had not realized that having one's own offspring would be so demanding.

Yesterday's events were still the talk of the valley. The noise of excited Nouma running here and there greeted my ears as I walked toward the brook.

Normal calm and orderliness was replaced by a loud disarray of agitated Noumaso seeking answers.

Drinking quickly, I hurried toward Mystery Grove and found Likeness and Image huddled near the two trees. Both were distracted and looked as if they had not rested. Other Nouma were also moving by, attempting not to stare at the changed appearance of the Likeness couple. I returned to Lhaloo with the news and settled down to a meal of my favorite herb. *Strange*, I thought. *It doesn't taste the same.*

Later in the morning, a hush spread across the valley. The unnatural silence quickly became unnerving. I stretched my neck to see what might be the cause. As I looked in the direction of mystery grove, Giver's voice shattered the silence.

Gather here, my Noumaso
To the valley garden
It is time to settle accounts
And find the way to pardon

The strange pronouncement startled me and the other members of the family. In instant obedience, we moved toward the area that Giver indicated. We were eager to see what Giver would say. I had a premonition of disaster, though I did not understand what it meant.

Giver descended in all his light and splendor and hovered above the valley floor. The Noumaso quickly assembled. I looked around but did not see Likeness and Image anywhere. *Very strange*, I thought. *They are always here when Giver comes. They usually run to meet him and laugh and dance for joy. I wonder where they are today.*

Giver was not long answering the thoughts in my mind as he spoke to Likeness and Image. "Son and daughter of dust, Image and Likeness of Giver, where are you?"

It was evident that Giver knew where they were. There was nothing he did not know. Giver waited for an answer. Not far to my left, a movement stirred the thick bushes of the grove.

The voice of Likeness answered. "Image and I are behind the trees. We knew you were in the grove, so we hid ourselves here. We were afraid because we are uncovered."

I remembered the scene from yesterday. The awareness on the faces of the couple, the quick hiding in the bushes, then the leaves held to their bodies. And now, the expression of fear: "We are uncovered." I looked at myself and at the other Noumaso. *We are all uncovered*, I thought. I saw nothing wrong in that.

Giver spoke again. "Who said you were uncovered? Did you bend my word and eat from the knowing tree? I told you not to do so!"

We Noumaso held our breaths in anticipation of Likeness's response. In what seemed a long time but must have been very quickly, Likeness answered. "It is the fault of Image, the one you took from my side. She gave it to me, so I ate it."

I was astonished that Likeness passed the blame to Image.

Giver spoke again. "Image, what is the thing you have done?"

Image replied, "Beaufang twisted my mind and changed my thoughts, so I ate from the tree."

I was now even more puzzled. Likeness, then Image, tried to pass blame for the bending to another. *They were not only bent*, I thought. *They were twisted almost beyond recognition.* I wondered, *what has happened to Likeness and Image?*

All the families of Noumaso waited Giver's next speaking. I saw Beaufang nearby. He stood tall and proud, the translucent presence wrapped around him like a royal robe. His manner changed as Giver turned in his direction and called him alongside the Likeness couple.

For your part in this disgrace
Shame will cover all your race
Cursed above all Noumaso
On your belly you will go
Until the day you feel the sting
Licking dust your food will bring
Between you and Image fair
Hostility will fill the air
War, your seed and hers will sway
From now until the final day
Your head He'll crush with mighty power
Striking His heel won't hold back that hour

The Noumaso watched in wonder as Beaufang, swaying and tottering, lost his ability to stand upright. He slowly coiled to the ground, his head falling flat in the dust. His long tongue flicked out in frustrated anger at his punishment. Hissing and striking out at the other Nouma, he quickly slithered away. The translucent presence that had covered him disappeared in the heavy air of the grove. Giver then spoke to Image.

> *What was easy will now be pain*
> *Offspring in suffering you will gain*
> *Likeness will rule over you*
> *His desire you will pursue*

Likeness, eyes turned away from Giver, awaited his fate. He seemed unable to look directly at Giver but peered uneasily from his contorted face. Giver ordered Likeness to look up as he spoke directly to him.

> *Because my voice you did not heed*
> *But listened to your mata's creed*
> *You ate the fruit from knowing tree*
> *Though I had said, "This must not be"*
> *This place is cursed because of you*
> *Life will be hard with labor too*
> *Thorns will grow and thistles sprout*
> *From this good place you must go out*
> *Your sweat will fall, your body reel*
> *The pain of toiling you will feel*
> *Then one day, you'll feel the sting*
> *Down to the dust your body fling*
> *I made you from the clay of earth*
> *Return you shall to place of birth*

We all waited in hushed silence as Giver then moved out among us. We felt the gentleness of his touch as he passed and caressed each one. He spoke words of comfort, though his voice carried implications of great sorrow and tragedy for us all. He explained some of the suffering we would share because of the bending of Likeness and Image. He told of the far distant day when results of the bending would be undone, but not before Beaufang and his spawn had worked their terror and destruction on all creation.

Likeness and Image stood silently in Mystery Grove as Giver hovered over the obedient Noumaso. They continued to clutch their now-dry leaves to their bodies. Shame and remorse were etched on their faces, still turned down and away from the shining radiance of Giver.

What happened next went far beyond my comprehension. One of the larger Nouma couples, beautiful white unicorns, stepped from among the others and slowly moved forward. They approached the center of Mystery Grove and stopped near the Likeness couple.

All the family grew silent as Giver, in his glorious swirling splendor, descended and covered the Nouma with his presence. He lifted them up and placed them on a flat stone. I realized that this was the stone where Likeness and Image had been presented as sovereigns over us all. Speaking into their ears, Giver made them know the importance of what they were called upon to do. Giver then parted his shining presence, leaving open access to the Nouma lying on the stone.

Beaufang emerged from behind the tree where he had hidden. The malevolent presence reappeared and hugged itself around him. The Noumaso watched in stunned silence as Beaufang, wrapped in the presence, slithered to the stone where the innocent Nouma waited. He opened wide his jaws to reveal long, curved fangs. The eyes of the two Nouma registered fear as they realized their fate. Giver quickly spoke comfort and they regained their composure.

The strong smell of hate I had perceived earlier permeated the grove. The hair stood on my back as Beaufang lunged toward the first Nouma. His fangs penetrated deeply as he struck with all his force. His shiny body rippled as if to inject even more of his vile poison. He quickly withdrew and repeated his attack on the other Nouma. Inside the misty malevolent presence, the Nouma trembled and then slumped in excruciating pain.

The translucent presence quivered with delight. Unearthly hideous screams and laughter erupted from the presence as it detached from Beaufang and disappeared in the heavy air. Beaufang moved away, scattering Noumaso as he went. Giver let the two Nouma feel the full force of the sting.

Giver wept as the now lifeless bodies of the two Nouma sprawled grotesquely on the flat stone. He then tenderly removed their Nouma coverings and, behind his swirling presence of light, fashioned coverings for Likeness and Image.

Giver called the Likeness couple forward and blew their leafy cloaks away. He placed the still warm, damp Nouma coverings around them. The sweet smell of fresh, sticky blood was nauseating to me. Likeness and Image looked at their new coverings and at the bloody, lifeless bodies of the two Nouma. They bowed their heads in shame as Giver moved up and over the assembly.

I felt compelled to lead my fellow Noumaso in honoring our two departed family members who today accepted the sting. I was especially touched to realize that they were the only two of their kind in our valley. I wondered if the inno-

cent Noumaso family would be forever incomplete because
of the price paid to cover the willing bending of Likeness and
Image. Even though I did not understand why, I knew their
sacrifice was to satisfy the requirements of Giver and to meet
the needs of Likeness and Image. I lifted my voice.

Giver made us for his glory
Sing we now his worthy story
Likeness and Image who bent away
Brought sting to Noumaso today
Noumaso both far and near
See the glory of these here
Selflessly laid down their being
Covering Likeness's reckless fleeing
Innocence plead we in this crime
And long for days before this time

I stopped my lamentations as Giver spoke inside my head
and gave me understanding. I was made to know that this
was only the first event in Giver's plan to regain the alle-
giance of the bent seed of Likeness. I accepted my role
and that of all Noumaso in the great plan of Giver.

Giver spoke from inside his swirling presence of Light.
"Likeness has become as we, knowing the good and the
bad. He must now depart from this place before he eats
from the life tree and avoids the sting. We must banish
him forever from this valley."

Likeness listened sorrowfully to this pronouncement
because he loved the valley home. The Noumaso were his
friends. Everything here was sheer delight, but his bending had changed it all in an instant. With heavy hearts,

he and Image were led away by Giver. They were taken to the end of the valley and shown a pass among the peaks through which they must leave.

Giver then called down from the heavens two stunning, shining creatures. They moved swiftly amid flashing light and great rumbling noise. They carried long, glittering weapons that turned in every direction. Giver stationed them at the pass and gave strict orders to never permit Likeness or his seed to re-enter the valley and eat from the life tree.

Likeness and Image wept aloud at this order. They looked back with great longing at their now-forbidden home. Pleas and appeals fell on deaf ears as they begged for pardon and sought to turn back to the valley. The shining beings towered high over the pass and stood in their way. Likeness and Image were then gently pushed toward the neighboring valley.

The translucent presence that had covered Beaufang glided from behind a large boulder and followed the Likeness family through the pass and down into the next valley.

We members of the Noumaso family remained in the valley for a time to mourn the passing of innocence and to see what would be next in our efforts to obey Giver's orders. My thoughts were whirling and tumbling inside my head. I knew that the others and I would never be the same again.

Returning home by way of Mystery Grove, I saw that the two lifeless Nouma bodies still lay where they had fallen. Filled with pity and sorrow, I stopped and began trying to scoop out the sandy soil under the edge of the flat stone. Other Nouma who had been standing silently in the shadows moved to help. The Simian members easily completed the work.

When the opening was large enough, they tenderly placed the stiff bodies side-by-side in the soft soil. The dried leaves Giver had blown from Likeness and Image were then laid over them, along with fresh leaves picked from the knowing tree. Small stones were placed to hold the leaves in place, and then the sandy soil was mounded over the bodies. I knew that this was the right thing to do. I raised my voice to the heavens and sang.

> *The sting has entered this new world*
> *Lord Likeness on us it has hurled*
> *In innocence you were first to know*
> *Sting's dark embrace and be laid low*

I could not continue. For the first time since my becoming, I was unable to put together words and thoughts. Deep sorrow swept over me as I turned slowly away and headed toward home. The stillness of the night was broken only by the sound of weeping from the Noumaso.

Naados's Proposal after the Bending

I awoke with a start. It was already full light. Lhaloo and the twins were some distance away. Lhaloo nibbled the dew-covered grass while the twins frolicked in the fresh morning air. I had never experienced such a long night. My own sorrow kept me from a sound, satisfying sleep. Nouma had been moving here and there all during the night. The entire valley was in turmoil.

Some of the family who had been staying near the rocky area occupied by Beaufang and his kin sought other resting places. The horror of the sting drove them to disregard the difficulties of the darkness and seek new areas. With the trauma of the events heavy on them, some gave up finding new places and fell to the ground to await first light. This was the first time since the becoming that the family was not all contentedly together. I wondered how Likeness and Image fared in their new valley.

I wished that yesterday had been a bad dream, but ongoing tumult and noise in the valley told me it was real. Cries came from every direction as the impact of yesterday's events remained the focus of the Noumaso. Giver's good world was gone. What today would bring was totally unknown. Would Giver abandon us? What about our valley home? Should we follow Likeness to the next valley? Would other Nouma be made to feel the sting? Could we ever feel safe and secure again?

I knew that the Noumaso should be gathered to make decisions about these things and many other concerns not yet considered. Mystery Grove, as the central point of the bending, would probably be the best place to gather. Others thought so too. As I moved in that direction, the confused voices of Noumaso could be heard.

Likeness, our lord, had been the unifying power in the valley. Now that he was gone, concern about who would fill that role was a heavy uncertainty on us all. I saw small groups of Nouma all around the grove in animated discussion. They were, I noted with interest, in groups with others most like themselves. Two main ideas were being considered. Some wanted to remain in the valley and hope that Giver would come and make another lord over us. Others argued for following Likeness and serving him in his new home.

It was evident that some Noumaso felt most at ease when near Likeness and Image. Among these were many of the fowl and four-footed grass eaters. Others of the larger Nouma needed vast ranges for grazing. Some, because of sheer size, needed great expanses of forest and plain to adequately meet their needs for food and exercise. The largest of our family favored marshy areas along slower-moving rivers for their homes. Here, they could float their heavy bodies as they grazed on abundant foliage along the waterway.

I withdrew from the assemblage, found a shady spot, and stretched out to think about a solution. I'm not sure how long I lay there when an idea entered my mind. I was sure it had come from Giver. I quickly returned to Mystery Grove and got the attention of the Noumaso.

"Fellow Noumaso," I began formally, "we are all here from Giver's good hand. He made us for himself and gave each of us special abilities and needs. We know that we are not all alike. Our needs are varied. Our thoughts are different. We will never all be happy with one decision about where to live. Here is what I propose. Let each Nouma family talk about what Giver has put in their thoughts about life. Let that be the guide for choosing where each will live.

"Some may wish to lie at Likeness's feet."

A nearby canine wagged his tail in agreement.

"Others may need to roam the vast plains or forests. Let us not make hasty choices. Take time to find what is right and best for you. Remember, we all came from

Giver's hand. We are to share the bounty he placed here. In obedience to his decree, let us fill up the mountains and valleys of our world with offspring. Let us look with hope to Giver. Life is beautiful, even with the sting."

Everyone was satisfied with my idea. Most hesitated to move away from Mystery Grove. We chose to spend what could be the last complete family gathering quietly feeding and talking.

Naados and the Life Tree

Late on the evening of the family gathering, I paused to eat one of my favorite herbs and made a painful discovery. As I cropped a mouthful and then chewed, something long and sharp pricked the inside of my lower lip. I cried out from the pain. Astonished, I stopped and let the food fall from my mouth. Several long, pointed stems were in the food. I cropped another clump and made another effort to chew. Once again, sharp objects stuck the inside of my mouth. Then I remembered Giver's words to

Likeness. "*This place is cursed because of you... thorns will grow and thistles sprout...*" I realized that the bending was not only affecting Likeness and Image. It also changed our lives in ways we could not imagine. I quickly went to warn the others about this new danger.

I visited Mystery Grove every day. I walked silently around the stone where my fellow Nouma lay buried and contemplated the two trees. What would have happened if Likeness and Image had eaten from the life tree? That kind of thinking always brought me to a dead end.

It will probably not be long, I thought, *before this grove will be completely* hidden *in the forest.* I was right. The trees were becoming very large and growing at an incredible rate. Something about the climate and environment made quick growth possible. Underbrush was already much higher than my head in places.

How will the fruit and leaves of those trees taste? I pondered. I knew the tragic results from eating the fruit of the knowing tree and had no desire to partake. *But what*, I thought, *about the life tree?* I looked around to make sure no other Noumaso were present. *What caused me to do that?* I wondered and then impulsively cropped a mouthful of young, tender leaves from the life tree. They were deliciously tender and sweet in my mouth, so I savored them as long as possible before swallowing.

Surprisingly, the leaves turned bitter in my stomach. I shuddered, looked around again, and waited for something bad to happen. I had a strange sensation that Giver was not unaware of my action but was not present in the way he had visited in the past. I tried to put my actions out of my mind.

As the weeks and seasons passed, many Nouma joined Likeness and Image in Far Valley. Many of us had already produced numbers of offspring. I realized that the great numbers of Nouma would require seeking out other valleys and plains if we continued our rapid reproduction. Home Valley would soon be overflowing as Noumaso families increased.

It seemed that Lhaloo was always swollen with life. There were now numerous sets of twins, many already grown and producing their own miniature likenesses. I wanted to leave Home Valley and explore our world. *How big is it?* I thought. *Are the other valleys and plains identical to our own? How long does it take for the golden sky orb to pass over all creation? What shape is our world? Are there other Likenesses and Images in other places?* These questions drove me to leave Lhaloo in the care of our offspring and discover more of the world outside Home Valley.

Exploring Eastward from Home Valley

I did not rest well the night before leaving Home Valley. Long before the feathered Noumaso started their morning serenade to Giver, I slipped away from Lhaloo and my Nouma family. Lhaloo stirred slightly, letting me know that she too passed a restless night. Once away from my family, I grabbed a mouthful of dew-covered, tender leaves. I decided to pass by Mystery Grove, hoping Giver might be there. It was no surprise that he was not.

I looked to the high country where sky orb rose in the morning and spotted the flashing lights of Giver's life tree guardians. Using the lights as a beacon, I moved toward them at a fast but unhurried pace.

The third day after visiting mystery grove, I arrived at the pass just as the golden sky orb peeked from behind a distant range of hills. I hurried on, not sure what to expect as I took one last glance at Home Valley, still wrapped in the dim light of early morning.

The shining guardians let me pass without incident as they had on other occasions when I left Home Valley. I suppose that today I expected some sort of encounter after my life tree experience. As I slowly descended the heights, I scanned the horizon for evidence of Likeness but saw nothing to indicate that he or Image was anywhere near.

As before, there were many Nouma in this valley. I sought out a nearby grazing group and paused to speak with them. Stopping made me realize how hungry I had become. They gladly shared the bounty that Giver had placed in the valley. As we talked, we spoke, of course, about Home Valley. These family members had left soon after the sting. They talked of others who also sought homes after Likeness' bending. The conversation always turned to Giver. They had not seen him since the sting and wondered if he had returned to Mystery Grove. Likeness and Image were on all our minds, but none from this Nouma family had seen them since their expulsion. We discussed the sting. None of their family had experienced it.

Once again, I realized my limited ability to grasp the vastness of Giver's creation. This made me more determined to explore our world. There were, no doubt, unknown vast regions where Noumaso could flourish under the good hand of Giver.

I crossed another long plain and climbed a range of high hills. I yet had not seen any indication of Likeness. Darkness was near as I found a small bubbling brook and stopped to drink the cool water. Food was everywhere, and a small copse offered shelter for the night. Unfamiliar night sounds caught my attention for only a moment. Tired from the long day's journey, I fell almost immediately asleep, but not before thinking of Lhaloo and the family.

I hoped to see Likeness but was more determined to explore our world, so I sought the nearest high point from which to plan my travels. I could see behind me in the far distance the hills that ringed Home Valley. This was in the direction where sky orb disappeared each evening.

Looking east and slightly south, in the far distance, I could see a river glistening in the early morning light. It flowed on a broad plain and seemed to come from the direction of Home Valley except to my south. High hills kept me from knowing its source. Looking east and slightly north, but at a greater distance than Southeast River, I glimpsed what was perhaps another river.

I chose to go toward Southeast River and follow its course. This would give me opportunity to explore the rolling hills and valleys between me and the river. With a long-stride pace, I started my adventure. Small members of Noumaso scurried among the grass and trees when I passed. Occasionally, in the distance, I watched larger Nouma and heard their normal feeding sounds. Since none of the Nouma seemed surprised by my presence, I chose to hurry on and cover as much distance as possible. I felt light on my feet and had remarkable endurance, which kept me from pausing to eat or drink.

River Valley Meetings

I covered a great distance before sky orb passed the mid mark in the sky and my shadow moved from behind to in front of me. Reaching the valley floor and finding luscious leaves in a vast, marshy area, I paused to refresh myself.

I heard sounds of movement and felt a trembling on the damp ground under my feet. Standing still, my ears turned in the direction of the sound. I waited. The vibrations under my feet increased. The sounds became loud, swishing thumps like heavy objects striking the ground. I felt no fear, just intense curiosity as whatever creature produced the sounds moved closer. Then the sounds stopped.

I looked all around and spotted only a few paces behind me and to the right a huge Nouma. Its legs were large, like tree trunks. It had a massive body over twenty times the length of my own. It towered high over the small trees from which I had been feeding and had sensed my presence but had not seen me in the shadow of the small trees.

I paused and then stepped from the shadows and spoke a greeting. The giant lowered its long, majestic neck and looked directly at me. It dropped the leaves it had foraged from the tree tops and made a sound that could only be laughter. Friendly eyes came very close as its head moved in my direction. I tried not to stare, but this fellow creature was doing so with no apparent hesitation.

I decided to speak again, so I moved slightly forward and said, "I'm Naados."

A deep voice answered and said, "I'm Behemoth, of the valley giants. My closest kin and I live along the swampy river areas. Smaller and different of our Noumaso prefer the grassy, tree-covered plains nearby. Welcome."

Behemoth asked me to follow him a short distance through the marsh to a small inlet off the river. He slipped into the water and moved far enough from the bank to let his heavy body float in the water. He looked like an island of skin with a long neck rising out of it. I glanced across the inlet and saw numerous others like Behemoth floating in the calm waters near the shore of the river.

Now much more comfortable, he questioned me about

my home area. A long exchange followed from which I learned that he and his kin were not part of the Noumaso from Home Valley. This was amazing to me, for I had assumed that we in Home Valley were the only Noumaso who came from the hand of Giver during that special time. This was evidently not so and increased even more my desire to explore our world.

After a lengthy exchange, I asked Behemoth about Giver and Likeness. He knew nothing about them. He and his Nouma had realized there must have been a cause for their being. They only knew that they all awoke and found themselves in this beautiful valley alongside the river. They found everything they needed to live and reproduce their own kind. They had no direct knowledge of either Giver or Likeness.

This provided me the chance to speak to the now gathering numbers of Behemoth's kin. I told them what we from Home Valley knew about ourselves, Giver, Likeness, and Image. They listened with rapt attention. When I spoke of the bending, the news brought cries of astonishment from the increasing numbers and kinds of Noumaso. Behemoth, as spokesman, expressed the question that was on all their minds. "How could Likeness and Image have done such a horrible thing?"

I explained more completely about Beaufang and the evil presence that enveloped him. They shuddered to think that a Nouma could have played such a role. Agonized cries filled the air when I told them of the first sting. It was difficult to continue because of the groaning and weeping from the Noumaso. I relived in my mind those now-distant events and was torn by the harsh reality of what the sting would ultimately mean to all of us.

Evening was near when I spoke more of Likeness and Image. The Noumaso were unaware of this part of creation and eagerly asked about them and their seed. I admitted that I knew nothing about them since they were banished from Home Valley. I promised to let them know when I found out more.

I spent one more day with Behemoth and his kin in order to give them as much information as possible before moving on down the river valley. These Nouma brothers showed me a choice place to spend the night and indicated their most delicious foods. I settled in to rest, but it came slowly. The events of this day made my head whirl as I thought about the possibility of many other Nouma who knew nothing of the fateful events of Home Valley. Was there something I should do to let them know? Lhaloo and my offspring were once more my last waking thoughts.

On to River's End

After another satisfying day with Behemoth and his kin, we spoke our parting words. I turned slightly away from the river and traveled for a short time before settling down for the night. I needed to be alone to rethink the impact of my last two days with the river giants.

Behemoth and my other newfound kin had agreed to spread the news of Giver everywhere they went. They were eager to prepare the Noumaso for the arrival of Likeness's offspring in their home areas. It seemed likely that Giver had only made one Likeness couple. I hoped to either verify or disprove this assumption during my travels. I was determined to follow the river to its end.

The river turned slowly toward the south and continued to grow in size as more streams flowed into it. Large numbers of Behemoth's kin lived in the marshes and low areas along the stream. I stopped and gave them the same news I shared with Behemoth. The response was always the same. There should now be dozens if not hundreds of Noumaso giving the news to their fellows.

Interestingly, in most places I stopped, the Noumaso called me "the messenger." It gave me a peculiar feeling, as if my role had great significance. During one such experience, I thought again of eating from the life tree. I wondered if my desire to visit our world was linked to my inability to feel the sting. I made every effort to leave those thoughts behind and enjoy the adventure of every new day's discoveries.

Three of Likeness's years passed during my travels. The entire landscape around me had flattened to include low, rolling, tree-covered hills and the now-slow-moving river. I do not try to remember all the hundreds of contacts with Noumaso of every kind and description during the journey.

I feel satisfying oneness with Giver's good creation. It is evident to me that Likeness and Image are the only members of their kind of creature. The realization pushes my desire to return to Home Valley but is not stronger than seeing where Southeast River ends.

A few days later, another unrecognizable sound with a strange, recurring tempo reached my ears. It had a slight roar followed by a peculiar swishing sound.

Thousands of feathered Nouma, unlike those I had encountered during my journey, filled the air. Their cries were shriller than any I had heard except that of the mighty eagles.

There had been a steady breeze for the past two days coming from the direction the river flowed. It had a damp, pungent smell that was both pleasing and penetrating. At about midday, I decided to hurry my pace and satisfy my curiosity about the new sounds and smells.

I topped a small rise in the sandy ground and could hardly believe my eyes. As far as I could see, straight ahead as well as to my right and left I saw nothing but water. It was a shiny, crystal blue with a rolling motion coming toward the ground where I stood.

Thousands of feathered Noumaso filled the skies above, and others moved on the ground along the edge of the water. The sounds I had been hearing were the pulsations of water reaching the land. The roaring was a short distance from land, and the whooshing sound came from water climbing up the ground, losing momentum and then rolling back into the vastness of the watery world.

Never lacking curiosity, I waited only a moment and then moved forward and waded into the rushing water. It felt slightly cool and refreshing to my legs. I moved a few paces farther and was almost knocked from my feet. Scampering to turn, I quickly regained the solid ground and puzzled over what had happened.

Reaching down to lick my now-wet upper leg, my brain registered surprise. The water was not sweet but had the same sharp sensation and taste as the white earth where my fellow Nouma and I licked to create thirst. As the wind dried the water from me, white, shiny crystalline flecks remained imbedded in my coat.

I backed away from the foaming water, found a small shade under a low bush, and pondered what I was seeing. *What an amazing world,* I thought as the rhythm of the water caused me to sleep.

Some unknown sound awakened me and caused me to focus again on the vast waters before me. At some distance into the water, I saw several huge creatures swimming—diving, jumping from the water, and splashing nosily back in again. Closer in toward me, smaller water Nouma darted and splashed. The waters swirled with life.

I knew that it was impossible to go forward beyond this point, so I made my way back from the edge of the water and sought the best way to cross the wide river.

Vast numbers of Behemoth kin fed along the banks and told me that the water was not deep but very wide. Small islands were scattered across the wide expanse. This made it possible for me to swim from one to another and cross the slowly flowing water.

I made it to the other side just before the sky orb slipped behind the horizon. Nouma feeding nearby directed me to a suitable place to spend the night. The discoveries of the day had drained me. A few quick bites of juicy grass, and I drifted into a sound, satisfying sleep.

RETURN TO
HOME VALLEY

I wanted to find a more direct way back to Home Valley, so I followed the river, but not along the banks as before. Confident that the behemoth clans would spread the news of Giver all along the river, I sought a direct northerly route.

It was a good decision. I stopped following Southeast River where it intersected with a stream coming from the west. Noumaso were everywhere. When I met groups who were unaware of the news about Giver, I took the time to tell them before moving on.

The diversity of life in our world is incredible. This discovery gave me an increasing devotion to Giver for his creative power.

One year and six night-sky orb cycles passed. The small river I followed split into two branches. I followed one until I realized that it had turned west and was taking me away from Home Valley. I stopped and rested for the night and when the sky orb rose, I turned east. In a few days, I was on my way back north toward Home Valley.

Nouma were scattered throughout the areas I crossed. I recognized most kinds of them and often found my own Nouma kin. It was a special pleasure to tell them of Giver and Likeness. One or more often wanted to travel with me, but I thought it unwise at this time.

After traveling five cycles of the night sky orb, the stream I followed began climbing steeply. The area was increasingly hilly. I had to move away from and then back toward the stream to follow it. Before many days, the stream had become small brooks flowing from every direction. I stopped, passed the night and thought about another way to find Home Valley.

A night of rest helped me think clearly. I remembered that several streams entered Southeast River from the west. I decided to wait in my resting place each day until the sky orb could be seen in the east and then travel as directly north as possible, which was not always easy.

The country I traveled had many shadow-filled ravines. I often waited until the sky orb was high in the sky to find my way north. Some days, I made little progress. Crossing a stream flowing in an easterly direction, I knew that I was moving toward home.

Scattered groups of Nouma lived in the remote areas I passed through, but not in the large numbers I found along the big waterways. I always took time to visit with them and tell them the news about Giver. They were eager to know of the vast numbers of Noumaso in other parts of the world.

Over three of Likeness's years had passed since I left the great, salty waters. This was not a short way to Home Valley. I could do nothing now but press on. Retracing my path would be impossible.

The next fifteen cycles of the sky orb were difficult for me. I wondered if I had overestimated my abilities and knowledge. This would be a great learning experience if I made it safely back to Home Valley.

Two evenings later, I walked past my normal stopping time. In the distance, I thought I saw a faint flash of light. I turned in that direction and stared until my eyes ached. My hope to see the flashing lights from the guardians was to no avail. I saw nothing else and finally gave up and rested.

There was no physical danger, but I experienced something that must have been loneliness. I made a long mark on the ground point toward whatever I had seen. I planned to continue in that direction. My rest was troubled, and I awoke tired the next morning.

Using the rising sky orb and my mark on the ground, I set off at a fast pace, trying to keep my eyes on the distant high hills. By the time my shadow had turned to face east, I was quite tired. Finding tender leaves and a water source, I stopped to refresh myself, but not before marking my direction of travel. That was fortunate, for after eating, I fell asleep.

The sky orb was settling in the west when I stirred. I was not pleased with myself. The rest period had kept me from a considerable time of travel.

I snatched a few mouthfuls of grass and chewed as I thought. *This is the time when the night sky orb shines brightly. At times, it is possible to travel during the night.* I waited until the sky orb had disappeared in the west and the sky turned black. In that short time before the night sky orb appeared, I hoped I would see the flash again.

In the far distance, I saw a quick, faint flash of light. I continued to stare at what had to be the flashing weapons of the guardians. Holding the spot with my gaze, I waited until the bright night sky orb was high enough to make shadows. I selected two peaks slightly west of the light flashes and walked toward them.

My night journey disturbed several groups of resting Nouma; but I pressed on, determined to reach Home Valley. As the sky orb lighted the eastern heavens, my endurance waned. I took water and a few mouthfuls of food, found a sheltered grove, and fell asleep at once.

It was the middle of the sky orb crossing when a noise awakened me. I thought someone was calling my name. Still dazed with sleep, I muttered a response and then heard it again clearly.

"Naados! Naados!"

I jerked awake and saw a small group of Noumaso standing around me. When my eyes were fully opened, I recognized two old friends from Home Valley and could hardly contain my joy.

We all talked at once. Questions flew, and I attempted to answer all the queries. Of all my days of being, this had to be one of the best. I was almost back to Home Valley.

Eight of Likeness's years had passed. Lhaloo thought I had felt the sting and would never return. Our offspring were grown and had produced many of their own. Mystery Grove was completely overgrown. A group of Nouma had traveled northeast and seen Likeness. He and Image had several offspring. On and on the news was given as they led me the short way back to Home Valley.

I would never have found this entrance on my own. Rivers in Home Valley flowed out in four directions. This one came out of the valley under a mountain. A huge cavern almost hidden by the face of a cliff was the channel through which it flowed. Outside the valley, it sprung forth as a river from the rock.

My friends had explored and found a path alongside the river that ran all the way through the mountain. This had become their favorite way to go and come. The drawback was that it was a great distance from where most of the Noumaso migrated. They used it to reach the high mountain groves where their favorite foods were abundant. This was where they found me. I am glad for their curious nature and overjoyed to be back in Home Valley.

LIFE WITH LHALOO

I was overjoyed to re-enter Home Valley after such a long absence. During my years of wandering, the valley had undergone serious changes. I could hardly believe the size of the trees down the center of the valley, especially those next to the streams. Their tops reached heavenward with branches intertwining forming an almost solid overhead canopy. This in turn created a shadowy resting place for countless Noumaso.

It was yet a one-day journey to Mystery Grove. Leaving my guides, I hurried toward home, eager to see Lhaloo and our offspring. I now had the luxury to feel a bit anxious about my long absence. Perhaps guilt also played a part in my feeling the need to hurry. I had not planned to be away so long.

The glow of the night sky orb enabled me to travel late. Tiredness and hunger finally caused me to stop, eat a bite, and find a resting place. Familiar night sounds lulled me to a quick and restful sleep.

Scintillating light eased me awake just as it had the day I became. I quickly snatched a bite of dew-covered grass and hurried toward Mystery Grove.

Near midday, I spotted the now dark and dense growth of trees and vines. I headed for where I remembered the two special trees only to be quickly turned away. The growth was far too thick and tangled for me to spend time getting there now.

I turned and headed for the grove where Lhaloo and I started our lives together. The area was greatly changed but recognizable. As I approached, a familiar form stepped out of the shadows and looked in my direction.

In an instant, we were both running toward each other. Lhaloo bumped into me, and we both fell to the ground, laughing from sheer delight. Regaining our feet, we joyously pranced and danced around, loudly greeting and talking. I felt as if life was starting anew and I was the most fortunate Nouma in all of Giver's creation.

Lhaloo was overjoyed and began recounting nonstop the news since my leaving. She told of our offspring and their exploits. Many had migrated to other valleys with their own matas and offspring. Others chose to stay in Home Valley with Lhaloo, awaiting my return. My offspring numbered in the scores and were constantly increasing.

During this telling, Lhaloo let me know in no uncertain terms that she was ready to obey Giver in producing more offspring. This said, she returned to telling the news of our friends and brothers of Home Valley.

We stood shoulder to shoulder for much of the day as I listened and soaked up events of the past years. Only as the sky orb slipped low in the west did Lhaloo become quiet. She nudged me toward a grove of young, tender bushes; started cropping leaves; and motioned for me to do the same.

We savored our first meal together for many years. As I eased my hunger, I noticed that Lhaloo was bigger and heavier than I remembered. Her sleek coat had an occasional area of lighter-colored hair. I observed but did not think much about it.

As night sounds filled the air around us, we moved to a secluded resting place and renewed our intimacy. I slept long and well, rousing at times to listen to the contented breathing of Lhaloo at my side. Life is good, even with the sting.

The sky orb was peering over the distant hills when Lhaloo and I took a morning run to one of our favorite grazing places. Friendly greetings from Nouma friends gave me a feeling of fulfilled contentment. We later rested, and I told Lhaloo about my journeys. She could hardly believe some of my stories and was intrigued by the tale of great salty waters. I promised to take her there if she ever wanted to go so far from Home Valley. She was pleased that there were other Noumaso like those in Home Valley. I told her that I had not met other of the Noumaso whose kin had felt the sting.

Beaufang and his spawn were in the valley, but the

strange translucent presence had not been seen again. The Noumaso now avoided Beaufang's kin. The once complete harmony of the Noumaso was forever destroyed. I wept at that thought, but it made me more determined to follow the will of Giver.

I sought out Beaufang, hoping to talk with him. He evidently carried great shame, for when I tried to approach him he quickly slithered away into an opening in the ground. After numerous efforts, I decided to leave him to his ways.

Home Valley was a comfortable break from my travels through the Southeast River valley. For now, familiar was what I needed. The days passed quickly, and before it even seemed possible, Lhaloo was once more swollen with life waiting to be born. She had a remarkably royal bearing during these times. I asked her about it and was pleased with her response.

"Giver's word to fill our world is sweet to my heart," she said. "I do not know when we will feel the sting, but I want to obey him until that time." I did not have the courage to tell her of my life tree experience.

The sky orb had not yet topped the eastern hills when Lhaloo presented me with two more offspring. The newness of this creative act never ceased to amaze me. I took the occasion to go to Mystery Grove and offer a canticle to Giver. Even though he did not appear as he had done in the past, His presence seemed to be in that special place.

Now that Lhaloo again had offspring to occupy her time and interest, I considered the possibility of another journey. I could not get Likeness and Image off my mind.

Where are they? How many offspring do they have? Does Giver visit them? Will they remember me? With this state of mind, I told Lhaloo of my desire to find them.

Lhaloo was amazing. She insisted that I leave at once. She knew that our dozens of offspring were more than capable of helping in whatever way she might need. I determined to seek out Nouma who had left Home Valley before leaving to search for Likeness. Perhaps some of them knew where to find my old friends.

Part Two

Lord Likeness's
Long Life

FINDING LIKENESS

One of my close Nouma kin told of sighting the Likeness couple within the past five Likeness years. It occurred during a trip seeking his offspring who had migrated. The Nouma had traveled east and then north a ten sleep-cycle journey. Passing along a high ridge above a wide valley, he had seen areas cleared of normal vegetation. Stopping only long enough to verify that this was not something that Giver had created, he continued the quest for his kin. I hurried to locate the traveler who gave me directions toward where the near-Likeness sighting had occurred.

With a quick goodbye to Lhaloo, I headed once

again for the pass. The life tree guardians were there with their shining weapons. As before, they paid me no heed. I passed between them and descended into the neighboring valley.

Shadows were long and the air cool when I stopped to eat and sleep. Long after I found the grassy grove where I passed the night, the excitement of my new adventure and missing Lhaloo prevented me from satisfying sleep.

Noumaso were plentiful in this valley, and I stopped often to ask about Likeness. It was not until after my third sleep that I found a Nouma with information. The Nouma was excited that I had undertaken the challenge to contact Likeness. He wanted to do so but did not feel adequate to talk with him. It appeared that the impact of the bending had already changed the relationship between the Noumaso and Likeness Kin. *Was I the only Nouma who spoke directly with them*, I wondered. He directed me a two-sleep journey north to a river that then flowed east. It was another of the four rivers flowing out of Home Valley. Just as he said, I reached the river after my second sleep.

The river moved swiftly along between low-lying hills. Numerous behemoth kin sheltered and fed along the banks just as others did along Southeast River.

I stopped to talk with a small group and discovered that one of them, with his mata, had followed the river out of Home Valley and found their kin located here. He had given the news about Giver to the Noumaso in this area. I had no need to spend time, for those living here were aware of events many years ago. They urged me to continue my search for Likeness. They seemed to think that for my fast pace he was probably a two-sleep journey away.

Encouraged by the thought that Likeness might not be far away, I redoubled my efforts to reach him and Image. Urged on by the hope of seeing them, I traveled until after full darkness and only halted when I could no longer safely travel.

First light found me heading east along the river, hoping this new day would bring me to my old friend from Home Valley. I longed to see Likeness, the bent sovereign of all Noumaso.

When the sky orb was directly overhead, I stopped to crop a mouthful of leaves and drink from a bubbling brook. As I chewed and sniffed the air, I heard a distant sound. I trembled with excitement, swallowed my food, and focused on locating the direction of the sound. The sound came again, a bit to my right and down the long valley. I did not recognize it since it was not like the normal Nouma sounds. I stretched my neck and rushed quickly toward the sound.

After a quick dash down the incline and into the valley, I rounded a grove of large trees and saw an area that had been cleared of vegetation. Instead of the normal grass, shrubs, and trees, some kind of green plants had been placed in long lines. They stretched across the large clearing. Curious as always, I stopped to check the plants.

Tentative sniffing let me know they were good to eat, so I bent to crop a mouthful. Before my mouth reached the first plant, something sharp and stinging struck me low on my right flank. I jumped straight up from the pain of being hit by this unexpected projectile. As I turned in the direction from which it came, another whizzed by, nearly clipping my right ear. I jumped from among the plants and ran for the nearby tree line.

From the shadows of another clump of tall trees, I heard a Likeness voice. "Out of my field you, greedy, four-legged Nouma. There is more than enough to eat elsewhere."

Catching my breath, I gazed from the concealment of the shadows and looked for the Likeness who spoke. Some distance down the clearing, I spotted the speaker as he emerged from beside a large tree. "Likeness," I cried out without thinking; then I stopped abruptly when the tall figure looked in my direction.

"Who is there?" he shouted.

I remained quiet.

He spoke again. "Come out. Let me see who you are. I mean you no harm."

The burning sensation on my flank gave me reason to think otherwise, but I decided to take the risk.

Stepping out of the shadows, I said, "I'm Naados from Home Valley. I'm looking for Likeness."

In an instant the figure was rushing toward me, excitedly speaking my name. "Naados. Yes. I know of you. I'm Likeness-Possessor, firstborn of Likeness and Image. I hope you are not injured. I thought you were a rogue Nouma determined to destroy my field. Come with me to our family home."

And so my first contact with the seed of Likeness was successful. It had been nearly seventy of what Likeness calls years.

We passed a succession of clearings with plants I had never seen. Possessor explained that they were part of his experimental food projects. He had searched out new varieties growing across the hills and valleys and took great pride in cultivating them for maximum production. He considered it part of his way to use the great diversity of Giver's creation for Likeness's kin's good. Now that he knew who I was, he offered samples of some of his favorites as we moved toward his home.

Possessor was eager to learn about me and why I had come. He quickly asked me about Home Valley. I gave a brief account of the becoming and the nature of that first beautiful home we all shared. He asked me about the bending and how it changed my life. He asked about Beaufang since many of his kin were also found here. He was intrigued by my telling of the guardians at the pass to Home Valley and inquired how I managed to slip by them.

The distance was far too short to answer all his questions but proved to be enlightening to me. It was evident that Likeness was teaching his offspring well. As was my habit, I could not resist asking about Giver. Possessor told me that Giver came often to visit the Likeness clan. He did not indicate that it was a pleasant experience for him.

After we skirted the edge of another grove of tall trees, the Likeness village came into view. I'm not sure what I was expecting, but nothing in my thoughts prepared me for this. I was astonished at the bustle of activity and impressed as scores of Likeness's offspring were busily occupied with what to me were curious activities. I noted that there were both males and females. They talked animatedly as they rushed about.

I noticed that all except the very young were covered. It

was only then that I realized that Possessor wore something that did not appear to be made from a Nouma covering. It had a textured pattern with various colors throughout.

Shame must still compel members of Likeness's kin to cover themselves, I thought.

When some of the smaller offspring pointed in our direction and cried out, all activity stopped. We moved toward a central tree. When we arrived there, Possessor presented me to his kin.

I spotted Image almost immediately. She was swollen with new life waiting to be born. Image had regained some of her royal bearing from before the bending, but clearly a degree of shame haunted her mind. It was difficult for me to read her emotions as she recognized me. They seemed to flicker between joy and apprehension. She greeted me warmly as she did to all Noumaso back in Home Valley and welcomed me to her home village.

I decided to say nothing about the bending that would embarrass her in the presence of her offspring. Image saw the small wound on my flank and told a young female offspring to care for it. She applied a soothing, good-smelling liquid that stung for just an instant and then brought complete relief.

Likeness was away checking on several new projects. Two of them were agricultural, and one involved the domestication of various Noumaso. I settled down to await his return.

REUNION IN LIKENESS'S VILLAGE

Possessor excused himself to return to his fields. Since my presence had been accepted as normal, I decided to look around Likeness's village as I waited Likeness's return.

There were numerous large, well-built structures—several made from stones stacked one on top of another. These were held together by some sort of clay that had hardened and made them very solid. They had an ascending access to the top, where dried grain and other kinds of food were placed. I ventured a step onto the surface and found it as solid as the ground below but with a strange hollow sound. There were tall, wide openings through which to enter all the structures.

Other structures were made from large trees which were covered with straight branches and topped by skillfully woven dried thatch. Open sides served as storage places for harvested food. I peered into several of these curious Likeness creations and saw carefully arranged sleeping places. There were also objects on which Likeness's kin could sit. Why anyone would want to sit in a shadowy structure was beyond my understanding. The open air of Giver's creation was much more satisfying to me.

Something I saw in one of the structures caused me instant interest. It was inside some kind of container and glowed like the sky orb but flickered like the weapons of the guardians of Home Valley. This would require further study on my part.

Image had entered the largest structure near the center of the village. I counted at least thirty of these curious places made by the Likeness clan.

Small, domesticated Nouma were scattered throughout the village. Sheep and goats rested in the midday shadows of tree-filled lanes. Many varieties of fowl, followed by their tiny offspring, scratched, pecked, and made their Nouma noises among the loose grain provided by the Likeness clan.

A grove of trees grew in the middle of the village. After studying it awhile, I knew why it seemed familiar. It looked like Mystery Grove back in Home Valley. The

Likeness family had placed a large, flat stone at the central entrance to the well-kept grove. Alongside the flat stone stretched a pile of uncut stones about the length of my body and half again that wide. I stood by it, and it reached the tops of my legs. The soil around had dark stains and evoked the memory of a smell from long ago.

I trembled as I remembered that it was the sickly bloody smell from the Nouma who first felt the sting. On top of the stones and scattered about the ground near them lay small pieces of what looked like parts of trees. They were black and had a strange smell. They had been badly damaged by something unknown to me. I hoped it would not be long before the meaning of what I saw would be clear to me. I quickly left this place that generated painful memories and continued my village walk.

Four lanes crossed the village. They passed from east to west and from north to south. Smaller paths branched off each of the larger access ways and led to individual structures. The entire area was beautiful and well-arranged.

I moved from place to place, observing small groups going about their tasks. The activity of several young females was intriguing. They carried fluffy white balls in a container. I bent to sniff one of them and put my nose too close. The ball stuck to it and tickled me causing a huge sneeze. This in turn almost emptied the container and scattered a great number of the balls across the ground. My hosts giggled and scurried to gather them again. They assured me that no harm was done.

As they chatted and laughed, they showed me how they separated the individual strands of the balls and then twisted them to make long, single strands. They showed me how their own coverings had been skillfully made from these strands.

I knew that Likeness could not create new things; only Giver could do that. I was amazed at how the knowledge Giver put in Likeness and Image enabled them to make useful things from what he had created.

Feeling the need to be alone to think, I took the north lane and headed out of the village. I found a place nearby to nibble tender buds from young trees and ponder the curious things I observed since finding the Likeness dwellings. Dropping to the shade, I dozed in the warmth of the afternoon sky orb.

I awoke with a start as Likeness noises rapidly approached. Hurrying from the direction of the village was an excited group of Likeness's kin. I stood, stretched, and waited their arrival. I immediately recognized Likeness and bent at his feet. He laughed and reached to lift me up. "Naados. My dear Naados," he said.

This began a long, happy time of talking, laughing, and crying as we caught up on events of the past years. Urging me along back toward the village, Likeness asked of my travels. He was eager to hear about Home Valley, although he could not speak the name without weeping.

We reached his home and sat to continue our talk. Image brought Likeness a container of water to drink and quickly returned with a much larger one for me. The night sky orb had finished over half of her journey when fatigue caused us all to stop and seek a time of rest. I was given a choice place to rest in Central Grove. Likeness wanted me to remain nearby since we were all eager to continue our visit.

New light came too quickly, but the joy of our reunion drew us from our rest. Likeness accompanied me to a nearby stream, where we refreshed ourselves. We then returned to Central Grove. Several of Likeness's older offspring gathered nearby to listen as we resumed our asking and telling.

Likeness's first questions dealt with Giver and Mystery Grove. I explained that Giver had not returned to visit with the Noumaso as he had done before the bending and Likeness's expulsion. My only explanation was Likeness's special relationship to Giver—the fact that he resembled him in ways that the Noumaso did not.

I then made my confession to Likeness about the life tree. He was surprised that I had been so bold and even more that Giver had not spoken a punishment on me. I told him of the strange sensation that Giver was not unaware of my action but that he had not appeared to speak to me. I reminded him that we Noumaso do not share the Likeness quality that makes it possible for us to question and disobey Giver. We only want to obey and please him. I yet have to deal with the thought that any of Giver's creation could question him.

Likeness was curious about the effects I felt from eating the life tree leaves or any results I now noticed. I told him about the sweet taste in my mouth followed by the bitterness in my belly. He seemed as puzzled as I.

"I noticed only recently," I said, "that some of the other Nouma seemed to be undergoing gradual changes that cause them to be less energetic. Others have stopped reproducing and have perceptible changes to their appearance." I mentioned the color change I noted in Lhaloo's covering.

I told him that my actions had not interfered in any way with my leaving or returning to Home Valley. The guardians paid me no attention as I passed between them.

I explained about trying to talk with Beaufang but not being able to get his attention. Then I shared one very important bit of information. I told of seeing the malevolent presence follow him and Image when they were banished from Home Valley. He insisted that we talk more about that at a later time.

Likeness asked about my travels. He was eager to hear stories of the Noumaso seeded all across the river valleys where I traveled. We talked about the amazing diversity of Giver's creation until the sky orb was directly overhead. He too had discovered other groups of Nouma scattered over the hills and valleys when he came to this new home.

I expressed my intent to travel to the very end of the four rivers flowing out from Home Valley. "Since none of us know how long life will be before we feel the sting, I have hopes that the life tree leaves will provide me adequate time to see a great part of Giver's handiwork."

I explained that in all my travels and contacts with different groups of Nouma, there was no hint of any of Likeness's kin, apart from those he and Image had brought forth. We marveled at this and talked of how important it is to obey Giver. We are compelled to fill up this great world with our own kind. This reality contributed to my deepening love and devotion to Giver for his wonderful plan.

We passed the entire sky orb journey until darkness

came without eating or leaving Central Grove. We satisfied those needs before going to rest. I insisted that after our sleep Likeness tell me how he came to this place. He agreed to tell me more fully about Image and the offspring. My mind was filled with rapidly tumbling thoughts as I attempted to sleep. Lhaloo was heavy on my mind.

Likeness's Story

I awoke as faint light from the sky orb colored the eastern horizon. Moving quickly from Central Grove, I found a copse of young trees with tender buds drenched with morning dew. I quickly satisfied my hunger. A drink from the nearby brook completely met my needs. I paused to utter praise to Giver and then hurried back to Central Grove.

Likeness was waiting my arrival. He carried a container with a dark, steaming liquid and a portion of some sort of food I did not recognize. I later learned that it was made from a kind of grain that the Likeness clan cultivated. He dipped it into the warm liquid and then thoughtfully chewed it as he prepared to speak of his departure from Home Valley.

"Naados, my friend, listen to me well. Perhaps the Noumaso are unaware of what I'm about to say. We Likeness-Image creatures are strange indeed. We have a tendency to not appreciate what we possess until it is no longer available to us. I suppose that this was our situation in Home Valley. How could any creature from the good hand of Giver have longed for more? Every provision for all our needs was met even before we became. When our eyes opened, we had only to reach and take what we wanted and needed.

"I have relived thousands of times what occurred there at Mystery Grove. Giver had not failed to clearly tell us what we should do. He spoke to me before Image was drawn from my side. He spoke again to the two of us when all was complete. Giver is innocent. I am the guilty one. How I could have permitted my beautiful Image to fall into Beaufang's deception remains a hurtful memory to this very day. See how I weep with the remembering?"

Likeness wiped tears from his eyes before continuing. He laid his hand on my head and then quietly resumed the telling.

"I never expected retribution to be so soon and all encompassing. I try to reason with myself and ask how I could have known what the sting would really be. I never get far before knowing that it is only another attempt to pass blame for my own actions. My poor Image, body of my body, accused as guilty of what was my crime. I thought that Beaufang deserved his punishment, although I have to understand that he was not alone and that the evil of the other went far beyond that of Beaufang.

"When Giver made His pronouncement to Image of her punishment, I was crushed in the center of my being. I had robbed her of the pleasure and ease that Giver had created. What had I done to my poor, beautiful mata? I bear the guilt of my evil each time Image brings new life into this world I bent.

"She slips toward the door of the sting. And in her anguished suffering, all I can do is watch helplessly. Great is my guilt. I deserve the sting. Giver speaks of our future forgiveness. I cannot think far enough to see it. I only trust that it is so because it was Giver who spoke it."

Likeness paused to clear his throat. He seemed to struggle within himself as he gathered his thoughts. Then he spoke in a strong voice his words full of resolve.

"My own punishment is just. The sting should have been my own that long ago day. I vainly try to remember the time before that day and the ease with which Image and I lived and enjoyed being. It is an incomplete memory. My body was strong and my garden tending a pleasure. My brow remained dry and my hands smooth as the skin of our newly become offspring.

"My eyes now weep from the salty drops pouring from my brow. Thorns and bad herbs ruin my fields. My hands are coarse and bear the marks of cuts and scrapes. They scratch the tender skin of my Image when I reach out to comfort her. My back aches with the lifting and strain-ing required keeping my fields productive. My mind is troubled; my heart heavy; and I know that in Giver's good world, the sting is my destiny."

Image had been standing silently a few paces behind Likeness and now moved forward. She tenderly placed her hand on his shoulder and whispered into his ear. Likeness looked into her eyes, patted her hand, and then turned to resume his telling.

"My mind is haunted by the coverings that Giver prepared for us. I never thought that my evil could cause the sting to come to innocent Noumaso. Image and I were terrified when we saw that we were uncovered. That which was so beautiful had turned to unbearable shame and remorse.

"What must Giver have thought when he saw our feeble efforts to cover ourselves with leaves? Now I understand that he knows everything even before it occurs. We were foolish to think we could deceive him.

"I am tormented by the memory of those two beautiful Nouma who did not flinch before the sting but bore it bravely. When Giver blew away our leafy coverings and replaced them with the fresh, bloody Nouma coats, my pride and self-glory dissolved. Image and I felt unworthy to be sovereigns over such innocence.

"The stern order from Giver to leave Home Valley overwhelmed us. How could we live apart from the Noumaso family and the good presence of Giver? Our resistance was futile. The terrifying image of the beings from above and their flaming weapons is etched forever in our consciences. We could never return."

We paused to take refreshment before he continued

the telling. Likeness waited, lost somewhere in long ago memories. He smiled sadly at me before speaking.

"Our minds were so confused that Image and I hardly knew what to do as we were forced from Home Valley. A few of our Nouma friends followed at a distance, but we were alone as we walked down the hillside, away from our only home since becoming.

"I wanted to put some distance between us and the guardians in the pass. Maybe it was out of fear. I do not know. I determined to travel until the sky orb was halfway in the westward journey and then find a place to pass the sleep time. This took us well into the valley just east of Home Valley. We saw numerous Nouma before we stopped beside a brook that flowed through a grove of trees. Food was abundant, so we ate and settled down to sleep. We felt terribly alone and did our best to comfort one another."

Likeness reluctantly focused on the grief and despair that accompanied the telling. His words seemed to come from deep inside, carefully selected to explain what had occurred after the bending.

"We traveled a five-sleep distance before seeking a suitable place to establish a new home. The spot we first chose lay against a gently sloping hill with a beautiful valley spread out before us. I prepared a sleeping place under the edge of trees like the ones we loved in Home Valley and began gathering our favorite foods.

"Several of our Nouma friends joined us and were a great comfort to Image. I began experimenting with growing certain of our favorite plants. It was hard work, just as Giver had said. We passed two night sky orb cycles before we realized that Image was carrying our first offspring. This caused me to think more seriously about where we should live.

"Before Image was unable to travel easily, we decided to move farther east, away from our beloved place of becoming. It was during that time of searching that we found this beautiful valley. Image was two night sky orb cycles from giving me our first offspring. I set to work making an adequate place for her and the coming little Likeness. I tried several kinds of shelters and finally built the first of many like the ones you see here in our village.

"When we were settled and awaited Image's time, Giver came to visit us. We were overjoyed to see him but very ashamed. He enfolded us with his presence as he had done so often before and spoke comforting words to our fearful hearts. Image and I wept a long time but were consoled by the nearness of Giver. He talked about the future and the difficulties we would encounter. He promised that he would not be far away, even when we could not see him.

"During the sleep time after Giver's visit, Image made her first trip toward the sting. Our first offspring, Possessor, entered our world just as the golden sky orb peeked over the eastern hills."

I remembered the arrival of our first twins and the amazing changes that occurred for both Lhaloo and me. I could imagine the topsy-turvy world of Likeness and Image with this first confirmation of Giver's good hand through the arrival of Possessor.

Likeness continued. "Just over three years later, Image again neared the sting to deliver our second child. He is called Morning Mist. Offspring have arrived with regular frequency after our first little Likenesses. We now have forty offspring, and some of them have become two-one creatures. They will soon produce their own offspring.

"Life is beautiful, even with the sting. As you can see, the years have passed quickly. I did what was necessary to provide for Image and our little ones. This cultivated valley and our village are the result of those years of labor and toil.

"We knew that Giver should be the object of our adoration, even if he was not always present. Many years ago, I made a replica of Mystery Grove here in our new home. Here in this place, the entire Likeness family gathers to meet with Giver. Even when he is not present, the family meets to give him worship."

I took the opportunity to ask about the structure beside the flat stone at the entrance to Central Grove.

Likeness considered his answer and then said, "We knew after the sting in Mystery Grove that Giver had strict requirements for his bent creation. As I met with him, I asked how we could please him and let him know we were sorry for our evil. He explained the tragic long-term effects of the bending and the extreme price to be paid one day to straighten the way of Likeness. He said it was necessary to shed innocent blood as a covering for our evil. I was horrified. Only after asking many more questions and hearing Giver's explanations did I understand.

"Certain members of the Noumaso were designated by Giver as innocent victims to roll back the penalty of our evil. This is accomplished as they give up their lives. The shedding of their blood and burning of their bodies is a sacrificial covering for our evil. The dark materials on the stones and the ground are remnants of the burnt wood on which the Nouma were offered. The Nouma remains that do not completely burn must be taken to a special place outside the village and left there."

My mind was reeling after this new information from Likeness. I became physically sick over the loss of innocent life. I started to question Likeness but hesitated. He could tell how distressed I had become and suggested that we stretch ourselves before continuing.

I took the opportunity to run from the village into a thicket, where I became violently ill. That seemed to relieve some of my distress. After wading into a small stream to refresh myself, I returned to Central Grove.

TWO OFFERINGS

I regained my composure as we all returned to Central Grove. Likeness asked Possessor and Morning Mist to join us near the flat stone as he continued his story.

"Our two firstborn offspring, Possessor and Morning Mist, realized that they too should be personally involved in honoring Giver. We discussed how to best do this, and it was agreed that each would prepare something to offer Giver when he next visited. I explained Giver's expectations. Each was to choose his offering.

"Possessor has been quite successful with his

crops, his produce lush and beautiful. We all enjoy it as part of our regular diet. He decided to gather the best of the harvest and offer it to Giver. We were impressed with the bounty and beauty of what he brought for that special gift. Our oldest female offspring, whom Possessor chose to become his mata, was especially proud of the hard work of her soon-to-be two-one partner. She was eager for Giver to come and receive this special gift.

"Morning Mist is different from Possessor, spending most of his time in the fields with the Noumaso. He has domesticated many Nouma and often brings special ones to the village. He had a difficult time choosing his gift. One day, he came from the pastures carrying a young Nouma over his shoulders. It was from his prize flock. He discovered that their kin had a soft, fleecy coat that could be clipped from time to time. Others take the fleece and pull it into single strands to be woven into coverings."

I nodded agreement, faked a sneeze, and said, "Just like those fluffy white balls I suppose."

Likeness smiled and continued his telling.

"Morning Mist placed the young Nouma in an enclosure and gave it food and drink. He carefully cleaned its covering and spent much time talking softly with it.

"Two sleep cycles later, Giver returned to our village. He appeared just before the sky orb disappeared in the west, descending to Central Grove and filling the area around the flat stone with his shining presence. I called Image. She sent word for our offspring to gather.

"We put on the Nouma coverings Giver provided for us at Mystery Grove. They were stiff, and the blood stains yet spotted the beautiful white of the covering. We felt that by wearing the coverings we continued to express our regret for bringing the sting. They remind us of the effects of the bending on us and all Noumaso. Giver called me into his glowing presence and spoke at length. By the time I returned to Image, our entire family had assembled.

"Image and I spoke thanks and praise to Giver. We offered a canticle, and most of our offspring joined us. I then told Giver of our two firstborns' desire to offer him a gift. He expressed pleasure and waited as they slowly approached. They were uncertain how to proceed, but Giver gently urged them forward.

"Possessor was first to move to the stone platform along-side the flat stone where Giver waited. As he approached, he signaled two helpers to come forward. They carried containers of his best produce and at his direction placed the gifts on the end of the platform nearest Giver. Silence was complete as Possessor briefly waited. Then he and the two helpers slowly backed away.

"Morning Mist hesitated long enough to reach for the Nouma at his feet. It remained silent as he swung it onto his shoulders and moved slowly forward. He also had two helpers. One carried a basket filled with pieces of wood topped by a bunch of dried herbs. The other had a clay container filled with glowing coals and a sharp knife."

My mind was spinning with this telling. The glowing coals were what I had seen inside the Likeness dwelling. Thinking about the innocent Nouma over his shoulders brought shivers along my spine. I remembered the two Nouma in Mystery Grove. I could not get the memory of how they received the sting out of my mind. I regained control and listened as Likeness continued.

"The helper with the basket of wood placed the dried herbs on the end of the platform away from Giver. He then carefully placed pieces of wood over the herbs and backed away.

"Morning Mist moved to the platform and gently lifted the Nouma from his shoulders. He placed it on the wood and pushed its head back, with the neck turned upward. He looked toward Giver and said something so quietly that none of us understood it. He then reached for the knife that his second helper carried and drew it across the neck of the Nouma. Bright red blood splashed on the wood. The Nouma quivered but made no effort to resist. The crimson flow passed through the wood and pooled on the platform. A small trickle moved down the side of the stone platform and dripped to the waiting ground. The silence was intense.

"When it was evident that the Nouma had fully tasted the sting, Morning Mist reached for the glowing coals. He dumped them on the platform and with a small stick pushed them under the wood and into the dried herbs. He bent and blew softly on the glowing coals. The herbs burst into flame, and soon the wood was burning brightly."

I felt faint at the picture Likeness described to me. I could imagine the fear in the eyes of the Nouma, the feel of the sharp blade on my own neck. I quickly looked to make sure no blood was flowing.

This was the first time the effects of what Likeness called fire were described to me. Remembering the burnt chips of wood from around the platform, I understood what the fire did to the Nouma. First, the searing heat igniting the fluffy fleece burning it almost instantly; then the intense flames starting to consume the body probably produced a sizzling, crackling sound.

Likeness spoke me back to reality as he continued recounting the offerings.

"Satisfied that the Nouma was being consumed by the fire, Morning Mist backed away and joined the others. We all waited silently to see what Giver would say."

I glanced at Possessor as he said something under his breath and looked sharply at Morning Mist. For a moment, I thought I faintly detected the malevolent presence from Mystery Grove behind Possessor. I glanced at Morning Mist and then back to Possessor. There was now no indication of that terrible presence.

"When the remains of the Nouma were almost consumed on the platform, Giver spoke from his shining cloak.

Likeness's seed brought forth today
First offerings to Giver
From their hearts out through their hands
Their thoughts are shared forever
Morning Mist has chosen well
The way to endless living
He understood my just demands
True offering is giving
Possessor's pride in his own work
Displays no understanding
Likeness's telling he heeded not
Ignored my just demanding

But do not fear, I AM here
When you turn to the good path
Live out my ways for all your days
You need not suffer my wrath

Possessor was not pleased when Likeness told this part about Giver's visit. He noisily left the group and walked away from the village. Likeness continued.

"Giver saw that Possessor was very angry. His expression and appearance completely changed. Giver assured him that he would be accepted if he did what was right, but the choice was his.

"I realized again, Naados, what a gift free choice is for us as Likeness-Image creatures. Being made like Giver is a gift you do not have, but you also do not carry the weight of your forever being determined by your choice.

"And so, Naados, we go from day to day. Giver is near. He is not always visible. We are, and we do what we must. Image and I daily ask Giver for strength to instruct our offspring well. They are bent, some more than others. We know it is because of our choice in Mystery Grove. We endure the pain of our own doing. We also enjoy the bounty of Giver's good hand. Life is beautiful, even with the sting."

First Sting for the Likeness Clan

I decided it was time to return to Home Valley. Finding Likeness and Image was rewarding and enlightening, but so much information at one time wearied me. My mind was filled with conflicting and confusing thoughts, especially about Possessor's and Morning Mist's offerings to Giver.

I said my goodbyes to Likeness and Image as they took refreshment for the new day. They urged me to remain for a while but understood my desire to return to Home Valley. With their best wishes for Lhaloo ringing in my ears, I headed west out of the village.

Passing between two great groves of trees, I heard Likeness voices. One sounded loud and angry. I started to call out but thought better of it. Instead, I moved silently toward the voices. Stopping under some low-hanging branches, I spotted two likeness males in an adjoining field. It was Possessor and Morning Mist. Staying in the shadows, I moved forward to better hear the discussion.

My ears hurt to hear Possessor's language. He spoke harshly to his brother, calling him words unfamiliar to me. From the look on Morning Mist's face, they were not good words. I detected a darkening, subtle change in the trees behind Possessor. Hardly believing my eyes, I saw the malevolent misty presence that had surrounded Beaufang in Mystery Grove detach from the trees and rush to envelope Possessor. Possessor immediately hurled insults and curses on his brother and then shook his fist at the heavens and said wicked things about Giver.

Morning Mist turned away, but Possessor rushed after him. As he pursued his brother, he stooped and grabbed a large stone. The presence darkened around Possessor as he reached Morning Mist. I could not move. Possessor shouted in rage as he reached Morning Mist and then swung the stone with all his strength, striking Morning Mist above his right ear. Blood exploded from the wound, and Morning Mist dropped to the ground. Possessor leaped toward him and continued pounding with the stone. The blood and gaping wounds made it clear that Morning Mist had felt the sting.

Uncontrollable weeping and a feeling of utter helplessness overwhelmed me. I had witnessed a Likeness creature take the life of another of his kind, his own brother.

The violence of his actions nauseated me. Possessor stood over the lifeless form, still clutching the bloody stone. The dark, malevolent presence melted away. Possessor shuddered, looked at the bloody stone in his hand, and then threw it to the ground as he realized the horror of what he had done.

Guilt filled his face as he quickly looked all around to see if any other Likeness kin was near. Seeing no one, he dropped to the ground and put his head in his hands, moaning softly. "What have I done? What have I done?" he said repeatedly.

I shivered, remembering that Beaufang said the same thing after his role in the sting. I was too traumatized to move. I could only look on the unfolding tragedy and imagine the consequences. Giver's punishment for the willful disobedience by Likeness and Image impacted all of us. Their act had destroyed a life made by Giver. Would we all now feel the sting as punishment for this evil action?

Possessor realized the seriousness of his actions and moved to hide the lifeless body of Morning Mist. He found a shallow dip in the edge of the field and dragged the body into it. He hastily gathered small stones and threw them around the body and then began scooping loose, sandy soil over them. Sweat dropped from his contorted face as he leveled the spot and then remembered the bloody stone. He found it and put it into the shallow burial place with his brother's body. He dragged a tree limb with leafy branches over the burial spot until the ground looked undisturbed except for the absence of grass growing on it. He sat down in the shadow of a nearby tree and wiped his brow. I wept softly.

Giver descended to the field and hovered over Possessor, who looked shocked by his appearance. Giver spoke.

"Firstborn seed of Likeness and Image, where is your brother, Morning Mist?"

"How should I know?" Possessor rudely retorted. "Is it my job to watch out for him?"

I was astonished at the way Possessor spoke to Giver. His bending went far beyond that of Likeness and Image. His act of murder had turned his heart to stone.

Giver spoke again. "Morning Mist's blood shouts to me from the shallow grave where you buried him. Your hands are bloody with the life of your brother. Now listen well to me. You are condemned to roam the earth. When you plant crops and harvest them, you will get very little."

Possessor argued with Giver. "That's not fair. The punishment you give is not just. I am not able to bear it. Here you are pushing me away from this good part of the earth. I cannot settle down and live a normal life. If any of my kin find me, they will surely deprive me of my life."

I could not understand Possessor's argument with Giver. He had given the sting. The only just punishment was to forfeit his life in return. He showed no remorse for his brother, only for himself. How far from Giver his wicked bent heart had gone.

Giver spoke again to Possessor. "I am capable of making sure you are not killed by your kin. I'm putting a mark on you to warn all others that I am responsible for your judgment. They will be afraid to touch you. Now get up. You must go with me to tell Likeness of your deed. You will be given your mata and chased far away from the east of this valley as part of the punishment."

I remained hidden for some time after they left. I could not bear to face Likeness and Image as they received the news of this tragic loss to their family.

Goodbye to Lhaloo

My memory of the return to Home Valley was clouded by grief and the pain from watching Morning Mist brutally feel the sting. Night fears haunted me when I tried to sleep. Rushing toward home as the sky orb passed overhead, my troubled mind replayed the horror over and over again.

When I reached the pass leading into Home Valley, the presence of the shining guardians jerked me back to reality. It was comforting to know that they were always there and always the same.

Not knowing where to find Lhaloo, I headed for Mystery Grove as quickly as possible. Fatigue caused me to stop and pass a short and agitated night. After rest, my quick pace brought me to Mystery Grove after the sky orb passed the midway point overhead. The relief I began to feel was immense. Even seeing the flat sacrificial stone seemed to calm my troubled spirit.

For the first time since starting home, I relaxed and cropped a few mouthfuls of my favorite food. Putting the horror of the events from my mind, I listened to comforting sounds of Nouma going about their Giver-assigned tasks. For a short time, it was almost as if the becoming had just occurred.

Eager as I was to find Lhaloo, my tired body again took control and responded to the pleasant warmth of the sky orb. I dropped to the ground and slept. Sometime during the passing of the night sky orb, I half-awoke, saw my surroundings, and returned to my first peaceful rest since leaving Likeness's home.

Cheerful morning sounds stirred me to consciousness. Sweet smells of my home reminded me that I had not adequately eaten for some time. I moved to a grove of young trees and eagerly stripped tender buds from the branches. I ate until satisfied and then turned to seek Lhaloo.

Lhaloo was not at the last resting place we shared before I left to find Likeness. I saw some old friends nearby and inquired about her. They told me of the last place she and our kin had been seen. I was eager to see my beloved mata, so I ran quickly in the direction indicated. Even at a distance, I knew her. She was among a group of our offspring and their offspring grazing near the shade of a grove of young trees.

Unable to hold my excitement, I rushed forward, shouting her name as I ran. She raised her head and looked toward me and then jumped from among the young offspring and bolted in my direction. We were one again.

News of my return quickly spread through the valley. Nouma were excitedly talking about my time with Likeness and Image. The Noumaso eagerly awaited my report about Likeness. The following day, they gathered at Mystery Grove and I told the entire story.

The Noumaso were overjoyed to hear of Likeness's offspring. Tales of the village and strange sleeping places intrigued everyone. Few could grasp the concept of food that had to be gathered and changed before eating. We all simply ate from the bounty around us.

No one seemed surprised that Likeness had made a replica of Mystery Grove in his new home. News about the platform where Nouma were placed and made to feel the sting caused great distress. I found it difficult to explain why such offerings were necessary. The mysterious thing Likeness called fire intrigued everyone. They were awestruck as I described how it was used to consume sacrifices offered to Giver.

I found enough courage to tell them about Possessor and Morning Mist. The entire gathering fell silent and then broke into uncontrollable mourning. The sorrow expressed when our Nouma brothers felt the sting was deep, but nothing compared to this news. We all somehow understood that Giver's reason for our becoming was closely tied to Likeness and his kin. The tragic sting of Morning Mist left the Noumaso of Home Valley unable to fully express their grief. We felt terrible sorrow. *Her* time had now been born. Many questioned what price we would now pay until the sting took us away.

Subdued by the unexpected news, the Noumaso slipped away. All we could do was ponder what would become of Likeness's kin. Lhaloo and I returned to where she had been resting and quietly talked during most of the passing of the night sky orb. We didn't go far from the resting place for many days. I wanted to be with her. She wanted me to retell every part of my adventure.

I decided to stay in Home Valley. My visit with Likeness had lessened my desire to travel. Twenty-three more of what Likeness calls years passed contentedly. Lhaloo and I produced fourteen more offspring. Each time she brought another new life was more difficult for her.

The passage of years was taking a great toll on her stamina and appearance. Her once sleek, shiny coat changed from a glossy, healthy tan to a dull gray. It had hard, dark splotches that became irritated and seeped a foul-smelling liquid. She had a poor appetite and moved slowly and deliberately. Rarely did she frolic in the fields and forests as before. She remained near our resting place, often passing extended periods of time lying on the ground, gazing into the distance. She wanted me nearby and called out if she lost sight of me. She had difficulty seeing me if I stood in a shadow or near a tree.

I became especially concerned when Lhaloo started forgetting past events. It was almost as if some things had not occurred, and I had to remind her over and over.

Some of the effects of passing time on Noumaso included drastic change in the body and mental processes. I did not have the heart to tell Lhaloo about eating from the life tree so long ago. It appeared much too late for anything to help her. I wondered how much she noticed the difference in her appearance and my own. I chose not to speak about it, matching her slower pace and feigning lapses in my memory. I'm not sure if that was proper, but I did not want Lhaloo to feel alone as she neared the sting.

Perhaps at a later time I will learn Likeness's term for what I was feeling. It must somehow have been wrapped up in what Giver felt toward his Likeness-Image creatures. I only knew that my thoughts were often captured by memories of when Lhaloo and I were much younger. These were thoughts far too deep for me as I consoled my beloved. She was slowly slipping away from me, and I could do nothing about it. My sorrow was deepening. Even so, Giver was good and life is beautiful, as we awaited the coming sting.

Not many days later, Lhaloo slipped and fell while reaching to crop a mouthful of tender buds. She was in intense pain. Her tired face contorted, and she uttered grunting cries with every strained breath. I stooped to speak comfort to her and then lay down against her and tenderly licked her face. Lhaloo sighed deeply and nestled close. We remained there all through the passage of the sky orb. She finally relaxed and indicated that her pain had eased. She nibbled at nearby clumps of herbs as I stayed close by her side.

Just as the sky orb slipped toward the distant range of

hills, she struggled to stand. I stood near to steady her. She spoke of Giver and his goodness. She started to speak to me but stopped as her eyes filled with tears. We touched faces in silence as we had done so often in the past. No words were necessary. We understood that the sting was the eventual destiny of all Givers' creation.

Lhaloo insisted that I take a short walk and graze on tender buds. She knew that I had not taken enough nourishment. I resisted, but she gently nudged me away. I reluctantly moved away, pausing to look back from time to time. Lhaloo kept silent sentinel where I left her. I will remember that moment forever.

I trotted down a small incline, stopped to drink from a brook, and then cropped tender buds nearby. It did not take long for me to be satisfied. I was anxious about Lhaloo, so I quickly turned to retrace my steps. I tried to spot Lhaloo as I started up the incline, but she was nowhere to be seen.

I ran quickly to where I left her. I looked anxiously around and spotted where she had headed deeper into the dense growth. Descending darkness caused me to move slowly. I stopped often and called out to her but heard no response.

I had gone no more than fifty paces when I saw her on the ground. I rushed to her side and spoke. She did not respond. I knelt beside her and saw her eyes open with a blank stare. My heart broke as I recognized that she had felt the sting.

I fell to the ground beside her still-warm body and nestled close. I remained there while the night sky orb passed overhead. I had not strength to move even when the eastern sky turned crimson as the sky orb climbed to his daily journey. My beloved Lhaloo was no more. I wept.

After pushing leaves and twigs around her body, I rose to say a word to Giver. The word would not come. How does one say goodbye to his mata? My heart was crushed with the realization that she was gone. I walked several paces away and lay down across the small trail. I remained there long enough to relive in my mind much of my life with Lhaloo. The memories were sweet, but the reality was bitter to my spirit.

What Next?

I sought our remaining offspring in Home Valley and told them of Lhaloo's final days. They had been uncertain how to react to her obvious decline. One after another told me of the special times they had grazed and enjoyed the one who had carried them to their becoming. I realized how much I did not know about my offspring. Guilt slipped across my thoughts. My choice to explore the world had kept me from much normal Nouma interaction. I keep kept these musings to myself.

Following my loss of Lhaloo, I became much more aware of the effect of the sting on the whole of Noumaso. I learned that the sting had been taking Nouma away since my first river trip. The length of living for Noumaso varied greatly. The smaller of our kin had short times of being. I was an exception because of the life tree. It appeared that in my own Nouma, Lhaloo had a long period of being. For me, it was far too short.

I passed another ten Likeness years exploring Home Valley. Occasionally, one or more of my offspring accompanied me. These times gave me the opportunity to tell them of the becoming and of my wide-ranging travel. It also permitted me to pass on knowledge given for our Nouma, the special things Likeness had spoken in my ear at my naming. During the early part of these years, my memories of Lhaloo remained strong.

I awoke one day and realized that I no longer continually thought about Lhaloo. I felt shame at that realization. Giver must have given me the next thought, for it rang strongly in my head. *Being is for now and tomorrow. The good and bad from yesterday must not dominate my days in Giver's good creation.*

Unsure what to do next; I explored the sources for the four great rivers flowing out from Home Valley. For whatever reason, I had never thought to seek their origin but was always interested in where they were going. I climbed the side of a northern slope to look out over the valley. I had done this many times before but never to seek the source of our abundant water. Halfway up the slope, I was able to see parts of all four rivers. Far to the northwest, they appeared to come together. This became my destination.

A three-sleep journey brought me to the area where

the rivers separated to flow in different directions. The source was a large lake. Far to one end of the lake was a huge cavern in the side of the mountain. I made my way there, awed by the wide rush of sparkling water gushing out. I guessed it to be several hundred paces wide with a depth I could not determine. It flowed only a short distance and then formed the large, beautiful lake. Two streams flowed from the lake in an easterly direction, the other two toward the west. The lake was some distance above the floor of the valley.

As I looked out over the lake and valley, I decided that I would continue to explore Giver's good creation. Nothing remained that required my staying in Home Valley.

There must be Nouma who do not know about Likeness and Image. Maybe they do not know the story of the first sting. Because of the life tree, I am as strong as the day of my becoming. Since my beloved mata has felt the sting, I have no Nouma who require my presence. The thought was disturbing but exciting. I returned one last time to visit the grove where my mata had returned to the soil.

I never left Home Valley without going by Mystery Grove. I was probably the only Nouma who could now find it. It was nothing like it looked on the day of becoming. The grove had grown into a large, dense forest. Trees reached skyward, the undergrowth a single tangled mass.

I walked carefully around until I found a small opening. Thorn bushes and briars were everywhere, but I was determined to return to the center. My body was scratched and bleeding when I pushed through the last obstacle to the flat stone. It was dark because of the trees' branches overhead. Vines twisted around everything. My eyes adapted to the darkness, and stepping to the overgrown stone, I tried to see the life tree and the knowing tree. To my surprise, when I spotted them hidden among thick growth, they were the same size as the day I cropped leaves from the life tree. I stored that detail away in my mind for future reflection.

No Nouma had been here since my visit several years before. I stopped to think about Giver and the becoming. I was held captive by memories of the first sting. My mind sped through events until the present. Cries of feathered Noumaso from the trees overhead drew me back and reminded me that darkness was quickly descending. I turned and worked my way out of the grove. The night sky orb was peering over the horizon. I quickly cropped a mouthful of tender leaves and settled in for my time of rest.

Frosty Breath, and Furry Coats

A last few goodbyes in Home Valley, and I headed toward the lake and the source of the four rivers. Excitement helped me cut the three-sleep trip to two long days of travel. I swam across two frigid streams to reach the banks of the river flowing northwest. I paused to strip tender buds and let my wet coat dry in the heat of the sky orb. The blue sky overhead felt close and protective. Sweet smells from Home Valley filled my senses. I once more turned my back on what was familiar to seek out the unknown.

Three more sleep times were necessary before I reached the gorge where Northwest River flowed from Home Valley. Noumaso of many kinds lived along the way. I stopped for brief conversations on my way to the gorge. Until the time I left Home Valley, all Nouma kin I met knew what happened since the sting. They had done a good job telling their offspring and reminding one another of past occurrences.

Wide plains spread to the valley walls on both sides of the river where it entered the gorge. Half a day's journey downstream, the water deepened and narrowed. Rising timbered hillsides crowded the river but left enough room to travel the banks. The river here became a rushing waterway. I did not like the feeling of being closed in by the narrowing walls of the hills. Fortunately, the narrow passage was not long. After a short distance, the river emerged from the gorge and slowed. The grassy banks widened into a lush, green paradise for grazing. I paused to rest and eat.

Darkness approached when I found a group of my Nouma and spent the night with them. They welcomed me and shared the best of their food sources. We talked of Giver and his good creation. Some of them knew about me. My travels were evidently being told in more heroic ways than they occurred. I resisted the temptation to correct the exaggerations and tried to be humble telling the events as they had happened. We spent half of the rest time in pleasant conversation.

Being with my own Nouma helped me pass an enjoyable time of rest. At first light, most of them scattered across the valley floor, seeking food. Several remained and led me to sample their favorite dew-covered morning delicacies.

One young female had remained closeby during our conversations. She now grazed nearby. She was sleek and beautiful like my former mata, Lhaloo. She was not yet attached and made that clear to me. She had no way of knowing that I may have been one of her earliest ancestors.

Her interest reminded me that I would face this kind of situation often. My long ago lunch from the life tree kept me young. My Nouma feelings from Giver caused me to be attracted to this unattached female kin. At some point, I would probably take another mata since I was a healthy specimen of my Nouma, preserved just as I was when I ate from the life tree. But this was not the time. My determination to explore Giver's creation was more demanding than settling down with another mata. I pushed the interest aside, said goodbye, and moved toward the river to continue my journey.

Members of the behemoth kin were numerous in the slow-moving portions of the river just as they had been in Southeast River. These were not part of the behemoth that came from Home Valley and did not know of events since the becoming. My behemoth kin gathered their clans and settled in for several days of the telling. In addition to those who lived in the water, Nouma land kin were also invited. I must admit that I did not remember all of the Nouma from the becoming. Of course, we Nouma are more aware of our own personal kin than others different from us.

Some of the dry land behemoth kin are strange indeed—their size incredible. I'm glad we are all family.

Their appearance would be terrifying if we were hostile. Young Nouma always crowded in close when I did the telling but sometimes proved disruptive. They were often sent away so that older Nouma could listen without distraction and ask questions about the events.

As always, members from every Nouma kin agreed to carry the story to others in their valleys. This permitted me to explore more distant groups and places.

Days and seasons merged into multiplied years as I traveled the Northwest River valley. Nowhere in this vast region did I encounter any of Likeness's kin. I'm now certain that the only ones who became were my two friends, Likeness and Image. Thinking about this causes me to marvel at Giver's good plan. He is, so we are. Likeness and his kin bring good and evil on all Noumaso. We do not have the possibility of choice as do he and his kin.

Giver, you alone are all my hope.

I often considered my destiny. Unable to feel the sting, I wandered the vast expanses of Giver's creation. Joy, peace happiness—they all expressed my inner feeling as I faced each rising of the sky orb. Sorrow, pain, uncertainty—these crowded the corners of my mind as I sought to make each new situation one that would honor Giver. My journeys as a messenger for Giver and his purpose gave me contentment.

This journey soon became different from others I had made. As the river turned to flow north, the temperature underwent a big change. Each day after the sky orb disappeared in the west, the air became increasingly cool. Instead of sleeping in the open or in a small copse, it was more comfortable to seek shelter in dense growth with soft, dry grass on the ground. Before the sky orb appeared in the morning, my breath sent silvery billows into the cool air. It resembled morning mist in Home Valley during the times the sky orb no longer passed directly overhead but much farther to the south.

The appearance of most of the Noumaso was also different. They had heavier coverings than my own and lived in dark, snug caves. I stopped often and spoke with them about Giver and the becoming. They were unaware of how they had become. It was with great joy I gathered the eager Noumaso and told them of our shared becoming. Huge but gentle woolly mammoths listened along-side white coated bears and vast herds of Nouma similar to my kin. I never ceased to be amazed by their vast numbers as they moved across the frozen earth. The story never failed to impress my Noumaso kin. They promised to share the telling of Giver with their fellow Nouma.

The closer I came to where the river flowed into the great salt water, the more noticeable these changes were. I later learned that Nouma appearance depends on how far north they live. I am slowly learning the amazing adaptations Noumaso make as they scatter over Giver's creation.

After many more Likeness years, I reached the vast, salty, roaring waters. I did not remain long. I wanted to become better acquainted with the strikingly different kinds of Nouma but the cold breeze blew off the water and made me long for the warmth of Home Valley.

How marvelous were the works of Giver. In every place and by all Noumaso, his name was revered. The thousands of Nouma encountered on this river again showed me the vastness of his creation.

I turned back toward Home Valley and traveled the opposite side of the river. The farther away from the frigid northern waters I went, the more comfortable the journey became. Visits with Nouma groups were routine, but my return took less time than going.

When I next see Likeness, he will need to tell me of the exact number of his years since our last meeting. I focus more on remembering meetings with Nouma than counting days.

Unsurpassed beauty is how I always describe Home Valley. Nothing is better than what is your own. Giver made Home Valley mine. During my years of travel, many changes occurred in my home. Old friends left behind felt the sting and joined my Lhaloo in the dust. Others replaced them. Hardly anyone remembers me. Home is no longer fully home, for I have become a stranger to its inhabitants. This must be a preview of what my life will be from now on. I hope to see Likeness's kin again soon. Maybe that will give my life a greater sense of continuity and purpose.

NORTHEAST RIVER
The Search for Likeness's Kin

My stay in Home Valley was short. Locating
Mystery Grove was becoming increasingly difficult.
For whatever reason, the Noumaso had abandoned
a large area around Mystery Grove. This permitted
the encroachment of rapidly growing forests. Most
of the nearby grazing areas were crowded with a
dense cover of new trees. It took me two days to
locate the grove, and it was evident that no other
Nouma had entered there since my last visit.

I did not want to forget this part of my past, but
I found it increasingly difficult to reach the center

of Mystery Grove. I supposed that the danger of others eating from the life tree or knowing tree was now almost nonexistent and probably for the best. The shining light from the guardian sentinels on the mountain could still be seen. I wondered how long Giver would leave them on their lonely assignment.

I traveled northeast, crossing several small streams and then finally Southeast River. I passed to the left of the guardians' position. The next day's travel took me to the Northeast River, which I followed downstream.

This area was more difficult to travel than the southern route by which Giver had driven Likeness from Home Valley. It had a rugged sort of beauty. Steep hills lined the river as far as I could see. Sure-footed Nouma traveled the narrow trails, skirting chasms with rushing streams and plunging waterfalls.

Varieties of plants and trees not seen in Home Valley grew in profusion. Shiny stones in the riverbanks, cut out by the rushing water, sent flashing reflections back to the sky orb. Swimming creatures splashed and jumped in the streams. No behemoths inhabited these waters, but certain of their small land kin roamed the lower ranges of the hills.

As usual, I stopped and talked with Nouma everywhere. Most did not know about Likeness and his kin. I never grow tired of the telling but am overwhelmed by their reactions upon finding out about the origin of the sting. I constantly looked for Likeness's kin but did not find any until after many cycles of the night orb.

I did not expect to see Likeness and Image in this area. My hope was to find Possessor's kin. With all his faults,

Possessor had been kind to me. I remembered him with sorrow and disgust I also remembered the role that the malevolent presence played in his actions. My hope was that he turned from his bending and was truly seeking to please Giver. Even with my desire to find him, I took all the time necessary to tell the uninformed Nouma of our story.

I slept high on the side of a rugged peak, hoping to see the sky orb peer over the eastern horizon. I awoke just as the velvet night lightened with the promise of the coming sky orb. As the first rays shot toward the sky, I noticed a subtle color difference near the earth that looked as if light from the sky orb was passing through a colored mist. Since the river I followed flowed in that direction, I cropped some tender shoots and headed east toward the sky orb.

From time to time, I thought I saw the color difference but could not be certain. I moved from the riverbank to cross hills and valleys as I traveled eastward. After two more sleep times, the rising sky orb showed the large, hazy covering over a distant valley. I was puzzled by what I saw and pushed ahead to reach the valley.

With the sky orb directly overhead, I topped a hill that fell away to the wide river valley. I would have arrived here by following Northeast River but had cut travel time going across country. Spread out before me lay a vast Likeness settlement.

The pathways traversing the settlement were not like those in Likeness's village. They turned and twisted in all directions. Fields surrounded the settlement, as did groves of fruit-bearing trees.

Some outlying dwellings had fields alongside. Others

near the center of the settlement were close together. A few were stacked one on top of another. They had stone layers on the ground with earth-colored material placed on them. Many reached up several times higher than Likeness's kin's height. I slipped into the shade of nearby trees as I considered my discovery. Memories of the wound from Possessor's weapon reminded me to be cautious.

I turned my focus to Likeness's kin scattered through the settlement. I had been away longer than I realized. There were more than I took time to count, busily going about their activities. Domesticated Nouma moved among Likeness's kin.

Unfamiliar sounds reached my ears from the large number of inhabitants, many of them unnatural sounds. Some were sharp and hurt my ears. Others were more gentle but not recognizable. I decided to stay under the trees and wait before going down into the settlement. I grazed and then settled down to observe.

So much was new and different that I found it was hard to understand. We Nouma preferred to be with our own kind. We preferred things the way Giver made them. Likeness' bent kin evidently preferred changing Giver's good creation. What they had done with it was not pleasing to my Nouma eyes.

The longer I looked into the valley, the more I understood the strange color I detected in the sky. All through the settlement, I saw the glow of the thing Likeness called fire. It flamed in places where various activities were taking place. I saw several round domes made from earth with flames inside. From openings, there emerged rapidly rising, swirling, dark plumes clouding the air around. It was the great number of these sources that combined to make the strange color hovering over the settlement and the long valley.

Possessor and His Kin

After a less than satisfying rest time, I decided to enter the valley. I encountered young Likeness kin soon after emerging from the forest rimming the valley. Cautiously, I called out as I approached them. They responded by shaking their hands at me and shouting, "Hey, Nouma! Stay out of our fields!" One whistled to a canine by his side and sent him running and barking in my direction.

Resisting the urge to turn and run, I waited until

my canine Nouma kin was nearby and then said, "Is this the way Nouma treat one another?"

He slid to a stop and said, "Sorry. We Nouma around here don't speak to one another much anymore. The Likeness kin no longer wish to associate with us in that way. Welcome, my brother but be careful where you speak."

We talked briefly, and I saw that the Likeness kin seemed puzzled. We moved to where they stood, deep in conversation.

"Offspring of Likeness," I said, "the Noumaso call me Naados. I come from Home Valley and know both Likeness and his offspring, Possessor." When I said *Possessor,* their manner changed at once. They introduced themselves and asked me to follow them into the settlement.

They called to one and then another of their kin as we moved from the fields into the maze of pathways. From a distance, I had not realized how wide the walkways were in the settlement. The ground under my feet was hard, and no herbs grew in it. Some of the pathways were, I realized, made from flat stones placed side by side.

There were places where water flowed from small, Likeness-made channels into holding basins. I asked if I might drink and was led to a low, long basin where other Nouma were drinking. They had fouled the water, but my thirst overcame the disgust I felt drinking the unclean liquid.

I saw some of the domed places with fire inside and recognized the kind of prepared nourishment that Likeness had so long ago eaten in my presence. It was being heated and was turning deep brown in the fire.

I also saw places where fire was being made white hot.

I glanced into it and quickly turned away, but not soon enough. My eyes filled with pulsating flashes of brilliant light. My guides laughed as they saw me shake my head in an attempt to regain my sight.

"It will be all right in just a bit," one of them said. "Just stop and close your eyes."

He was right. The sensation quickly passed, and I could see normally.

I watched workers reach into the intense heat with long implements and pull out glowing pieces. They placed one piece on another large, hard object and began to pound it with something large they held in their hands. I was astounded. My guides thought it quite amusing.

We went some distance into the settlement and then stopped before a large Likeness resting place. I was instructed to wait while one of the young Likeness kin went inside. He soon emerged with an adult Likeness male. I studied him carefully as he approached. I thought that it was probably Possessor, but his appearance made me unsure. His head was covered with long, dark hair that continued down the sides of his face, joined under his nose, circled his mouth, and continued below his chin.

He paused, stared at me, and then threw his head back and laughed. "Naados, is that you? But your Nouma feel the sting long before the age you must be. The life tree story must really be true."

Possessor dismissed my guides and led me to an area covered by branches of a beautiful flowering tree. He called, and his mata came from the dwelling. I recognized her from long ago in Likeness's village. My mind flashed back to her part in presenting the two offerings. She kindly welcomed me and brought a basin of fresh water for me to drink. She invited me to eat from a budding bush nearby, but I refused. My excitement at finding this couple took away all hunger.

It was time for the telling, and I could hardly wait to listen to Possessor. I stayed in this place for many sky orb crossings. What follows is Possessor's short telling of events after he came away from Likeness's village.

"I know you were nearby, Naados, when I let the evil presence take control of my passions so long ago. You must have hated me when you witnessed my brutal killing of Morning Mist. Not one passage of the sky orb has occurred without my thinking of that terrible time. The pain that it brought to Likeness and Image is more than I can bear. Sorrow and remorse cover me. I cannot tell you how I dreaded facing those who gave me life with Giver standing alongside. No sleep is ever deep enough to give me complete rest.

"Not only do I bear the shame of my deed, but Giver put a mark on me to keep others from taking my life in vengeance. Out of shame, I try to cover the mark, but everyone sees beyond the hair on my face and knows the truth. Being forced away from my home was pain beyond belief. I understood some of what my givers of life felt when they were forced to leave Home Valley.

"Oh, the constant burden of the bending. I came to this place after being chased away to the east. We are such a long distance from Likeness's village that until recently, no others have come here. Life is hard, but Giver made our world to have all we need. Hard work has been a constant part of our lives.

"Offspring came quickly and now come frequently. My mata has been near the sting many times and always emerged with new life in her arms. She is a wonderful two-one partner from Giver. Our offspring and their offspring now add to our world.

"Giver has placed many special abilities in them, but they do not recognize that it comes from him. They also choose to follow my stubborn path. This city is named after our firstborn, Branded. He shares my marks and many of my characteristics. Unfortunately, they are not all good.

"Branded has a firstborn known as Wild Donkey. He could never be kept confined to the city. Even while very young, he caused us great anxiety by taking frequent trips alone into the forests and mountains. His wanderlust has now taken him far to the southeast with some of his offspring. Wild Donkey's firstborn is called Giver's Combat. We all acknowledge that Giver constantly makes efforts to regain his rightful place among us. Most of us are not heeding his appeals. Giver's Combat's first offspring is Giver's Man. He bears this name as an expression of our hope, but he is not fulfilling it in living."

I was amazed at the direct meaning in the names of the Likeness offspring. They told much of the nature and character of each individual. I was happy that we Noumaso had only to remember the simple names given us by Likeness at our becoming.

Possessor continued. "Giver's Man's first offspring is called Overthrower. He has rejected all efforts by Giver to bring him back from the bending. As proof of this determination, he has taken two mata. One carries the name

Pleasure. He took her to satisfy his own base desires. The other is called Protection. She has the oversight of the household and the offspring.

"We know this is a serious violation of Giver's plan because it breaks the bonds of Likeness relationships and creates confusion for the offspring. Overthrower is so determined in his twisted thinking that he took the life of a young Likeness male who spoke to one of his mata. He speaks against Giver by declaring that he will carry out more serious punishment to his enemies than even Giver could do.

"Overthrower's mata, Pleasure, gave him two male offspring. River is the firstborn. He is always moving, never still. He is a nomadic herdsman, wandering the far valleys and plains. Her second born is Celebration. No two offspring could be more different. Celebration has the making of music in his being. He has devised instruments of music and shows others how to use them to make pleasing sounds.

"Protection, Overthrower's second mata, gave him an offspring called Forger. He knows how to take stones from the earth and with great heat turn them into glowing liquid. This liquid can then be changed into useful objects."

I could not resist asking about this marvel. Possessor told me that the fiery object that had caused distress to my eyes was a place for turning stones to flaming liquid.

"Protection also gave Overthrower a female offspring. She is called Pleasant Sweetness. From time to time, an offspring brings great enjoyment. She is one such."

Possessor's offspring continue to multiply and scatter into many parts of the east. He told me that some of them are moving back to the west and encountering other of Likeness and Image's offspring. He said that several of his kin's beautiful female offspring had been taken as mata by Likeness's male offspring. He seemed pleased that the mark put on him was not hindering the uniting of the clans of Likeness.

I was treated with kindness during my stay in Branded City. That kindness did not take away my feeling ill at ease. It was not because of what I saw but what I did not see. There was no evidence of any effort to meet with Giver in Branded City.

While there were no places where Likeness's kin gathered to talk about Giver or instruct their offspring about him, there were many gathering places where loud talk and riotous laughter could be heard. In some of the dark, narrow passageways, there always seemed to be male and female Likeness kin engaged in improper activities for public places.

I said what I could about Giver when the opportunity presented itself, but how could I take the role of messenger to Likeness-Image creatures? I knew much about them by observation and by my friendship with Likeness, but I did not possess their unique relationship to Giver. Neither did I have the capacity to choose to disobey Giver. *I thank you, Giver; that I only desire to obey you.*

After two cycles of the night sky orb, I started back toward Home Valley. As I thought about my return, it occurred to me that this was a good time to visit Likeness again. I said goodbye to Possessor and his growing clans. He indicated the most direct way to Likeness's valley and gave his blessings for my departure. I wondered what would become of this part of Giver's bent creation.

Visiting Lord Likeness

Possessor had been right about his offspring scattering back to the west. In the many crossings of the sky orb required to find Likeness, it was rare that I did not encounter scattered groups of Possessor's kin. They always showed me kindness and extended hospitality. They lived in villages, usually near a stream or small river, and were accompanied by members of the most commonly domesticated Noumaso. I found this part of Giver's world becoming more populated than was to my liking.

Everything looked different than from my last visit. I was approaching Likeness's home from the east instead of the west. As I came nearer the area where he lived, I found small villages of his kin scattered throughout the rolling hills.

These villages were easily distinguishable from the Possessor clan's villages due to the placement of the passages through them. It was comforting to me to find the east-west, north-south lanes running through the villages. I could be reasonably sure that there would be some sort of central place, made to resemble Mystery Grove in Home Valley.

It had been far too long since I had seen Giver or known that his presence was near. But as quickly as that thought passed through my mind, I understood that it was inaccurate. Giver is always near; he is just not always seen. I was comforted by that realization.

The sky orb was directly overhead when I reached a Likeness village. What I now knew to be called smoke coiled upward from fires used for food preparation across the village. I saw several young Likeness offspring working in nearby fields. Others followed a flock of fleecy Nouma.

One of the latter saw me and ran in my direction. "Hello, Nouma," he said. I responded, and he started a rapid series of questions, as was the habit of Likeness kin who had only his short time of being.

"Who are you? Where are you from? Why have you come here? What do you want?"

As he paused for breath, I quickly said, "I'm known as Naados. Likeness is my longtime friend. I have come from Possessors' domain, and I want to see Likeness. Can you help me?"

The young male chuckled at my mimic of his way of questioning me and stepped up beside me. He put one arm around my neck and said, "No problem, Naados. Just come with me."

He gave a quick wave to his companions and started through the village at a fast pace. We emerged on the other side, entered a small forest, and followed a well-worn path through the middle. Neither of us spoke as we emerged after a short time. I saw a large village in the far end of the valley.

"Just follow your eyes, Naados," said my young guide. He laughed, patted my flank, and quickly turned and ran back into the forest.

I followed him with my eyes until he disappeared down the path. *Oh, the joy of newly being,* I thought. *May that young Likeness kin experience the good hand of Giver throughout his journey.* I moved quickly down the incline to the valley floor and hurried toward the large village. I thought I recognized landmarks but was not sure.

Numerous Likeness kin worked in the fields along the path I was taking. From time to time, one would straighten his back and give a long, friendly wave. When they were near enough to hear, I gave a greeting in return. By the midpoint in the sky orb's descent to the west, I arrived in the outer edges of the village.

The familiar layout of lanes was comforting, so I proceeded at a comfortable pace. Ahead, in the distance, I spotted the central grove of trees. Out of pure excitement, I increased my speed until I was running toward the grove. The closer I came to the grove, the more of the Likeness clan I saw going about their activities. Most paid me little or no attention.

I slowed to a comfortable walk as I reached the outer lanes circling the large central grove. I found the flat stone and the platform on which Possessor and Morning Mist had placed their offerings to Giver. My eyes flooded with tears at the memories. Alone in my remembering, I did not notice the approaching Likeness kin until he was a few paces away. I shook my head to clear my dripping eyes and looked straight at him. I started weeping all over again. It was Likeness.

We rushed together, and Likeness wrapped his arms around my neck. We wept, laughed, and then wept again. The continuity of life I lost when my Lhaloo felt the sting was restored in this wonderful reunion. Likeness walked me to the flat stone, sat down, and gently nudged me to the ground at his feet.

Silence is often the best form of communication. We remained for a long time before Likeness spoke. "Naados, old friend, welcome back to my home." We then began a long series of telling. My tale was short compared to that of Likeness. It did not take me long to tell of the sting taking my beloved Lhaloo. My loss seemed small compared to that of Likeness. The killing of Morning Mist will surely trouble him all his time on Giver's good earth. I hoped he would gain some comfort in my telling what I saw that long ago day. The fact that I had been present and could recount the event would hopefully help him.

He immediately asked about that terrible day. With great reluctance, but at his urging, I told all that occurred from the time I left him and Image. I wept frequently because of the pain my telling was producing in Likeness.

He insisted that I continue and tell all. This was the most difficult thing I had ever done.

Other Likeness kin gathered quietly while I spoke. Frequent sounds of weeping filled the silent gaps between my speaking. And then I had finished. Settling such major heartbreak through the telling opened the way for us to move on. I was eager to talk of those now living instead of focusing on those departed through the sting.

Likeness started his telling. "I can never describe the horror of seeing Giver coming with Possessor from the fields. I knew from the expression of anguish on Possessor's face that my worst fears were true. Giver's presence was a paradox that sad day.

"He stayed slightly above and between Possessor and me. While he was all comfort and nearness to me, it was evident that his presence was painful and disagreeable to Possessor. Giver required Possessor to make full confession and ask my forgiveness. Had Giver not wrapped me in his presence, I never could have accepted the truth. I now understand that goodness and judgment are both part of his nature. Giver helped me understand and restrain my response to Possessor.

"Comfort was almost impossible to give to my dear Image when she arrived. She who had carried the becoming life, now extinguished, could not be consoled. I held her close, as Giver had held me, and we wept together for what seemed forever. As our other offspring gathered, they too shared our deep grieving over the violent way the sting came on Morning Mist.

"Giver then spoke his curse on Possessor and put the

mark on him. It was a terrible thing to see. I knew that it condemned him to banishment forever. I shuddered and remembered our banishment from Home Valley. Possessor was forced to take his mata and leave immediately for a land far to the east.

"Giver remained with us for many passages of the sky orb. He kindly did so to help both Image and me. When he finally withdrew, Image and I clung in desperation to one another for many cycles of the night sky orb. Our other off-spring understood and took care of the necessary things for living. They grieved with us but much more quickly realized that those remaining must continue life. They reminded us that life is beautiful, even with the sting.

"Image and I returned to near normal after she was once more heavy with new life. Our ability to have off-spring is what gave us courage to go on from day to day. When Image finally approached the sting and brought another new life into our world, we were on our way to healing from the loss of our gentle Morning Mist."

LORD LIKENESS'S OFFSPRING

The night sky orb was well above the horizon when Likeness paused and suggested that we take nourishment and rest. Even though I was eager to hear the telling, my exhausted body agreed with Likeness. I asked to pass my rest time in Central Grove. Likeness was pleased by my request. The night sky orb traveled much too quickly. The rising morning sky orb sent pulsating rays that blinked me awake. I went to a familiar place outside the village to refresh myself and then quickly returned.

Likeness resumed his telling. "The new life that Image brought was special to us. We decided that his name should reflect our hope but not forget our deep sorrow. We chose to call him Substitute. We know that Giver provided him to replace our departed Morning Mist. He lives his name well. His gentle spirit and desire to please us and Giver provided a healing balm for our bruised spirits.

"Substitute and many of his kin have chosen to remain near this village. At first, it was to provide encouragement to both of us, especially to Image. By his remaining near, I had opportunity to teach much about Home Valley; the sting; and, of course, Giver. Several of his more recent offspring have moved to the south and east as their kin multiplied. Many return often to visit.

"Substitute produced a male offspring who carries the name Likeness is Frail. We all recognize that the sting is no more than a breath away for any of us. There is no guarantee that we will see the sky orb rise tomorrow. We choose to not pass our lives with constant dark thoughts. We are reminded of our frailty each time his name is called.

"Since his naming, many of our kin have started calling themselves by the name of Giver. You notice, Naados, that this is reflected in the names of many of my kin. This reminds us to recognize how fragile we are and how we constantly need Giver's touch. Several of this line of our Likeness kin moved to the south and west of this village. They are near the river you first explored.

"Acquisition is the firstborn of Likeness is Frail. Our recognition that all being and living is acquired from Giver causes us to seek constant reminders. Acquisition is skilled in many special ways. He has taught great numbers of Likeness offspring to construct dwellings and make their villages a good place for their offspring. He thinks new thoughts and invents new things. His skills will one day be useful to all Likeness kin. Most of his clan dwells to the south. He travels often to help others.

"Acquisition's offspring, Giver be Praised, is another kin whose name carries witness to our absolute reliance on Giver. The speaking of his name brings worship to Giver. May he always live his name to the full. His kin have scattered among other lines of our offspring. They often are the leaders in celebrations to remember Giver."

I could not help but notice how Likeness and his kin considered the designations of their offspring. This, and the way their villages were organized, shows a clear pattern. Likeness's kin through Substitute are different from those who come from Possessor.

I chose this time to tell Lord Likeness of the chaotic way that Possessor villages and cities are built. I informed him of my difficulty navigating the passageways. We thought much and discussed at length what this could mean. We then returned to the telling.

"How favored I am to have such notable offspring," Likeness said. "Even with the bending, many of them look beyond our limited time of being to the never-ending days of Giver.

"Descending is the offspring of Giver be Praised. I do not fully understand Giver's good plan, but it must involve those who are to come in the distant times we cannot see.

Descending reminds us that the final resolution to the sting may be far away, but Giver is able to bring it about.

"You met the latest in my line of offspring. The young male who directed you to this place is called Dedicated. He is the offspring of Descending. I must tell you that he is a special Likeness kin. He sees and acts far beyond the days of his being. When we gather to meet with Giver, he is among the first to arrive. He remains in rapt attention long after others have returned to their activities.

"We all know that he takes solitary walks in the fields and forests. Some have heard him speaking with someone when no other of our kin was nearby. When questioned about this practice, he smiles and says very little. In all other ways, he is normal for a young male. He is often spoken of as a good example for proper Likeness behavior."

These times of telling were sweet to my ears. I saw more clearly how the design of Giver had been woven into the rapid increase of Likeness' kin. There was one thing that Likeness had not said. Feeling a need to know, I asked, "And the sting, has it been felt among your kin?"

Likeness responded without hesitation, "No Likeness kin since Morning Mist has felt the sting.

"I'm sure that is not all you wanted to ask," Likeness said. "For the Noumaso, it is different. From long ago, members of the Nouma families have felt the sting. We noticed that certain Nouma kin have short times of being. Others such as you have much longer times to be. Yes, the sting is among us. But up to this time, it is only your Nouma kin who feel it. And you, Naados, had you not tasted the life tree, would have joined Lhaloo in the dust long ago."

I confirmed his observation by telling my own experience among the Noumaso. Everywhere I traveled; my eyes saw the results of the sting on my kin. I'm not certain why, but I have come to accept it as expected. This must be a gift from Giver so that all my living is not troubled with anguished expectation of the sting. It does not take away the pain. Life is beautiful, even with the sting.

Likeness insisted that I tell him more about my travels since our last meeting. I reluctantly did so, in short form. The telling was made easier by the uniformity I found in our world. It is good, even after the bending.

He was interested in my river journeys. The Likeness kin around us were fascinated by my experience, especially the climate difference that caused my breath to be seen far out from my mouth. I did not have words to adequately describe it. I don't know why, but I paused and told of the young, unattached female Nouma of my kin who had shown interest in me.

Likeness slapped his leg and laughed. "Why, Naados, an old Nouma like you thinking such young thoughts? But then, I suppose you are as young as when you tasted the life tree. That may not be a bad idea, my friend."

What was I to say? I had recently entertained the thought.

Likeness was relentless in drawing out information about my travels. I remained several more passings of the sky orb before feeling it was time to move on.

My visit was encouraging, but Likeness was not surprised when I spoke of returning to Home Valley.

"How I would like to go with you, Naados. You must

be my eyes and ears in that distant paradise. Promise you will return and tell me all you see."

With that statement in my ears, I said goodbye and headed northwest toward Home Valley. I was a great distance from Likeness's village when a disturbing thought came to me. All during my stay with Likeness, Giver had not appeared. Likeness had said nothing about a gathering of his kin to talk about Giver and the sting. I had no way of knowing if he and Image continued to wear the old Nouma coverings when meeting with Giver.

HURRYING HOME

My intention had been to take the most direct route back to Home Valley. I decided instead to head west to Southeast River. I wanted to see how the Nouma living in that area were doing.

The nearer I came to the river, the more Nouma I found—especially the large varieties of behemoth. Just beyond a high range of hills and some distance from the nearest Likeness kin villages, I saw large valleys full of behemoth kin. The lushness of their world provided more than enough food for them and as many more. I thought that Giver must smile when he looks on his creation.

The movement of the masses of Nouma feeding reminded me of something I saw on my Northwest River journey. The patterns were like the rhythmic swaying of the tall grasses on the vast plains. I stood watching far too long and remained on the peaks for the passage of the night sky orb instead of in the valley. It was worth the time.

The night sky orb showed only a single sliver of light. The near darkness caused the masses of twinkling objects above to brightly shimmer like new leaves on mountain trees in a midday gentle breeze. I rested well and dreamed good dreams.

I descended toward the river and once more sought the shortest way back to Home Valley. I greeted the Noumaso encountered along the way. When told that they knew of the sting and Likeness, I continued my journey. Excited by the prospect of seeing Home Valley, I hardly noticed the passing cycles of the night sky orb.

Late one evening, I saw the familiar flashing of the Home Valley guardians' weapons. Just two or three more sleep times and I would be home.

The changes in Home Valley did not surprise me. The Noumaso had greatly increased in number as they had everywhere I traveled. There were none, even of my own Nouma, who knew me. That caused me to begin thinking differently about Home Valley. My feelings had not changed, but Home Valley was becoming like any other place in Giver's creation. My life tree episode had turned me into a stranger in my own world.

With confusing new thoughts, I decided to seek out

Mystery Grove one more time. Taking my bearings, I moved in that direction.

Fortunately, Nouma had continued to graze the hillsides nearby, and the encroaching forests had not completely hidden the grove. I paused, grazed until satisfied, and then picked my way through the tangled growth. Before long, I knew that I would require a sleep time on my way in. I pushed on until the sky orb disappeared behind long, dark shadows and found a comfortable place to rest. Frequent cries of Nouma seeking food interrupted my rest throughout the night.

Dim, diffused light greeted my eyes. I stripped a few tender leaves, chewing as I walked, and finally spotted the overgrown trail leading to the flat stone. I arrived there with great difficulty.

A sniffing examination told me that only my scent was on the stone. The life tree and the knowing tree had not grown or changed. I took time to offer up my thoughts to Giver and turned to retrace my steps.

My feelings were not as intense as during past visits. Perhaps it was because of the years of my being. Maybe it was the result of my visit with Likeness. The thought of Likeness caused me a new unpleasant sensation. I expressed it by asking myself, *how long before he will feel the sting.* I tried to think on other things and rushed out of Mystery Grove as fast as possible.

The sky orb had almost disappeared when I emerged and trotted toward the place where dust from my Lhaloo now nourished the herbs. I visited with two Nouma kin and then spent a satisfying sleep time in the edge of the small forest.

It was now clear what I would do. I moved at fast pace toward the lake from which the four rivers flowed. Southwest would be my next journey of discovery.

As I traveled, I thought about Likeness's comment. *Why, Naados, an old Nouma like you thinking such young thoughts; maybe that is not such a bad idea.* Perhaps I would again spend a lifetime with a mata. I repeated it several times to no one in particular and then laughed at myself.

Southwest River, and Another Mata

With a spring in my step, I headed away from the lake feeding the four rivers. The cave source for the lake flowed just as much as before. What wonders Giver has worked to provide an abundance of water for his creation. I followed the stream flowing southwest with no idea if my journey would be long or short. I laughed at the thought that it did not matter. He is, we are, life is beautiful, even with the sting.

Southwest River did not flow through a restricted opening as the other three did, but it moved in a long, gentle curve where it exited Home Valley. No hill of any size was near. Far to the west, I saw a high range of hills. Another lower range could be seen to the south; but the flow of the river appeared far from them. Nouma grazed on both sides of the river, and behemoth kin were more numerous the farther along the river I traveled.

As was my habit, I talked with the Noumaso along the way. During the first days of travel, they were all aware of Giver, Likeness, and the sting. I wondered how far downriver this would be true since most Nouma are territorial. I, of course, am the great exception to every rule about Noumaso.

I moved at a leisurely pace and explored everything along the way. Many of my Nouma kin lived in this wide valley. I usually drifted in among them with nothing more than a polite greeting. This proved to be the best way to listen rather than talk. It was only possible with my own Nouma kin. Were these descendents of my own offspring? I had no way of knowing.

There was never a shortage of unattached young females. I determined to go far from Home Valley before permitting myself to think about settling down with a mata. It somehow seemed the right thing to do.

Three cycles of the night sky orb took me a good distance from Home Valley. From the east, another large stream intersected with Southwest River. Just a five-sleep journey beyond that point laid a beautiful, wide valley rimmed by majestic timbered hills. Numerous small streams flowed through the valley and into the river.

Ever the explorer, I left the river and traveled up the valley, which was rich with herbs and trees. My favorite foods were there in abundance. The Noumaso were friendly, so my decision to remain for a time was easy. When I asked what they knew about Giver, Likeness, and the sting, they had no answer. They said that they had not been told the story.

Since this was another untouched part of Giver's creation that needed the message, I decided to stay as long as necessary to tell all the Noumaso in the valley. I stopped counting the cycles of the night sky orb and settled down to enjoy my time there.

It took me ten cycles of the night sky orb to fully explore the valley. The more I saw, the more I wanted to stay. I put thoughts of other journeys out of my mind and told the story all through my newly adopted valley home. The sky orb cycles were sweet. I enjoyed my living, just as I had as a newly become Nouma.

No Likeness kin had ever been here. The sting was among them, but not like the horror of the first sting in Home Valley. They accepted it as a normal part of the cycle of being. I did not have the heart to tell them differently.

During my exploring and telling the message, it was natural to become part of a group of my Nouma. They were kind and gentle and accepted me with no question. *This is where I belong,* I thought. It was not long before I was sure.

It had never occurred to me that another female Nouma would cause me to put memories of Lhaloo far in the back of my mind. It happened. She was young but ready to become a two-one creature. I will not attempt to do more than say that our joining was as natural as breathing. Her name was Lohaa. From the time we met, she gave me great joy. Being united with her put all thoughts of further travel far from my mind.

Days flowed into years as Lohaa and I lived and added to the Nouma kin of our valley. She regularly approached the sting and walked back with miniature replicates of herself. My life was complete. After our offspring were producing their own offspring, we moved away from our original group.

We went to a far part of the valley near a distant range of eastern hills. This gave me the opportunity to climb to the heights and study the surrounding hills and valleys. Lohaa enjoyed exploring and often went with me. We spent wonderful times together enjoying the bounty of Giver. I took every opportunity to tell her about Giver, Likeness, and the sting. She had a tender young spirit and wanted to know everything.

I struggled inside myself about telling Lohaa my entire story. How could I make her understand that which was both a gift and a curse to me? How would she react? I could never truly know her feeling about living and the inevitable final decline to the sting. In the end, I decided not to tell her. Instead, I chose to help my beautiful Lohaa live every day to its fullness. I found no other practical solution.

Our offspring and theirs which followed numbered in the hundreds. Giver was good to the Noumaso in our valley. I kept my secrets locked inside. Were it possible for everything to remain forever just as it is now, I would be the happiest Nouma in Giver's creation. I knew that was impossible. By the goodness of Giver, it remained so all through the lifetime of my dear Lohaa. Seventy-five Likeness years passed as a single night, and Lohaa became dust.

After an adequate time with our offspring, I drifted away to resume my exploration of Southwest River. I suspect my Nouma kin thought I had felt the sting and joined Lohaa in the dust.

TO THE END OF SOUTHWEST RIVER

Southwest River became wide and moved more slowly, just as Southeast River had done. Well-watered plains extended as far as I could see and teemed with vegetation and Noumaso. The converging river valleys were filled with behemoth kin. *What was Giver's purpose for these numberless gentle giants?* I often wondered. The thought was beyond my Nouma ability to understand.

The roaring vastness of salty waters greeted me at last. Now knowing what to expect, I settled down to learn as much as possible about the Noumaso in this unique setting. Giver's creative wonders amazed me.

Winged Noumaso filled the skies, singing their high-pitched songs. Creatures on the wet, powdery expanse where the water met the land scurried about with animated delight. They were doing what Giver designed them to do. I spent many passages of the sky orb with my head down on the ground, eyes at their level, observing their busy activities. I wonder what they thought about me.

Journeys end. I headed back toward the source of Southwest River. Every day was a new adventure as I met more and different Noumaso. Life was enjoyable. This time away from Likeness's kin provided relief from my troubled thoughts. I was continuing to struggle about the full implications of the bending on all Noumaso.

One event on my return journey bears the telling. Just after the sky orb passed the midpoint overhead, I saw one of the most striking things I had ever encountered. Actually, I first heard it. A pounding sound snapped my ears to attention. I stopped and identified its easterly origin. Shaded by a small grove of trees, I watched and waited. The noise became louder, and I realized that it was the sound of running Nouma. They had to be large and were moving fast. Nouma frequently run for enjoyment, but this was not that kind of sound.

Just as I stretched my neck and started to step out of the shadows, they came into view. They were passing by at some distance and not coming in my direction, so I moved forward a few paces. They were four-footed Nouma, just as I am, but much larger. They had broad backs and majestic, sturdy necks. I felt the ground tremble as they ran.

I remembered this Nouma kin from the becoming but had not taken special notice of them since that time. Even with that remembrance, at this distance, they seemed different. As they came nearer, I saw Likeness's kin on their backs. These majestic creatures were being urged on by shouts of those sitting astride them. My mind struggled to understand what I was seeing. These were the first Likeness kin that I had seen this far west, and they were making Nouma carry them.

They disappeared behind a low hill, and the sound quickly faded. My surprise at seeing them and the speed at which they ran kept me from noticing how many there were—just several large Nouma and the same number of Likeness kin on their backs. What was our world coming to?

With more questions than answers about my latest observation, I continued toward Home Valley.

Goodbye to
Lord Likeness

Urged by an inner feeling from Giver, I turned and hurried east toward Likeness's village. My mind was troubled by thoughts of Likeness. My memory of our last visit reconstructed his appearance, and I was uneasy. In reflection, my delight at being with him kept me from realizing how much he had changed. Thinking these thoughts brought memories of the decline of my Lhaloo so long ago. I was struck by how similar the subtle changes in Likeness's appearances resembled them. Such thoughts gave me cause to hurry.

Likeness's kin were everywhere as I followed Southeast River. I avoided their villages and kept to the low hills. I drove myself on long after the sky orb disappeared in the west. I wanted nothing to keep me from reaching Likeness's village as soon as possible.

Ten sleep-times later, early in the day, I saw familiar landmarks and knew that Likeness's Village was near. Coming down a hill toward the valley floor, I stopped to graze and refresh myself. Satisfied, I started on and then heard a familiar voice. Pausing to listen, I realized that it was Dedicated. Not wanting to intrude, I moved quietly toward where I heard his voice.

Dedicated was walking along the edge of a small grove of trees. He was no longer the inquisitive youngster I had met during my last visit, but a magnificent, mature specimen of Likeness's kin. Imagine my surprise at seeing Giver with him. It had been far too long since I last saw Giver. Not wanting to approach uninvited, I stopped just outside the line of trees and waited. It did not take long for Dedicated to look my direction and cry out to me.

"Come here, Naados, old friend."

Without hesitation, I ran to his side and accepted his warm embrace. Giver made me welcome by extending his presence of light to include me.

I had forgotten the intensity of being with Giver. It was difficult to breathe normally until I started offering up my thanks to him for his wonderful creation. Being in his presence then became familiar and natural. I was almost embarrassed to be included as Dedicated continued his intimate talk with Giver. Time stood still as I savored the sweetness of the moment and the nearness of my Giver of being.

After a time, all talk stopped, and Giver moved up and away. Dedicated turned and give me his full attention. His first words were, "You don't know, do you?" He saw by my puzzled look that I did not.

"Likeness is near the sting," he said.

I sighed deeply. So this was why I felt compelled to rush to Likeness's village. Swirling emotions heavy with grief and sorrow prevented me from opening my mouth. Dedicated realized how heavy this news was and put his arms around my neck. I wept at the coming sadness.

As we slowly walked toward the village, Dedicated attempted to prepare me for seeing Likeness. "Do not expect Likeness to be as he was during your last visit. Years have come and gone, and we are all changed. You remember me as a youngster at that time.

"It appears that only a short time remains for Likeness to stay in Giver's good world. He has made every effort to prepare his kin to accept his time for the sting. This is especially difficult for Image. She remains faithfully at his side. All those times she neared the sting to bring new offspring into the world have prepared her. She knows that his time is near. Only occasionally, when others insist, does she take nourishment and rest. She then quickly returns to hold the hand of her dear Likeness."

I asked how Likeness's kin were dealing with his impending departure. Dedicated said, "It is an emotional time. Our only memory is from the telling of how Morning Mist felt the sting. No Likeness was present to witness how it happened. This is our first time to know that the sting is coming and to wait for it."

I made no effort to tell of how my Lhaloo felt the sting, for there is no comparing.

Necessary activities continued as we entered the village at a subdued pace. Groups of Likeness's kin from other villages had gathered and were talking quietly. Dedicated led me through the crowd to Central Grove. Likeness was there near the flat stone with Image at his side. His weakened, emaciated condition staggered me.

He gathered enough strength to glance in my direction and send a slight smile my way. Image also looked but then turned her attention back to Likeness. He had been placed in a half-sitting position on thick pads of what Likeness's kin used in their places of rest. Without the warmth of the descending sky orb, his body trembled. He had several coverings over his body. I observed the covering on top of all the others. It was from the innocent Nouma that Giver had provided at Mystery Grove.

Likeness whispered something to Image, and she called my name and beckoned me to her side. I hesitated, but Dedicated gently pushed me forward.

The scene was strange. Likeness, made by Giver to be forever, lay struggling for breath. His mata, Image, taken from his side, watched protectively over him. He who had chosen to eat from the knowing tree was quickly approaching the sting. I, servant to Likeness, had eaten from the life tree. My body remained strong and young as I was on that fateful day. This is a mystery too deep for me, a simple Nouma.

Image whispered a greeting and motioned for me to lie down alongside the flat stone. This position put my head at the level of Likeness's face. He watched my every move and smiled as I looked into his eyes. This was my first time to peer into aged Likeness's eyes. They looked back at me through a light, filmy covering. The brilliant twinkle they had in the past was gone. I wondered if pain was associated with this condition.

Likeness spoke. "Naados, old friend, I knew you would come. Our paths have crossed too many times for you to be absent for the most mysterious event of my entire time in Giver's good world. Thank you. Your presence gives me courage and pain. Courage, for you proved that the life tree is a good gift from Giver and it could have been mine. Pain, when I remember what could have been. If only Image and I had heeded Giver's instructions and chosen to avoid the knowing tree.

"I think often of Beaufang. I am sure he continually tries to deceive our offspring as he did Image and me. And this bloodstained Nouma covering, you know why I kept it, don't you? It is a reminder of what my bending cost all of Giver's good creation. My heart is bruised with the thought of lost life and innocence. I deserve the sting. Giver is just in all His actions."

With that, Likeness fell back, exhausted. His darkening, wrinkled face told the whole sad story.

Image breathed out a long sigh and tenderly patted his hand. "Thank you, Naados, for being a true friend to my dear Likeness. Life is good, even with the sting."

I spoke briefly with Dedicated and told him that I

wanted to be alone outside the village for a time but would return and remain inside the grove near Likeness. I went to a familiar place to think about Likeness and Image. Fatigue from my journey and the emotion of my recent visit with Likeness caused me to fall asleep. I awoke when the night sky orb was directly overhead. I cropped some nearby tender herbs and returned to Central Grove.

As I trotted toward the village, a glow like the night sky orb appeared over the trees. I stopped, looked straight up, and saw the night sky orb overhead. I looked again toward the village and saw the same glow as before. Puzzled, I hurried along the trail and wondered at the cause of the glow ahead.

As I topped a small rise, the village spread out before me. The source of the glow was not one thing but many small things. I saw it in most of the Likeness dwelling places. It spilled out the entrance opening as well as smaller openings along the sides of the dwellings. I had no idea what this shining in the dark time was. It made it much easier to see. I intended to ask about this strange new thing.

Central Grove had several glowing points, just like those in the dwellings. They cast dim shadows in circles all around where they were placed. I put the mystery out of my mind but admit that it was enjoyable to see clearly even when it should be dark.

Image was beside Likeness, where she had been when I went outside the village. Groups of Likeness's kin were all around. Some were seated. Others lay on coverings on the ground. More of them arrived through the night. I made for my favorite resting place in the grove and joined the waiting friends.

Likeness stirred occasionally, and Image always responded immediately to his needs. She gave water to drink or whatever else he requested. His rest was troubled through the night. As the sky orb lit the eastern sky with glowing color, the strange glowing objects grew dim and then turned dark. The Likeness family waited along with several Nouma kin. I was ill at ease as the sky orb turned the sky bright blue.

Members of the village served morning nourishment to the visiting Likeness kin. The prepared foods that I had observed long ago were among the things offered. There was also an abundance of fruit and fire-roasted grain. I nibbled leaves from a nearby tree and waited.

The sky orb was halfway through her morning climb when stillness settled over the grove. I sensed a slight movement down the lane leading north from the grove. I turned to look and saw, to my dismay, a slight outline of the malevolent presence. It floated slowly forward. My mind flashed back to Mystery Grove and replayed the terrible way my Nouma kin felt the sting. I was appalled that the presence was here. Relief was immense as Giver came between the presence and the grove and then descended slowly to the place where Likeness lay.

Giver quietly called for Likeness's kin to come near. I sensed that the Noumaso were also welcomed, so I moved closer to the flat stone. As he had done at the becoming, Giver wrapped his shining presence around Likeness and Image. He then spoke so that we all could hear.

Child of dust, creation fair,
Lord of all who breathe this air
Choosing brought you to this day
From this fair world you go away
Your spirit I reclaim my own
To dust must go your skin and bone
Likeness offspring follow you
Till all one day I shall renew

Giver then drew closer to Likeness and Image. He spoke to them alone. I tried but could not understand what he said. He then moved slightly above the couple and remained motionless.

Likeness struggled and sat up from his resting place. Image moved close to his side as he prepared to speak.

"Giver made us to be forever in this good place he created. Image and I chose the lie of Beaufang instead of the truth of Giver. Our wicked bending brought this horrible curse on us as well as all that Giver made. Since the bending, the dust is our destiny. For over nine hundred years, by the good hand of Giver, Image and I have avoided the sting.

"Today, it comes to me, the first Likeness to become. If sorrow could change our sort, we would have returned to before the bending long ago. Nothing we can do will make that change. It can only be when the seed of Image invades our world. Then transformation will come. My eyes are too dim to see that distant time. My body is too frail to endure. My spirit is tired and longs to fly free. I leave only my sad legacy of bending. Giver forever brings his promise of restoring. Giver, you alone deserve glory. It is your mercy I crave."

Likeness closed his eyes, took one deep breath, and then fell back on his resting place. Image's eyes filled with tears. She let them overflow and fall on Likeness's face. She bent and tenderly kissed his silent cheek. She then pulled the old Nouma covering up and over his face.

Image stood, raised her hands up to Giver and spoke. "Giver, source of all good that ever has been or ever will be, I make this request of you. You made me from my mata's side long ago. He has felt the sting and will soon become dust. We together shared life. May we now share the sting? In your good hands power to be and power to undo the being resides. I plead your mercy and ask for release from my frail form."

The silence seemed to shout after the request from Image. She placed her old Nouma covering on the ground beside the flat stone where Likeness's still form now lay. Looking around at all those who had gathered, she nodded. I was unsure if it was in acknowledgment of our presence or as an act of farewell. Then I knew which it was. She sat on the Nouma covering and slowly stretched full length on it. Reaching up, she touched the covered form of Likeness. She then slowly dropped her arms to her sides.

Giver spoke.

> *Mata of Likeness, Image fair*
> *Release I grant you from this care*
> *Since the bending you followed my way*
> *To dust you go with your mata today*

Image raised her head toward Giver and smiled. For an instant, she had the newly made glow from her becoming. Her eyes grew wide, and her head fell back to the covering. After a short sigh, she closed her eyes. Giver descended, swirled his presence around the couple, and then moved up and out of view. No one spoke for a long time, and then mourning began among their Likeness kin. I wept as I walked quickly away. No one would ever weep over me.

PART THREE

POSSESSOR AND
HIS CLAN

RETURN TO
BRANDED CITY

Just how long I sought solitude after Likeness's passing is a blur in my mind. I traveled two sleep times away from Likeness's kin and then roamed unfamiliar hills and valleys. I halfheartedly gave the sad news of Likeness and Image to Noumaso I met and then continued my wandering. Spiraling cycles of eating, sleeping, and reflecting took me north until I reached Northeast River.

I passed several sleep times on a beautiful plain beside a range of hills overlooking the river. My attempts to offer thanks to Giver were, at best, done out of habit. Alone, in the middle of a sleep time, when the night sky orb showed only a silvery rim as she passed, I considered the twinkling heavens overhead.

Giver spoke inside my head to my heart.

"Naados, time has not ended. It is very young. You must recapture the joy of being. I have not changed. The living must continue the doing. You will always be among them."

I awoke with the gentle internal rebuke from Giver urging me on. My body was refreshed, my mind clear. The magnificent river flowed eastward in the valley below. The air was fresh and clean. I grazed contentedly and then decided to swim the river and follow it east toward the cities of Possessor's kin. Life is good, even with the sting.

The north side of the river was new to me. A range of distant high hills watched over the river as far as I could see to the west and the east. Hills nearer to the river gave me a choice vantage point as I traveled east. As in all other places where I traveled, Noumaso had multiplied and filled the verdant valleys. My pleasure in telling the story returned, and I spent many wonderful passages of the sky orb talking with my kin. Thoughts of Home Valley came infrequently. When they did, I felt a twinge of guilt but quickly put it out of my mind. Living is far more than being in one location. There is nothing I could change if I were in Home Valley.

Early one morning, I grazed and watched my behemoth kin in the river below. They seemed to be making more noise than was normal for them. I soon saw what caused it. Not far from the south bank of the river, I saw an object with them in the water. The object made of wood was as long as the largest behemoth.

It was wide in the center and narrower on each end. On the top, toward the middle, was something similar to a low Likeness dwelling. Sticking out from each side of the object were things like small tree trunks that had thin, flat pieces attached at the end near the water. They moved forward and back, up and down, splashing as they went in and out of the water. That was the sound scattering the behemoth. The thing was moving slowly up the river.

I marveled at the sight; and as I looked more closely, I saw several Likeness kin on it. Some were standing near the middle. Two were on the end, heading up the river. Others were seated along the sides, moving the long things which extended into the water.

A Nouma nearby saw my furrowed brow as I gazed at the object in the river. He laughed and said, "Is this your first time to see the river houses of the Likeness kin?"

"Yes, it is" I replied.

"If you are troubled by it, you had better not go on down river," he said. "They fill the waters as you get near the large Likeness cities."

"What are they for?" I asked.

"They carry things made in the liquid fire up the river to the scattered Likeness villages. When they go back down the river, they take food to eat for their kin living in the cities," he replied. He told me that the nearest Likeness city was a five-sleep journey if I traveled throughout the sky orb's crossing. It is the city that Possessor gave the name of his offspring, Branded. I decided to stay north of the river and head for the city.

POSSESSOR'S KIN
Progress and Problems

My rest was disturbed several times by Likeness sounds coming from near the river. As the sky orb peered over the distant horizon, her rays passed through layers of unnatural colors. I remembered this spectacle from my last visit. It seemed to be larger and gave the morning sky an eerie appearance. For an instant, it reminded me of the malevolent presence. I put the thought out of my mind, but it would return later.

I continued east, seeing many river houses. Some were moving, and others stopped along the riverbanks. It seemed wise for me to swim the river soon. I had no way of knowing how difficult it would be when I came near Branded City.

I found a wide bend in the river where the waters moved more slowly, and I made my crossing. The sky orb was low in the west when I arrived on the south bank. I moved up a gentle slope and found a sheltered grove of trees, an ideal place to take my rest. My preferred foods were abundant, as well as a fresh water source. The view overlooked the eastern bank of the river. There were no high ranges of hills to block my view of the rising sky orb.

Possessor kin villages were all along the river. The passages through them followed the natural contour of the countryside just as they had in Branded City. I avoided going through them when possible. Instead, I followed the riverbank or the low hills outside the villages. The Possessor villages had the same glowing objects to give light during the passage of the night sky orb that I had seen in Likeness's village. I hoped to find out what made this marvel possible. The answer came unexpectedly.

Traveling near the river, I came to a place where the hills crowded in on each side and made the water flow fast. It was here I saw that a wall of stones put in the river ran downriver at some distance from the bank. As I traveled downstream, the wall came closer to the bank, causing the water trapped inside to move faster.

Rounding a small bend, I saw water funneled into several large objects made from wood and the hard thing made from melting stones. This is difficult for me, a simple Nouma, to describe. These circular objects were attached to a long, round central point. They rotated around that central point as the water flowed over them. The many attached flat parts caught the water and made it turn fast.

This created a great rumbling sound. The long, thin, whirling center part disappeared into a huge Likeness dwelling. High-pitched sounds coming from there hurt my ears, so I moved quickly away. At some distance, I could tolerate the noise and stopped to look back at the strange thing.

Several of what appeared to be large vines came out of the structure and were attached to tall trees. These went to a place where there were more trees, and many smaller vines were attached to the larger ones. They too were placed high above the ground on some sort of pole or tree. Many round, glowing objects were attached to the poles. They could be easily seen glowing, even though the sky orb shone brightly overhead. I must stop. My mind whirls with the telling. I will only say that I saw the vines all around the Possessor cities and villages.

I came to an outer part of Branded City and started making my way through the lanes. I wanted to reach the center of the city. For the most part, I was ignored by Likeness's kin. They went about their activities with only an occasional quick glance in my direction. Almost all the Nouma kin I saw were domesticated. These were the varieties that had chosen much earlier to remain near Likeness and Image.

In some groves of trees, I saw members of the Nouma clan who had been made to carry Likeness's kin on their backs, the ones I saw galloping near Southwest River. It appeared that they were being kept there for that purpose.

I reached a large, central place in the city and stopped in the shade of a tree. I looked around and saw a group of mature Likeness males sitting and taking food and drink. I moved slowly in that direction and waited to see if my presence would be acknowledged. A canine near the group trotted up to me and sniffed. He then lay down without a greeting.

I waited before I spoke. "Well, Nouma kin, have the city dwellers lost their voices?"

He jumped up, startled. "You speak our language?" he asked.

"Ever since my becoming," I replied.

He settled back down, placed his chin on his paws, and spoke quietly to me without looking in my direction.

"You best not speak openly, my brother. Many of the Likeness kin do not have good feelings toward all Noumaso. There are only a few of them that I can freely talk with. If you want to be safe, only speak when a Likeness kin speaks directly to you. Lie down, rest a while, and then I will take you to one of them."

I thanked him and dozed as I enjoyed the warm rays of the sky orb.

Giver's world has certainly changed, I mused as I half dozed. My new friend called me back to awareness.

"They are all gone now but my friend. Come with me and meet an offspring of Possessor."

The elderly offspring of Possessor nodded kindly and indicated for me to sit closeby. My new Nouma acquaintance spoke to him.

"Master, this stranger speaks the ancient tongue of

creation and has come to visit. I warned him of the danger but told him you would welcome him."

"Thank you, my faithful friend. Welcome, Nouma kin. I am Giver's Man and offspring of Possessor."

I was cheered upon hearing his name and responded by telling him my own. "I am called Naados by Nouma kin."

He breathed deeply and stared in my direction.

"Naados, you say? Not *the* Naados? You are doubly welcome to our city, friend of now-departed Likeness."

We talked at length of the sting and the departure of Likeness and Image. He told me that several of Possessor's kin had traveled to Likeness's village to mourn the passing of the two from whom all Likeness's kin came. I admitted to him that I did not have the courage to remain after they breathed their last.

He understood and then told me of the days of mourning. The difference between Noumaso and Likeness kin again became evident to me. We Nouma did not have the ability to choose or to reject Giver's way. We knew only to obey.

You poor likeness creatures, I thought. *You may pass your time in this good world with constant regret for choices made. This gift of free choice must be a heavy burden.*

Giver's Man took a long time to tell me about his kin.

"Possessor is now very old and probably not far from the sting. He wears the mark of the curse from Giver, but many of his kin no longer remember what it signifies. This is probably because the memory of Giver and honoring him is far from the minds of Possessor and his clans."

Giver's Man told of how he tried to remember Giver along with his immediate offspring. He wept while speaking. He bears great heartbreak because they refuse to follow Giver's way.

It is evident that the offspring of Possessor are bent and warped beyond imagination. I kept that thought as I commented to Giver's Man about the many things that had been discovered and developed by his clan.

"It is true. They are very creative," he said, "but they frequently use new things to hurt one another. Giver is never in their thoughts. It almost seems that every thought they have is turned against Giver."

I asked about the relationships between his clan and Substitute's offspring.

"The males come to our cities and villages to take our females away to be their matas," he said. "Our young females have an exotic sensual beauty that is very attractive to males from Substitute's restrictive culture. When males visit here, they are introduced to pleasures not known or practiced by most of Substitute's kin. Many of them choose to leave Giver far behind in order to experience all the freely given pleasures.

"In our cities are places to satisfy every desire of the mind and flesh. None here remain true to the promise made during the joining ceremony with their mata. Most of the females seductively seek joining with any male at any time. The males do not resist. There are very few remaining among us who practice Giver's two-one Likeness commands."

Giver's Man told me of a brief visit by Giver to Branded City.

"Giver appeared over the center of the city several years

ago. He came during the height of an annual celebration of sensual pleasure. Thousands of our inhabitants were engaged in drunken, vulgar behavior. Giver appeared with a shout so loud that drinking cups broke in the hands of the revelers. Complete silence ensued as Giver then manifested over the city and spoke."

Evil are you, through and through
You run from my good pleasure
You give no care to what you do
And throw away your treasure
I will call away from you
My Spirit's drawing power
Weep you will I tell you true
When you reach that hour

"Giver then said that life would become very short because of our wicked behavior. He spoke of disease leading to the sting. He told of evil actions taking the lives of many of Likeness's kin. He warned of changes among us and above us and beneath us. He spoke of terrible things to come. Very few paid any attention to his telling."

My mind reeled from what Giver's Man told of the total rebellion lived out by Possessor's seed. "Are there none who gather to honor Giver?" I asked.

"None who gather," he replied. "Some of us secretly speak of Giver and meet to remember Him, but we are few in number. If we are found out, we will probably be driven from the city."

"Is this true only here in Branded City?" I asked.

"If only that were the case," he replied. "I have traveled

through many of our cities and villages and have yet to find those who publicly gather to honor Giver. You have time, Naados. Why don't you travel through our area and see for yourself. Please return to tell me if you find what I say is not true."

I thanked Giver's Man for his honest telling of the state of Possessor's offspring. My mind was troubled by the potential for disaster with such a large part of the Likeness kin choosing to rebel against Giver. My canine Nouma friend offered to escort me south out of the city. He asked that I stay close behind him and reminded me not to speak as he led me through the twisting back streets. He asked that I observe carefully the behavior of those we passed on our way out of town.

I could hardly believe the open way wickedness was practiced in Branded City. The reflection of Giver and His good character was nowhere to be seen in these Likeness kin.

After we were safely out of the city, my Nouma brother dropped back to walk beside me. "Thank you for listening to my advice," he said. "Please be very careful should you ever return to Branded City. Go with Giver, my Nouma brother, and think kindly of us who stay with our Likeness masters."

I took Giver's Man's advice and traveled southeast to see Possessor's kin and how they were living. I have often regretted that decision.

The regions to the east and south of Branded City are filled with Possessor's offspring and their kin. There are vast herds of domesticated Nouma tended by Likeness's kin riding their sturdy Nouma mounts. It was an amazing spectacle to see thousands of these beautiful creatures grazing the lush prairies and plains.

The plains are mixed among the fertile river valleys and magnificent forests of giant trees. Even though there are many Likeness villages and cities, the open countryside filled with large fields dominated. The Likeness inhabitants could be multiplied by the thousands, and yet there would be room for all. Giver's world was far from filled.

Along all the large rivers and streams where there are cities and villages stood objects to create artificial light. In the area I traveled, it was nearly impossible to spend a rest time without seeing the glow of Likeness's night illumination in some direction. This was accompanied by the fouled air over the larger cities. I was amazed that the burning of wood to melt stones could make the pristine sky turn gray. It was that way in much of Possessor kin's world.

I saw another sad thing about Possessor's kin that involved their abuse of the good foods that Giver created. Luscious fruits and berries are found everywhere. They give delicious sensations to my tongue and mouth and are satisfyingly filling. It appears that anything that Giver made can be turned to bad use. I was surprised by what had been done with the sweet fruits. All across Possessor kin villages and cities lived those who took the fruit, extracted the juice, and changed it. They discovered how to change the juice from a sweet, enjoyable drink into a fiery, strong brew.

I observed that when taken in large quantities, the transformed ingredients caused Likeness kin's brains and bodies to act in unnatural ways. Even-tempered individuals became belligerent and hateful. Clear-thinking, sensible individuals became raving mad and did despicable things. Fights between kin broke out, and one or another would be seriously injured.

Males who were normally good to females became harsh and abusive. Some followed the path of Possessor and brought the sting to their own kin. Heads of families and clans were overpowered by the drink and failed to meet the needs of their mata and her offspring.

Under the influence of the malevolent presence, good became evil and evil became good to Possessor's kin. I traveled for many of Likeness's years among these corrupted offspring of Possessor. I wept often for their little ones who were growing up to become like their parents. Giver was not honored among them. They knew truth but chose to follow the deceiver to their own forever hurt.

I faithfully did the telling among Noumaso everywhere. For the most part, they avoided Likeness kin and lived out the lives for which they were created. I alone reminded them of why they were on their way to the sting.

Final Walk with Dedicated

Hardly realizing it, I had spent over fifty of Likeness's years traveling in the southeast among the kin of Possessor. The heartbreak of seeing Likeness's kin choosing to ignore Giver was a great mental strain. I decided to travel west toward Southeast River and avoid the large clusters of Possessor's kin. I then planned to travel north to see my friend, Dedicated, before a visit to Home Valley. There were many things I wanted to talk with him about.

My journey west was refreshing. The vast valleys

were filled with behemoth kin. Hills and plains teemed with swift Noumaso. My feeling that Giver was near made the experience enjoyable. I especially tried to notice Nouma less familiar to me. The long-necked, gangly-legged tree-top grazers were a treat to watch. Giver had equipped them with special lips capable of picking through the long, sharp thorns that emerged on their favorite trees after the bending. They always have abundant food and no rivals since it grows on top of trees only they can reach.

I traveled through an area where large troops of Giver's spindly limbed acrobats lived. Their antics are always entertaining. I smile even now as I remember their joy of being. How they scolded me for laughing at the entertainment they provided. I think they were appeased when I let great numbers of them cling to my back as I ran through their forest home. I marveled at the tall, heavy body and long neck of the feathered Nouma who did not have wings to fly but ran at great speed across the plains. I peeked into dark crevices where shiny eyes of creatures who feed while the night sky orb passes peered curiously back at me. I wondered what they look like.

I raced with black and white-striped Nouma who resembled those ridden by Likeness's kin. I watched a family of large feline Nouma lick one another as they lay in the shade during the heat of the sky orb.

I found an entire hillside bare of growth, sparkling with the reflection of millions of miniature sky orbs and wondered what use such things might be. I passed an enjoyable day with a group of my own Nouma, telling stories from the past. I hardly knew how to explain to the Noumaso how I knew the stories and why they were true.

I finally turned north and headed for familiar territory. This was my first time to enter Likeness's village from the south. I spotted it several sleep times later as the sky orb headed down toward the distant western line of hills. I stopped to rest and think about my coming visit.

The familiar destination had grown and changed during my years away. It looked to be almost twice the size it was when Likeness and Image felt the sting. Beautiful fields surrounded the large valley. Herds of white, fleecy Nouma grazed the hillsides. Smoke from cooking fires drifted upward, mingling with the dissipating morning mist.

Morning Mist. What memories that name brought swirling into my mind. I was concentrating on it so much that I almost ran into a Likeness kin who stepped from a nearby grove of trees into my path. I stopped just as I was only a step away from him. He looked familiar, but I did not recall his name.

He attempted a scowl but failed as his face broke into a huge smile. "Hello, Naados," he said.

"You probably do not remember me, Naados. I am called Between, the father of my father is your friend, Dedicated. My father's name is Cleansing Comes. I was near you when Likeness and Image felt the sting. Dedicated speaks often of you as a dear friend to the entire Likeness family. Come with me."

Between led me toward Central Grove of Likeness's village. He told me that it is now called Likeness-Image City. The name was changed after Image made the remarkable request of Giver to feel the sting with her beloved Likeness. We quickly arrived at Central Grove.

The flat stone was no longer at the entrance to the grove. It now was in the center. Several trees had been removed and replaced with places for Likeness's kin to sit around the central stone. The altar had also been moved here and was at the end of the flat stone. The main roads leading to the center of Likeness-Image City now converged at the flat stone in the grove.

Something had been chiseled into the top of the flat stone. I recognized a representation of Likeness and Image as well as Likeness's markings. Between approached and told me what the Likeness markings said.

"This is the remembering place for those who brought life to all Likeness kin. Likeness and Image were first to become, first to be bent, and first to feel the sting in the natural order Giver spoke it on all Likeness kin. They asked for mercy from the good hand of Giver."

"So this is how Likeness kin prepare their own for the dust," I said.

Between replied, "We wanted all offspring who follow to know how we became. This talk will remain on the stone long after we feel the sting and are dust. I will leave you for now to have your memories. If you want to see Dedicated, you will find him in the place he meets with Giver. You found him there the last time you came to Likeness-Image City."

I thanked Between and then settled down to remember my dear friends. Strange how the sweet and good seem to overpower the bitter and evil when I take time for remembering. My thinking about Likeness and Image brought joy to my spirit and a smile to my lips. *Thank you, my dear Giver of everything. You have the ability to put grief in the dark places of my mind and to display happiness in the places where the sky orb shines.* With that thought, I set out for the grove where Dedicated had his visits with Giver.

When I neared the grove, I moved as slowly and quietly as possible. From a distance, I heard the conversation between Giver and Dedicated. I always felt that I intruded on the most intimate communication that existed when I approached Giver and Dedicated during these times.

I knew that they were aware of my presence, but they continued as if alone in the universe. I remembered the last time that I was in Giver's presence and started to silently offer up thanks to him for all his wonderful works. I told him my heart and worshipped as best a Nouma can. The sweet joy of his presence enfolded me. Every care and concern fell away as nothing while he saturated me with his presence of light.

I don't know how long I stood enjoying the overflow of communion between my Maker and my friend. I sensed that this is why Likeness's kin exist. That this is what Giver intended before Likeness's wrong choice and the bending. I felt compelled to fall to the ground in the presence of a Likeness kin involved in pure worship to Giver.

The meeting grew in intensity. It was as if I was observing a cosmic, joyful, flowing dance. Swirling, spiraling light and color filled the grove and overflowed toward the heavens. Dedicated shimmered in the reflected light from Giver. Dedicated and Giver did not appear to be alone in the pulsating light and motion.

As a Nouma, I do not have words to tell it completely. It seemed that heavenly helpers joined the joyous celebration. The entire area vibrated with energy. Giver permitted Dedicated to look my way out of the swirling light. Dedicated waved in my direction, called my name, and immediately returned to the indescribable celebration. Astonishment and awe overcame me. I dared not breathe for fear of missing any part of what was happening before me.

Then the movement and heavenly sounds stopped. I heard feathered Nouma singing praises to Giver. A breeze whispered in the undulating leaves of nearby trees. From somewhere across the valley, I heard the sound of young Likeness kin laughing. Giver turned in his shining presence of light and began to move away. Dedicated reached out to him, and Giver reached back, wrapping his presence around him. Dedicated looked at me once more, smiled, nodded, and then turned back to face Giver. Giver pulled him closer and started to step away. Dedicated kept pace, and then they suddenly started to rise over the grove.

I watched in astonishment. I had seen Giver come and go many times. He had never brought anyone with him; nor had he ever taken anyone away. Dedicated was going away with Giver. Dedicated was now completely wrapped in Giver's presence of light; and in an instant flash, they disappeared into the blue sky above.

I fainted away on the ground, dazed for a long time. My ears were ringing, and my heart felt as if it was trying to beat its way out of my body. I tried to breathe deeply and fainted away again. This happened several times before I started to regain my strength. Before trying to stand, I looked in every direction, hoping to see someone nearby. I desperately wanted a Likeness kin to have seen Dedicated go away with Giver. There was no one. I was alone.

I remained on the ground a while longer and then stood unsteadily to my feet. My head was light, and I was slightly dizzy. I reached for a nearby branch of tender leaves and chewed them to gain strength. I shook my head and snorted several times, attempting to feel normal. It took a while longer before I felt steady enough to move to a nearby spring of water. I bent and drank deeply and then raised my head and stared intently at the point above the trees where Giver and Dedicated had disappeared.

I could not leave without returning to Likeness-Image City to tell someone what had happened. Who would believe my story? After quiet reflection, I decided to tell Between. Perhaps it was no accident that he met me earlier coming into the city. That must be it. With Giver, there were no accidents—just appointments for those who desired to please him. I stopped that thought at once. It was far too heavy for consideration by a simple Nouma, especially after the incredible event that I had just witnessed.

I made my way back into the city and asked where to find Between. A young Likeness female led me to his dwelling. Between was busily engaged telling younger Likeness kin the stories from the becoming. I settled to the ground and listened with great interest.

How had the telling been preserved? I wondered. It was easy to listen to Between. He spoke with great animation and passion. The young Likeness offspring sat openmouthed as he took them through the telling from Mystery

Grove in Home Valley to this very time. I too learned much. There were many events from Between's telling that helped fill the gaps in my own understanding.

Between stopped often to answer questions from the young Likeness learners and then continued the story. I heard many things about Likeness, Image, and Substitute that were not part of my telling. I planned to add them to what I would tell the Noumaso.

Between finished the telling. The young Likeness kin thanked him and moved away, seeking other distractions. I waited quietly until Between took food and drink and then moved forward to speak with him.

"Between, my Likeness brother," I said, "I found Dedicated as you said I would. He was deep in conversation with Giver. It seemed as if I had returned to the becoming and was seeing Giver and Likeness at the beginning. Nothing since that time compares with what I saw today."

I paused and then continued. "Dedicated was wrapped by Giver in his shining presence. I had to drop to the ground from the awe of what I saw." I stopped again, unsure about how to continue.

Between saw my hesitation and moved his face closer to mine. He looked deeply into my eyes and smiled. "Yes Naados, Say it."

"I'm afraid you will not believe me," I said.

He laughed and asked, "Where is Dedicated?"

I glanced away and then turned and stared full into his eyes.

"Giver took him away!" I shouted. "They were swirling and talking and dancing. They stopped for just an instant, and Dedicated reached for Giver. Giver wrapped him in light and started to move away. Dedicated walked away with him. Together, they moved up above the trees and then immediately disappeared in a flash into the sky."

Between rubbed his chin with his hand as if contemplating my words. He then smiled broadly and broke into hearty laughter. "So, he finally did it. he finally did it," he said. "Giver just took him along."

I was puzzled by his words.

Between saw my furrowed brow and explained. "For many of Likeness's years, we have talked about Giver and Dedicated. Few Likeness offspring have enjoyed such a relationship with the Creator. My father, Cleansing Comes, often said that Dedicated would prefer living with Giver to being among his kin. 'Giver will take him,' became a saying among us all. We believed it would happen, but we were unsure when.

"You old Nouma; you did it again! There you were in the right place at the right time to see the unusual. I almost envy you, old friend."

I interrupted with, "It's a good thing I ate from the life tree or I would be a dead Nouma. My heart almost exploded in my chest!"

We laughed together as we talked of Dedicated and his times with Giver.

Before leaving Likeness-Image City, I had questions to ask Between. "Has the joining of Likeness kin males and Possessor kin females brought any change to this city?"

Between grunted, paused, and then spoke. "More than anyone is willing to admit, I'm afraid. Most of our males who return no longer desire to gather for our meetings with Giver. Their matas are hostile toward any mention of Giver's name. You probably have not noticed, but the Possessor females have established businesses selling images of objects they pretend to respect. In the same places, they offer themselves for joining with both males and females. They are corrupt and are corrupting our young offspring.

"This is one of the reasons I take time to do the telling for our offspring. I hope to help counteract the invasion of the malevolent presence among us. More of Possessor's kin are coming here every year. I fear that their aggressive ways will overpower our desire to be gentle as followers of Giver. I fear for my offspring and for theirs to follow. I know that Giver will not forever overlook their folly. I weep for the days before the bending."

Between asked me to remain in Likeness-Image City for a few passages of the sky orb. He was determined to show me the extent to which the offspring of Possessor had corrupted the city.

It did not take long for me to understand his reason for concern. New areas of the city no longer had the straight lanes through them. They twisted and turned like those in Branded City. Lustful behavior occurred in open public places. Very young Likeness kin constantly consumed the fiery drink. They fought with their fellows and from time to time brought the sting to others. It had become unsafe to walk through many parts of the city when the night sky orb was dark. Young Likeness females were attacked and violated.

It was with heaviness in my heart that I said good-bye and headed toward Home Valley. I felt helpless to do

EDDIE PAYNE

anything about the growing rebellion against Giver by the offspring of Likeness. Perhaps I could best help by encouraging the Noumaso. I was told that many of them were also victims of violence by bent Likeness kin.

HOME VALLEY
AND BEYOND

To my great surprise, I discovered Possessor and Likeness kin now living in some of the vast, open areas west and north of Likeness-Image City. Possessor's kin had traveled up the river into the undeveloped countryside.

Farther to the south and west, a mixture of Likeness's kin now lived. These settlements were a result of joining the two lines of offspring. I made some effort to contact them as I passed through but had no great success. Most of my information about them came from the Noumaso I met along the way. Some told tales of abusive behavior toward the Noumaso by Likeness's kin. Others chose to move away from the new settlements of Likeness kin. The Nouma kin always found undeveloped areas where they could live out their lives in peace.

I chose the northern route back to Home Valley. This permitted me to see how far the Possessor kin had gone in that direction. I was surprised that they had moved up the river to within sight of the guardians' flashing lights at the pass. This put the village at a five-sleep journey from the pass. I wondered if any had attempted to enter Home Valley.

It seemed best for me to return using the old trail into the valley. Likeness and Image traveled it when they were driven out. The trail went through the pass where Giver had placed the guardians. Enough Nouma kin used it that I traveled with no difficulty.

The morning I neared the pass, I found evidence that Likeness's kin had been here. Near the bottom of the long hill leading up to the pass, trees and grass were withered and burned. Large rocks had been dislodged from the peaks overlooking the pass. Many were scattered for a great distance along the trail.

The kinds of things usually carried by traveling Likeness kin littered the path. I stopped to think about what I saw. It looked as if Likeness kin attempting to follow the trail through the pass were stopped by the guardians. I could see no evidence that harm was done to the Likeness kin. In their haste to escape safely, it seemed they had dropped what they were carrying and ran for their lives.

I looked up at the silent guardians and hoped that I

would be permitted to pass. I need not have been concerned. The guardians watched me come up the trail and
descend the other side of the pass. Home Valley spread
her beauty before me. I stopped, choked with emotion.
"Is it possible I have lived more than fourteen hundred of
Likeness's years?" No one answered my question.

Hurrying down the pass into the valley, I sought
familiar landmarks. Some of the more permanent ones
were evident. Most were not. The years of uninterrupted
growth had turned the valley into a forested haven for
Noumaso. The absence of Likeness kin left the valley as
pristine as it had been the day of becoming. Hundreds of
years of growth turned the valley into the most magnificent forest in Giver's world.

Noumaso ranged through the valley. I greeted them
as I moved toward the area where Mystery Grove was
located. They responded kindly but had no idea who I
was. I should have expected their reaction. I have, after all,
outlived generations of Noumaso.

I stopped to graze with a group of my own kin. Were
these offspring of my own and my long-departed Lhaloo?
I blushed that I had not thought that name for a long time.
Then I remembered that it was acceptable. Life is for the
living. I stopped myself in the middle of that thought. *Relax,
Naados, old Nouma, you are home. Enjoy the peace of the moment.*
I realized that my life had become far too complicated.

I grazed and rested during several passages of the sky orb
and then set out to look for Mystery Grove. Surprisingly,
I found the area with little difficulty. The problem was the
size of the forest surrounding it. It had doubled in size since

my last visit. The newer growth on the outside was not as tall as the old familiar trees near the middle but spread over a wide area. I looked around the outside, trying to find where I had entered in the past. There was no easy way in.

As I pondered what to do, a heavy, furry Nouma kin approached. "Hey, Nouma," he said. "Are you lost? Do you need help?"

I had seen his kin many times but had never spent much time with them. I wondered if I should tell him everything or just give up on entering the grove. I chose to tell my tale. He munched nearby ripe red berries and listened, nodding from time to time. I told the essentials about my interest in Mystery Grove.

He grunted and said, "Follow me. If you don't mind, some new scratches on that sleek coat. I can get you to the older part of the grove." I followed willingly as he pushed a path through the undergrowth.

"I have a special place deep in the grove where I take long periods of rest. It is a comfortable, secluded cave, and I have yet to be disturbed there."

With that, he led me deep into the forest. We eventually reached a part of the grove I recognized. I thanked him. He turned and lumbered away to spend time in his special sleep place.

I carefully worked my way toward the center of the grove. As the sky orb slid behind the western hills, I found the flat stone. Nothing had changed but the growth around the stone. The tall trees overhead were now so thick that direct light could no longer reach bushes and vines underneath. The area around the stone was cluttered with old, dried vines and bushes. One thing remained unchanged: the two special trees from the becoming. They had not grown. They were as green and tempting as on the first day of creation.

When light penetrated the grove, I stood by the flat stone and spoke to Giver. He did not appear. I worked my way back through the tangle, following the path made by my new friend. I stepped out of the forest just as the sky orb slipped behind the western horizon.

After a satisfying time of sleep, I decided to move on. I paused only long enough to eat the delicious, dew-covered herbs from home and then trotted toward Northwest River. I wanted to follow the river west for at least three cycles of the night sky orb and then turn south. Vast areas in that region had yet to be explored. I wanted to know if Likeness's kin had arrived there. Knowing that they use Nouma to carry them great distances, it seemed possible that some had moved that far west and north.

Travel was easy and familiar through the Northwest River valley. Rivers and streams overflowed with behemoth kin. Plains were covered by vast herds of four-footed Nouma. Food was abundant. Giver's handiwork was untouched by the bent Likeness clans. How different this was from the areas east of Home Valley. The tranquility of the area caused me to take more time on the journey than I intended. I felt no guilt about doing it.

When I left the river and turned south, travel became more difficult. There were no longer any familiar reference points. I was spoiled by following rivers on my previous journeys. I remembered that when I stopped following the rivers in the east, I was still in familiar territory. The vast, western plains are different. Streams and small rivers are everywhere, but I could not always tell if they were headed toward one of the two rivers I had explored.

I learned to use my shadow as the most accurate way to be sure of my direction of travel. Overconfident on several occasions, I became completely disoriented. This usually occurred when morning foggy mist lingered until nearly the middle of the passage of the sky orb. I think that Giver permitted me to have that helpless feeling in order to remind me of my constant need of him.

Large groups of Noumaso filled the vast, grassy plains. Most of them had heard part of the telling and passed it down from generation to generation. It was exciting to see their response when I told them of more recent happenings in our world. During one such telling far south of Northwest River, they told me about the Likeness kin now in the area.

From what they said, it must have been shortly after I saw the Likeness kin riding Nouma that they started settling in the area. Some of the huge, shaggy Nouma of the plains were the first to see the Likeness kin.

They swept in on their Nouma mounts and frightened Noumaso everywhere. Five Likeness years passed, and then many came with their matas and offspring. Their arrival was not pleasant for my shaggy Nouma kin. They brought something no Nouma had seen before. They carried small tree branches that made a loud noise and flashed fire.

The Nouma telling me was upset by the terror of his story. I quickly understood why.

"When they chose places to live, they did not talk with the Noumaso. We made many attempts to welcome them and get their stories. The Nouma they had with them acted strangely and treated us badly. We could not understand why.

"They were not among us long before we knew they were hostile. They came among us riding their Nouma mounts and making fire stick noises. My kin fell before them. The Likeness kin brought the sting to my Nouma along with the noise of their fire sticks. They then took long, sharp objects and removed the covering from our fallen kin. They left the bodies of my kin where they fell to become dust.

"They took the Nouma coverings and fastened them together. These were attached to small trees to make shade from the sky orb. The Likeness kin brought the sting to multitudes of my Nouma kin. We learned to avoid them, but not before this great sorrow visited us. There are now many Likeness clans in this area. Most of them no longer live in the shadow of our Nouma coverings. They place stones on top of other stones and cover them with small trees from the forests."

It seemed that these Likeness kin were from either Possessor's offspring or the mixed Likeness offspring. Whoever they were, they no longer attempted to talk with the Noumaso. *They are very bent*, I thought.

I stayed several passages of the sky orb to make sure the Noumaso understood the telling and then said goodbye. I felt the need to return to Likeness-Image City. Between needed to know about the efforts of Possessor's kin to enter Home Valley. I also wanted to tell him about the Likeness kin on these plains in the west. Giver's Likeness creatures were changing and it was not for the good. How different they were from Dedicated.

Changes at Likeness- Image City

Traveling east was easier for me than the journey south across the forests and plains. I only had to wait until the sky orb came over the horizon to know the direction to travel. By heading that direction and making sure my shadow did not go north or south of me, I made steady progress toward Likeness-Image City.

Great numbers of Likeness's kin now lived in the valleys and plains of the areas that I crossed. For the most part, I skirted their villages and small cities. I felt no need to know more than I had learned on the western plains. What was to become of Likeness's kin?

When I crossed Southeast River, it had many Likeness river houses carrying things. With the passing of the years, the river houses had greatly changed. They were larger and belched plumes of black smoke. Spinning things on the back of them stirred the water and pushed them quickly forward. It must have been frightening and dangerous for the noumaso in the rivers. Cities were scattered along the banks. The familiar, dingy haze covered the cities and river valley. My breathing always became difficult in these areas. The glowing objects giving light in the dark were everywhere. *What are the Likeness kin doing to Giver's creation?* I thought.

Likeness-Image City had grown west and now overflowed into two adjoining valleys. I spotted it from a high hill and was surprised by its increased size. The original city was a great distance from my vantage point. New cities wrapped around it. Had I been gone that long? The small cities were joined together by lanes but separated by forested hills and cultivated fields. This was what I passed through as I made my way toward the old city.

The new outlying cities were made like Possessor City. For the most part, their lanes and passages followed the contour of the hills and valleys. Some old Likeness influence provided one larger lane coming into the city from the west. It was not straight like those in old Likeness Village but did go generally eastward toward the center of the old city.

I attempted to move at a pace that called no special

attention to my passing. From time to time, a canine ran to yap and nip at my feet. I usually ignored them, but now and again it became necessary to speak. I usually said, "Hey, Nouma born yesterday, where are your manners?"

They always slid to a stop and replied, "Sorry, elder Nouma," and then turned and ran quickly away. Evidently, even the Noumaso were not telling their own how to live correctly. They changed the old creation tongue. Their offspring resembled the Possessor Likeness kin more and more.

I passed one sleep time in a small forest on my way to the center of Likeness-Image City. Several smaller Nouma kin lived there. They listened with respect to my telling. They did not recall that the story had been told by those who gave them life. *So, even the Noumaso are leaving the old ways*, I thought. *Are we Nouma also being bent beyond recognition?* That was my thought as I closed my eyes to rest.

I reached the straight path in the old city early the next day. Changes had occurred throughout old city. Numerous Likeness dwellings were no longer occupied. They had become little more than piles of stones and decaying trees. Likeness's offspring were there but were more subdued than those in the past. I spoke to a few scattered Nouma, but they too were apathetic. What had happened to Likeness-Image City?

I soon reached Central Grove and was relieved to see that it looked just as I remembered. A few mature Likeness males sat and sipped some kind of beverage. The quiet of Central Grove was a contrast to the noise that assailed my ears as I passed through new parts of the city. How quickly we accept the noise that comes with change.

I spoke a greeting to the Likeness kin and would have passed on toward the center of the grove but was stopped in my tracks by a loud, "Naados, is it really you?"

The speaker jumped to his feet, spilling his drink as he rushed toward me.

"Naados, I can hardly believe my eyes," he said. "I thought I would never see you again."

I searched my memory but could not find a name to fit him.

"I am Cleansing Comes, giver of life to Between. Welcome, old Nouma. Come tell us of your travels."

By now, his friends had risen and were crowding around me, smiling and speaking. It was good to be among Likeness kin who remembered the old ways.

Cleansing Comes introduced me to his companions. I was so filled with memories that their names went in my ears but did not stay in my mind. Two of them were offspring of Dedicated. I'm not sure about the other two. Cleansing Comes called for water for me to drink and then insisted that I tell them how Dedicated went away with Giver. Even though Between had told them many times, they wanted to hear the story directly from me. I never had a more alert and attentive audience.

I began by saying, "Giver took him."

They glanced at me and then at one another and broke out in laughter.

They all spoke at once, saying, "You remembered. You remembered."

From that point on, they held on to every word and often stopped me to ask questions. It was as if they were all living that tremendous event for the first time. I cannot tell how pleased I was to give them answers to their questions. It was special for me to once more be among Likeness's kin who knew Giver and could speak with passion about Him. When I finished the telling, I asked Cleansing Comes to tell me what had happened since my last visit.

Cleansing Comes leaned back where he sat, placed a hand on his bearded chin, and began speaking.

"After you went away, Between called us together. He told us that you had seen Dedicated go away with Giver. It brought much joy but also sorrow. Joy because we knew that Dedicated passed each day wanting to be with Giver. We know that he now has his desire fulfilled. Sorrow because his presence gave so much to each of us. His optimistic spirit pushed us all to think good thoughts about Giver and His great plan for Likeness's kin. With him gone, we have no one with such a passion for Giver and His ways. Between fills in part of what is missing, but he knows he does not have all of Dedicated's gifts. Life must go on.

"We did our best, but life became increasingly difficult. When our males started bringing Possessor kin matas back to our cities, everything changed. I know you have observed the differences."

I stopped him long enough to agree and promised to tell them more about Likeness's kin in the west after he finished.

"Very soon, we who honor Giver became the objects of ridicule. It quickly went beyond ridicule. Numbers of us were designated as social misfits. Some of our more zealous kin were severely mistreated. Others were made to feel the sting by the merciless, overzealous Possessor kin. There are those of our kin now held in Possessor houses of correction who are designated as mentally deranged and dangerous to the social order. I tell you, Naados, we suffer for Giver. The malevolent presence controls most of Likeness's kin.

"We know that Giver is aware of what we suffer. We also know that he does not force Likeness kin to obey him. Most Likeness kin have taken the gift of free choice and twisted it to their undoing. The question that we who follow Giver now ask is how long will Giver tolerate such wicked disobedience? The few of our remaining Likeness kin who are wise in the ways of Giver believe some judgment is soon to come.

"When we tell these things to Possessor kin, they mock and scorn us. 'What has not improved for Likeness kin since what you call the becoming?' they say. 'If there were a Giver, why would he want to judge us for the good changes we have made?' They accept no answer we offer. They choose to continue their blind pursuit of pleasure. They spend their time dreaming up new ways to practice what they call full living. They mock the thought of a living Giver."

I could see that this telling had emptied Cleansing Comes both mentally and physically. Not wanting to bring him to the point of exhaustion, I suggested we finish the telling at a later time. One of his kin agreed.

Before leaving, I asked where I could find Between and his family.

Cleansing Comes said, "They are among those who have moved away from the center of Likeness-Image City. They have become part of a small group of Likeness kin who live north of the city. You should have no problem finding them since the settlement is near where Dedicated went away with Giver."

I thanked them and asked permission to go north to find Between and his clan.

"Be sure and ask about his offspring Rest Giver," Cleansing Comes called out as I walked away.

What I was told became evident as I headed north out of Likeness-Image City. There was no additional building in that direction. I soon found myself in familiar countryside. It was soothing to be outside the crowded confines of the city. I set a steady pace up the path. In short order, I rounded a familiar curve in the lane and saw the fields and forests from which Dedicated went away with Giver. To the east across a small valley and up the side of a hill was the new settlement of Likeness clan. I hurried in that direction.

Fleecy Nouma grazed in the valley and up the far hillside. Two small male Likeness offspring sat under a tree watching their flock. A canine Nouma kept the flock from scattering in the valley. The scene was a peaceful reminder of what had been normal long ago before most Likeness kin became so bent. I longed for those times.

The young Likeness offspring called out as I passed nearby. "Hey Nouma, why are you alone?"

Good question, I thought. "I'm a wanderer," I replied, "friend of Cleansing Comes and Between."

They jumped up and ran quickly toward me. "Have you ever met a Nouma like yourself called Naados?"

I paused and then replied, "I see him every time I drink from a still brook."

They glanced at one another and then caught on. "You are Naados?" one of them asked.

"Indeed, I am," I replied.

They laughed and then grabbed me around the neck. "Welcome, friend of our kin. Between will be very pleased to see you."

They took me into the settlement. I noticed at once that the trails leading in were just like the lanes in the old Likeness's village. I did not have to wonder if there would be a Central Grove. It was just where it should be in the center of the village. Two Likeness kin were seated there in deep discussion.

One of my guides called out, "Between, look who is visiting."

The older of the two Likeness males turned. He then leaped up and over where he was seated and lunged in my direction.

"As I live and breathe," he said. "If it isn't Naados."

"Your servant," I replied.

Between then called the other Likeness male to his side. "Naados, I want you to meet my offspring, Rest Giver."

Rest Giver stepped forward, politely nodded, patted my head, and then stepped back beside Between. Between glanced at me, looked back at Rest Giver, and then threw back his head and laughed. Rest Giver looked uncertain until he glanced at me. I snorted and then laughed. Rest Giver realized what he had done and then joined us in laughing.

"Sorry, Naados," Rest giver said. "I did not intend to treat you like a pet lamb."

"Quite all right," I said. "I much prefer it to the treatment I receive in some places." I thought, *This Likeness and I will get along very well.*

Between called for water and a basket of fresh herbs for me. We then talked until the night sky orb was half-way through her journey. I was invited to take my rest there in the grove. Between said that we had much to talk about and wanted us both to be well-rested.

Between and Rest Giver

After a refreshing snack in the grove where Dedicated always met with Giver, I was ready for a talk with Between. He and Rest Giver came to the grove, and we settled down for serious talk about the future.

Between wanted me to understand what was going on in Likeness-Image City that had caused his clan to move to this location. He told me more about the abusive behavior of Possessor's kin.

"They seem willing to do anything to erase the memory of Giver from the hearts and minds of

Likeness's kin. The conditions are terrible under which those they call mentally deranged are held. Their only crime is that they have cried out publicly against the wickedness of the clan leaders. They are locked away in dark places and given almost no food. They are tied by their hands and feet to the walls of a small room. Their keepers insult them and threaten to take the sting to their mata's or their offspring if they do not renounce all belief in Giver. Some do not last long under the abuse.

"Most of us are not treated this badly. We are considered simpleminded and deceived. They permit us to leave what they call *their* cities and remain isolated in areas such as this. We are fortunate that they almost all fear coming to this area. The tales of Giver's visits here have kept the superstitious Likeness kin from even passing through."

"What about Rest Giver?" I asked. "There seems to be something special about him."

Between nodded in agreement. "Even before his birth, Cleansing Comes said that Giver had a special task for him. He thinks it has something to do with a coming cleansing on all of Giver's creation. None of us understand what that *cleansing* means. Rest Giver comes often to this very place. He can speak for himself."

Rest Giver hesitated and then spoke. "Since I was young, Giver has spoken inside my heart. I listened to the Possessor kin talk, and thought I would resist Giver. One night, Giver spoke to me in a dream. His appearance was fearful."

I nodded in agreement. How well I remember those times in his presence.

Rest Giver continued. "He said that I should choose to

follow him. I already knew this. My life giver and others of my kin told me often. I asked why it should be me and not someone else. He said that my heart was bent toward him. He also said that he would give me abilities to work with him. I tried to understand, but I am young. He promised that at the right time I would know what to do.

"When I awoke, I spoke to Giver and told him that I would do what he asked. Not long after that, our family moved to this place. Between told me about Dedicated and his walks with Giver in this grove. Giver meets with me here, but also inside my heart and head. I sit and think about him. He gives me thoughts about how to do his bidding."

Between spoke, "Rest Giver, tell Naados what Giver has said to you about cleansing the earth and how he will do it."

Rest Giver lowered his eyes and furrowed his brow. "The words are difficult," he said, "but I know they are true. Giver has determined to destroy all life from this world. He knows the evil the offspring of Likeness and Image are plotting. He is pulled between mercy and justice. Likeness's kin are continually becoming more wicked and corrupted. Giver has determined to cleanse the earth and start with another line of Likeness's kin."

"Does this mean that He will do again what He did in Mystery Grove so long ago?" I asked.

"Tell him, Rest Giver," said Between.

"The telling is painful," said Rest Giver, "but I will say it. Giver said that I will have a mata and offspring. We are to be those who survive the catastrophe. Giver has said that water will fall from the sky and come up from the earth and take away all life."

This was too much for me a simple Nouma to understand.

"Morning mist now waters our world," I said. "I do not understand this thing about so much water."

"Nor do we," said Between. "It is a deep mystery."

Rest Giver continued, "Giver has not told me everything, but he has said that I must make a very large vessel to take my family and the Noumaso to safety."

"Noumaso?" I asked.

"Yes, Naados. Not only Likeness's kin but Noumaso must be delivered," said Rest Giver.

How can that be? I thought. *This young Likeness male has no idea about how many Nouma live in our world.*

My mind was now reeling, and I began to feel weak. "So, tell me more," I said.

Between said, "Show Naados what you have made, Rest Giver. Maybe it will help him better understand."

Rest Giver stood and indicated that we should follow him into the grove. Hidden deep in the small forest stood a Likeness dwelling. Between and I followed Rest Giver inside. He pulled back coverings from several openings to let light stream in. In the center of the dwelling, a large, flat surface lay on top of small tree trunks. A miniature Likeness river house almost filled the surface. But it was not a Likeness river house. It was very different.

Rest Giver explained what I was seeing. "This is the first thing that Giver has shown me about what I am to do. When the time comes, Giver will show me how to build this vessel."

I studied it with great interest. I had seen many river houses, but this was unlike any of them.

Between saw my furrowed brow and said, "Me too, Naados. I have no idea what this represents. Giver has helped me understand that he is doing it, so I have no fear for Rest Giver."

We returned to the open field overlooking the valley. Rest Giver stopped and studied the slopes leading down to the small valley. "I wonder," he said, "if the vessel will be big enough to fill the valley."

I looked from end to end of the expanse and laughed. I heard a small gasp from Rest Giver and turned my eyes in his direction. He was looking at me.

In an instant, he too laughed and said, "Naados, it is not difficult to know what you think. You say it even when you don't speak."

I looked away and thought, *I hope I somehow fit into the plan that Giver is showing to Rest Giver. I like this Likeness offspring."*

Between and I started back across the valley toward the settlement. Rest Giver said he wanted to go back into the forest. "Giver has started showing me special trees in the grove," he said. "One kind is strong and straight. It looks as if it could be used to build a vessel, but I have not been told so. Another he has shown me has thick, sticky fluid inside. I'm marking those trees in this forest so they can be easily found later."

Between and I talked quietly as we returned to the valley. I could not help silently counting my steps down the hillside and back up the other into the settlement. *How big will the vessel be?* I wondered.

I passed another refreshing sleep time in the settlement. When the sky orb rose, we took food and returned to Likeness-Image City to talk more with the wise Likeness kin. No one else was on the path south until we neared the city. "This part of the old city is avoided by many Possessor kin," I remarked to my friends.

They nodded as we approached Central Grove.

THE REPORT
OF NAADOS

The elder Likeness kin were gathered at Central Grove. We were warmly greeted and given places of honor. Cleansing Comes, the oldest of the group, said thanks to Giver. He then announced that I, Naados, would talk about Likeness's kin and their settling toward the west. I expressed my thanks and proceeded to tell what I had seen.

"Likeness's kin have multiplied far beyond what I expected. For many of your years, they were only east of here. In my travels, in the past hundreds of years, they have moved steadily to the west. I first saw only a small group of mounted Likeness kin near Southwest River long ago. My latest travels to Home Valley and beyond were a different story.

"Let me speak first of those who followed Northeast River toward home valley. I did not expect them to attempt to return to our place of becoming. I thought that the stories of the guardians placed in the pass into Home Valley would keep them from wanting to go there. That is not so.

"On my last travels, I saw Possessor kin villages within sight of the lights from the Guardians' position. They can be seen during the passage of the night sky orb. These Likeness kin are settled about five sleep times from the pass.

"Not only are the villages close by, but some of the likeness kin made an effort to enter. They did not realize the power of the guardians' weapons and were driven back when they went up the trail to the pass. I do not think that any of them felt the sting, but the things they carried were destroyed by the fire from the weapons and by great stones falling on them from the pass. The guardians let me pass without challenge.

"Mystery Grove in Home Valley is barely recognizable. A huge forest now covers the entire area. A Nouma friend led me toward the center, where I spent one sleep time. The two trees from the becoming remain there, unchanged to this time. I always wonder what will become of them. For now, they are safe, protected by the guardians at the pass and the thick forest surrounding them.

"I traveled Northwest River from home valley for several cycles of the night sky orb. My main purpose was to search for Likeness's kin. When I was well on my way to the great salt water, I turned to the south. There are Nouma everywhere I travel. I also see marvelous things that Giver placed in the dust of our world. I think that Likeness's kin search for shiny objects in the dust.

"My travels took me far south before I found the Likeness settlements. These Likeness kin had taken the coverings from Noumaso to make shelter from the sky orb. They did this before making the more solid dwellings such as you use here.

"They have weapons that the Nouma living there called fire sticks. The weapons make a loud noise and can give the sting from a great distance. Hundreds of Nouma felt the sting from these weapons. I was told by my kin that these Likeness kin are not kind to any Noumaso. My kin go far from any Likeness village to avoid contact with them.

"When I turned east to come here, I found that Likeness kin villages were scattered the entire distance. Most of the villages are along the rivers and streams. Southeast River has big cities and is full of Likeness river houses. My behemoth kin have moved away from the cities along the rivers and streams. Nouma seem to be forgetting normal behavior as they are influenced by the Likeness kin.

"The changed drink made by your kin is in use every-where. I saw no evidence of efforts to honor Giver in these settlements. They appear to be like those living in the outer reaches of Likeness-Image City. Thoughts of Giver do not seem to be in their heads or hearts. That is what I saw."

Plans for the Future

No one spoke for some time after my telling. The seven elderly Likeness kin and Rest Giver seemed to be deep in thought. I glanced from one to another. Rest Giver, the most recent to join the group, looked around the gathering from time to time. Our eyes met, and he quietly stood and moved to where I reclined.

In a whisper he said, "Naados, my kin are deeply troubled. They were already determined to try something to help our offspring. You're telling has them even more perplexed about what to do."

Movement among the seven broke the spell. Everyone waited for Cleansing Comes to speak.

"Since I have lived in Giver's world longer than any other present, I will begin our discussion. What Naados told us confirms and reinforces our concerns for Likeness's kin. There seems to be no way to turn the hearts of Likeness offspring from the bending. All our efforts up to this time have met with rejection. Possessor kin's influence has overwhelmed all attempts to keep our offspring looking to Giver and his good way.

"We are convinced that Giver is planning a cleansing. We think that this will take away all living things from this good world. Naados, I'm afraid that even the innocent Nouma will feel the judgment of Giver. I propose that we take measures to learn as much as possible about what the bent Likeness kin are doing. We must not be caught unaware of how they may attempt to prevent the success of Giver's plan."

Between spoke next. "Cleansing Comes speaks Giver's truth. I think that we need to secretly send some of our kin to Possessor City and observe what they are doing. We are all aware that Giver is showing Rest Giver things about the future. Rest Giver is young, and his knowing is incomplete. Our reliance is in Giver, but we must do our part to work with him.

"I propose that the two offspring of Dedicated here with us go to learn the secrets of the Possessor kin. He-Follows and True Heart are firm in the way of Giver. We will ask Giver to go with them and protect them from those who may want to do them harm."

Comments from one another confirmed Between's proposal. The two designated kin agreed to travel through Possessor kin's cities to the east. Javelin, offspring of Cleansing Comes, volunteered to go with his friends. After some discussion, it was agreed that he should accompany them. His skills and knowledge could prove helpful in dangerous situations.

Everyone expressed concern about the Possessor settlements east of Home Valley. We feared that bent Likeness kin, not understanding Giver's abilities, would make continued attempts to penetrate the valley and gain access to the life tree.

Cleansing Comes wondered if great numbers of them felt the sting that their kin would turn on those who follow Giver and seek to punish them. Everyone agreed that the ancient entrance to Home Valley should be visited. With one voice, they said I should be the one to go. Cleansing Comes said that I should not go alone. He suggested that Rest Giver and his sibling, He-Helps, go with me. This would help Rest Giver better understand the great challenge before him. We all agreed and planned our journeys.

TWO OF LIKENESS'S KIN AND A NOUMA

Those designated to visit Possessor territory spent ten passages of sky orb with Cleansing Comes and Between. They planned how to best obtain the needed information. I was called on to give insight into the attitudes of Likeness kin and Noumaso. I talked about locations I found during my last visit that provided secure places from which to observe.

The elders gave them instruction about the behavior of Likeness's kin who drank the fiery beverage. They were shown how to pretend to be controlled by the beverage. It was thought that mimicking the behavior could help them avoid detection. These things were outside my understanding.

After another five cycles of the night sky orb, they were sent on their way, wearing the kind of coverings used by Possessor kin. We spoke words to Giver as they departed and hoped to see them safely return.

Rest Giver, He-Helps, and I passed many of what they call days planning our own journey. They asked questions until my head was spinning. We wanted to be as well-prepared as possible.

Since I was the traveler and had taken the journey many times, they asked me to lead. I resisted but was convinced that in this situation it was best.

We determined to take a long route, avoiding all Likeness kin cities and villages whenever possible. We would travel during the passage of the night sky orb if necessary. What we would do depended on how much the Possessor kin had expanded into new areas.

I alone would speak to the Noumaso we encountered and explain the purpose of our journey. We would do everything possible to avoid leaving evidence of our passing. That was easy for me. My tracks blended with those of great numbers of Noumaso. For my Likeness kin, it would be more difficult. They devised special coverings to wear on their feet to disguise their identity.

These kinds of concerns had never entered my mind in the past. I was learning how difficult it had become for the Likeness kin to be followers of Giver. After that night of rest, we set out.

THREE TRAVELERS

We headed north just as sky orb started her journey upward. Dingy gray covered what had once been a pristine blue sky. Wispy spirals of morning mist and what Likeness kin called smoke mixed and drifted upward. Feathered Noumaso sang their spirited, high-pitched songs to honor Giver for another day. We stopped on a hill overlooking the village and asked Giver to take us safely on our journey.

With traveling companions unaccustomed to my fast pace, I moved slower than usual. It would require some time traveling together for me to gauge how fast to go. I was unsure how often they would need to stop for rest. They had strong, young bodies, so we traveled at my slow pace with no difficulty.

The first few days of travel, I had to remind them not to talk or make noise. By the end of ten sleep times, they were reasonably silent as they walked. I stayed far enough ahead of them to hear or see any danger in time to flick my tail in warning.

They had a problem with their feet. I helped them find soft, fuzzy herbs to put in the foot coverings they wore. This helped ease the pain. I tried to choose easy trails to travel because of my friends. This often took us twice as long as usual to cover the distance. We constantly came upon Noumaso. They kindly told us about anything unusual in their home areas. My traveling companions were welcomed with great kindness.

I hesitate to speak of another problem my friends encountered. They were accustomed to eating foods prepared from the herbs, fruits, nuts, and other delicious things that grew in our world. We carried none of these prepared foods with us. For some time, they talked every morning about the drink they took with their food. I do not understand. We Noumaso only drink from the abundant water that Giver provides.

We took extra time to find their food. They did not have the habit of eating what was available when the need for food was felt. For the first few days, we often did not find the kinds of food they enjoyed. I noticed that this caused some sort of problem that required them stopping often and finding a place to be alone. Maybe I would ask them about it later. I quickly began watching for tasty Likeness food.

It had been much easier traveling alone. By the end of one cycle of the night sky orb, we worked out the problems of traveling together. It was enjoyable to have companions.

The area we passed through had little evidence of Likeness kin. We decided that they must be staying close to large rivers and streams. I set our course to arrive at Northeast River, knowing that we would see Likeness kin there.

We topped a rise one morning and emerged from the shadows where we were walking. I saw the river in the distance and pointed it out to my friends. I snorted a signal for them not to move until told to do so. I moved slowly forward, ears high to hear any sound.

I saw the Likeness kin before hearing them. They were in the valley below but not yet near us. They traveled a well-worn Likeness path and looked to be about twenty in number. They rode Nouma mounts and pulled something behind them. Since they were distant, I called for my friends to move up beside me.

They saw the travelers. "What are two of the Nouma attached to and pulling?" I asked.

He-Helps shaded his eyes to see clearly and then replied, "That is one of the new objects they use to carry food and other supplies from one place to another. See, Naados. It has what we call wheels attached to long pieces of metal. The wooden box on top is fixed to the metal and carries the load." He-Helps used words that I had never heard before.

"What are wheels?" I asked.

He chuckled and said, "They are shaped like the sky orb. They move easily when joined by the long pieces of metal."

"Metal? That is another word I do not know," I said.

"Metal comes from the melting of stones. I know that you saw places where this is done in Possessor City."

"Yes," I said, "but this is all difficult for a simple Nouma."

We watched long enough to see that they were headed upriver toward Home Valley. I observed that those riding the Nouma carried long fire sticks. I wondered if they could give us the sting from that distance.

We moved away from the Likeness trail and followed the river from a safe distance. When the sky orb was down toward the western horizon, we saw a large Likeness city on the banks of the river. I was sure that this was the city not far from the pass into Home Valley.

We found a place deep in a grove of trees and planned for the next day. Late in the sleep time, when most of the light orbs from the city had dimmed, I searched the western horizon for signs of the lights from the guardians. I strained my eyes but only once thought I saw a flash. My sleep time was filled with dreams of Home Valley.

I awoke with a start and realized that I was alone. I jumped up and headed out of the grove. I saw He-Helps seated at the edge, looking out over the river and the city below.

I slowed and spoke. "You scared me, my friend. I was afraid that you had gone to the city."

He turned and said, "Now why would I do that, Naados?"

Then, before I could respond, he said, "Rest Giver went there at first light. We think there are many mixed Likeness kin living there. Perhaps some of them will give us information. Rest Giver planned to find some exotic foods on his way down and pretend to be a wandering food gatherer."

I gasped and fell to the ground. He turned and chuckled. "Don't worry, Naados. Rest Giver is very clever. He often visits the Possessor areas of Likeness-Image City to gather information. Cleansing Comes has no idea. Nor would he approve of it. This is how he has found out so much about river houses. He already knows the best wood for building. He is searching for the most effective way to seal the seams so that they will not leak."

I sat up and said, "But you should have told me."

"Sure," said He-Helps, "and you would have gladly told him to go."

I replied. "I have been too protective, my friend, and have not given enough thought to your intelligence and skill. The best thing for me to do is find some good food and wait."

"Thanks, Naados," He-Helps said. "Now don't worry about a thing."

Since I know that Giver has chosen Rest Giver for a special job, there is no need for me to be concerned. If only it were that easy. I tried to turn my thoughts to Home Valley. In doing so, I dozed in the warmth of sky orb.

I was jolted awake much later as He-Helps said, "He is coming."

I hurried to his side and saw Rest Giver walking up the hill, whistling. He carried something in his hand and acted as if he were the only Likeness kin in the world. He hurried his pace when he spotted He-Helps.

"Well," he said, "did you think I tasted the sting?"

"That is not funny," I tried to say with a serious voice. It sounded foolish even to me, so I laughed loudly. "You gave me a scare when I awoke and you were gone. He- Helps told me about your double life back in Likeness-Image City, so I decided not to worry about you. Tell us what you are carrying and then what you found out in the city."

Rest Giver spoke. "Sorry to have caused you concern. I was afraid that you might not approve of my visiting the city. When I arrived with the special herbs, I was immediately out of danger. They thought that I was an eccentric from the city who gathered special foods. I bartered what I had gathered for this."

He opened the packet, and out fell one of the containers in which Likeness kin store food. He also had a shiny, hard, empty container with two small drinking cups and two of the things I had seen his kin use to scoop food from containers to their mouths. He-Helps smiled broadly.

Rest Giver opened the container to show He-Helps. They both laughed. It was some sort of dark, smelly thing.

"Tomorrow, we will have a proper morning meal," said He-Helps.

They laughed at my puzzled look. I then realized that this must be what they use to make their hot drink.

"You risked your life for that?" I said.

They laughed and slapped me on the flank. I decided that I might as well laugh too.

"Now, what serious information do you have?" I said.

"Here is what I found out," said Rest Giver. "You are right, Naados, about their plans to go to Home Valley. They have been working for some time to get well-armed soldiers to this city."

"Wait," I said. "Explain yourself. Two terms I do not understand. *Well-armed* and *soldiers* mean nothing to me."

"Soldiers," said Rest Giver, "are Likeness kin trained to fight and even bring the sting to others. With the bending, Likeness kin want what belongs to others. Leaders among them gather individuals looking for adventure and provide weapons with which they can fight. They train them to do it well.

"*Well-armed* means that they have things like fire sticks. These enable them to take life at a great distance. They also have sharp, long knives they call swords. These are made from the melted stones. There are now a large number of soldiers not far from the pass into Home Valley. They think that they will be able to defeat the two guardians. They plan to go into the valley and find the life tree. Their leaders think that they can become rulers of the entire world if they possess that tree."

"But Giver will never permit that," I said.

"We know that, Naados," said He-Helps, "but the bent Possessor kin do not. They are blinded by the malevolent presence and believe that they can do anything they imagine."

"We must warn the guardians," I said.

Rest Giver gently reminded me that would not be necessary. "I'm sure that Giver is aware of their plans and will do what is necessary to keep them out."

"At the very least," I said, "I would like to be there when they arrive."

"As would we," said Rest Giver. "As would we."

We decided to rest and then head for the pass when the sky orb appeared.

My friends did not even take time for their morning drink before we started traveling. We skirted the city and pushed forward at a fast pace toward the pass. I knew that we needed at least four more sleep times to arrive there. We traveled all during the passage of the sky orb, snatched food and slept, and then resumed travel early the next day. The sky orb was slipping behind the horizon on the fourth travel day when I saw the peaks.

We moved well off any trails and settled in for rest. I had been watching the lights from the Guardians for the past three nights. Now it seemed that they were almost near enough to reach out and touch. My Likeness friends were excited by their appearance.

We rested. Then, before sky orb appeared, I led my friends up toward the pass. I stayed far to the side of the main trail. I watched the guardians and stopped when they glanced in our direction. I did not want to endanger my friends. When we stopped, the guardians paid us no further attention.

As the light from the sky orb peered into the valley below us, I gasped in astonishment. As far as I could see, there were long lines of Likeness kin. Over many of them, I saw faint wisps of the malevolent presence. It was unlike what I had seen in the past, but I did not take much time to think about it.

The soldiers in front were standing and wore special coverings. Something that looked like Beaufang was woven into the coverings. They carried fire sticks and other objects that I did not recognize.

They stood in lines that had about a hundred soldiers, maybe more. Far behind the lines of those standing were other soldiers riding Nouma mounts. Behind them were more soldiers on foot.

Rest Giver said, "Naados, below, you see how far the bending has taken Likeness kin. These are our brothers who follow leaders who refuse to acknowledge Giver. They seek to conquer and gain for their own benefit. The lives of these you see below mean nothing to the leaders. They are simply used for gaining wealth and power. They are here seeking the ultimate power, that of living forever."

"But, Rest Giver," I said, "I ate from the life tree and seek no power. I often wish I had not nibbled those leaves. You see me now as I was then, a young Nouma. I have not changed in these hundreds of years, but I have no desire for power or glory."

"Yes, Naados, I know," said Rest Giver, "but you also do not carry the gift of free choice. You were made for obedience alone and do not need to choose. We Likeness kin carry the seed of our own undoing. Giver made us with the power and ability to choose."

He-Helps nudged me and said, "Look. They are starting to move toward the hill."

Encounter at the Pass

We looked toward the valley below and saw the soldiers begin to move forward at a steady pace. Several tapped small branches on what they carried that looked like part of a hollow tree. Others chanted something that I could not understand. This tapping and chanting seemed to help the soldiers move forward together.

Rest Giver sighed and said, "I hoped they would not be so foolish."

He-Helps and I remained silent as we watched their progress across the valley floor. Those riding the Nouma moved into position on each side of the advancing soldiers. Others far in the distance fell in behind the last of those on foot. It was an impressive sight.

As the first soldiers reached the hill and started to move up the slope, I heard a strange sound coming from where the guardians were stationed. I glanced up the slope.

The guardians were stirring. I tried to watch both the soldiers and the guardians but found it impossible, so I chose to watch the guardians. From where they were, on either side of the wide pass, they slowly stood to their full height. Their appearance was fearsome. They each reached out across the pass with one of their wings and touched in the middle. It looked like a wall of black filling the opening. They then stretched their other wings out and slightly down toward the soldiers. This too gave the appearance of a dark barrier.

I looked back to the valley below and saw the malevolent presence deepen in color and spread over the entire army. The woven Beaufang symbols on the soldiers' coverings glowed brightly.

The soldiers advancing up the hill hesitated but were quickly urged on by shouts from those riding the Nouma. The rhythm of the tapping increased as the climb up the hill became more difficult. Most of the soldiers had not yet reached the hill when I heard another sound coming from the guardians. It started like the gentle whisper of a breeze through small leaves but quickly increased to a low roar. I looked again at the guardians. They were slowly turning their heads from side to side and blowing down the slope.

Out of the guardians' mouths came what looked like

heavy morning mist. As the mist swirled down the hillside and reached the valley, it became dark like a sleep time with no night sky orb. It raced quickly across the entire valley, covering the soldiers and continuing far beyond. The guardians continued to blow, and the darkness became more intense. Only a faint pulsating glow from the malevolent presence could be seen in the darkness.

Rest Giver and He-Helps had hardly breathed since the guardians began their defense of the pass. We were high over the valley so were not in the darkness. We were able to see the vast distance it covered. We huddled more closely together and watched the darkening valley below.

For a short while after darkness filled the valley, the soldiers' leaders shouted at them to continue up the hill. Then, just as quickly, the sound of movement stopped. Only the occasional clanging of weapons and snorting of Nouma could be heard; then even that stopped. We saw nothing from our safe vantage point except the deep darkness below. My ears were up and straining to hear any sound. There was none.

The guardians continued to blow the darkness down into the valley. Some confused shouting between the soldiers indicated that they were disturbed by the darkness. The shouts did not last long as their leaders quieted them. One of the guardians began making a moaning sound that tumbled down the hillside. It quickly became a deafening roar. The roar changed to noise like soldiers shouting and running down the hill and into the valley. My companions and I watched and listened in astonishment.

What happened next is hard to describe. The leaders of the

soldiers in the valley, unable to see anything, shouted out orders to defend against the enemy rushing on them. This started a loud roar and clanging, as they began to use the fire sticks and swords to defend themselves against the unseen enemy.

The guardians continued to make the sound of soldiers and Nouma pouring down the hillside. The noise in the valley increased to an incredible roar of screaming and cursing, mixed with the boom of fire sticks. It moved from what were the lines of the soldiers nearest the hill and continued through the valley.

Rest Giver said, "They are fighting one another. They don't realize there are no enemy soldiers. I can't imagine what slaughter is going on in the valley."

He-Helps stared wide-eyed and rubbed his hands together. We were all astonished at what was happening.

The sounds of fighting continued on and on and then slowly subsided at the bottom of the hill. Sounds of heavy fighting moved across the valley and into the distance. The dark covering sent by the Guardians remained over the valley for half the passage of the sky orb. When the only sounds coming from the valley were distressed cries of wounded soldiers, the guardians stopped blowing the darkness and sound into the valley.

Just as quickly as the darkness had filled the valley, it was cleared away by the Guardians. I watched as they calmly turned it into a fine mist and made it disappear. They then folded their wings and settled back to their original positions. The hillside was quiet.

I turned and looked down the hillside and out over the valley. My friends had been quietly staring in that direction since the darkness lifted. What had been a huge living Likeness army was now a vast, bloody plain piled full of the dead and dying. As far as I could see across the valley, not one soldier was standing. Both Likeness kin and Nouma had felt the sting. In the deep darkness, they had given the sting to one another.

Thousands of Beaufang spawn crawled over the fallen soldiers. They seemed to be moving away from the carnage toward the nearby forest cover. The malevolent presence was nowhere to be seen.

We sat and looked at the bloody valley until the sky orb was headed for the far western horizon. My friends were sickened by the carnage below. They knew that this was probably an indication of what was to come. I was unsure how to react.

The dead Likeness soldiers would become dust. They wanted what was not to be and shortened their time in Giver's good world. My friends knew that they were also offspring of Likeness and Image. They had been made to honor and worship Giver. They forfeited all that could have been.

Likeness's kin will weep when the telling of this encounter reaches the cities, I said under my breath.

"I know a way down the hillside that will take us far away from the valley of slaughter below," I said.

They agreed to leave the area as soon as possible. I knew that they were appalled by what had occurred. We went down the hillside to the south and were far from the valley of the sting when I chose a place to pass our sleep time.

We were exhausted but found it hard to rest. I napped through the passage of the night sky orb. Neither of them rested well. I rose just before the sky orb and sought a quiet place in a grove of trees to talk with Giver. He did not appear, but I knew that he was there. My mind was calm when I returned to my friends. They had awakened and held steaming cups of the beverage with which they greeted the new light.

It was only after several passages of the sky orb that we talked about what happened at the pass. We discussed it at length and finished with more questions than answers. It was agreed that we should return to Likeness-Image City and report the battle. I chose the route that followed Southeast River but stayed in the hills and forests, well away from the cities. We journeyed four cycles of the night sky orb before arriving north of Likeness-Image City.

PART FOUR

CLEANSING COMES,
AN UNKNOWN FUTURE

The Gathering

Our return to Between's village was uneventful but welcome. "Home has never looked so good," said Cleansing Comes.

He-Helps agreed, shouting, "No more trips like this for me!"

By now, news of our arrival had spread, and Likeness's kin were gathering. Everyone greeted me warmly, but it was nothing like the enthusiastic welcome given to my traveling companions.

Cleansing Comes had especially good news. His mata was heavy with waiting-to-be-born offspring. She looked as if it would be more than one. My kin usually have two or three each time they pass near the sting. I had forgotten what it was like to have a two-one partner waiting at the end of a journey.

Life is beautiful, even with the sting. How long had it been since that thought passed through my mind?

Food was prepared in abundance, and the celebration continued until well after the night sky orb rose in the east. I slipped away, crossed the valley, and found a comfortable place in the forest to graze and pass the sleep time. My dreams were troubled, but then they stopped and I drifted into secure, satisfying sleep. Leaves turning in the mild breeze whispered me awake as the sky orb lit my resting place.

I leisurely satisfied my hunger and thirst and then made my way back across the valley into the village. My friends were finishing cups of their steaming beverage and answering a stream of questions. I settled to listen and observe.

Painful as it was, the telling helped me rethink the events and their implications. I shivered at the thought that Giver would probably soon bring his cleansing to this world. What would become of my poor, innocent Nouma kin?

He-Helps jolted me back to the present by moving to my side and saying, "Our three friends have returned from their journey to the east. They are in Likeness-Image City, resting. Javelin was injured while defending his companions and is being cared for. He will carry scars from his encounter but should heal completely."

"So when are we going there?" I asked.

He-Helps replied, "It will probably be in two days. There are Likeness kin outside the city who will be called to the meeting."

I decided to pass the time in the forest across the valley. The solitude was welcome, and I had time to think about Giver.

From the shadow of the trees, I saw my friends start down the trail from the village. I walked out to join Between and my two traveling companions for the short journey to Likeness-Image City. We exchanged greetings and then remained silent until we reached the edge of the city. Three other of Between's kin traveled with us.

Most of the elders and other invited kin had gathered at Central Grove. Happy greetings were exchanged. There were no other Nouma present except two canine companions of Cleansing Comes. We spoke, and I settled down to observe and listen.

Cleansing Comes started the gathering by speaking to Giver. "You have met with our kin many times in this place, Giver of all life. Today, as we gather, we know our help must come from you. Your creation is bent almost beyond recognition. Our kin willfully turn from your good way. Help us think your thoughts as we hear talk of what our kin have seen to the east and to the west. You are just in all you do. We speak glory and honor to your name as we listen to you and the telling of our kin."

Rest Giver then told of our journey to the entrance to Home Valley. He called on me occasionally to fill in details of the travels and of the areas through which we passed. He-Helps made good observations about the Nouma we met and their thoughts on Possessor kin's conquest of the areas along the rivers.

It was a normal telling until Rest Giver spoke of our

arrival at the pass. In his excitement, he spoke eloquently about the awesome appearance of the guardians. His description of the army gathered in the valley below the pass sent chills across my back, even though I had seen it myself. When he spoke of the soldiers' coverings, he asked me to tell about the Beaufang image on them. This gave me an opportunity to talk about the malevolent presence and the role it played in the battle.

Rest Giver told of the guardians' defense of the pass. Since I had been watching them while he looked out over the soldiers, he asked me to tell how they produced the darkness.

I used all my telling skills to describe the way they filled the valley with darkness. He then told of watching the darkness overflow the valley. His description of the unseen battle should be told forever to Likeness's kin. I added only a comment on the terrible unnatural sounds coming from the darkness. I told of how it was like the sounds made by the malevolent presence in Mystery Grove at the time of the first sting.

Rest Giver ended his lengthy telling by describing the incredible carnage left by the Possessor army blindly killing their own. He wept as he spoke of the blood flowing in the valley. He shuddered when speaking of thousands of the spawn of Beaufang crawling over the bloody, dying bodies of Likeness's kin. Shocked silence greeted the end of the telling. They had never heard of this sort of slaughter of Likeness kin. Cleansing Comes shook his head in disbelief.

Between suggested that we wait for the next day to hear from our three brothers who traveled to the Possessor cities. "We have heard of sorrow too deep to add more at this meeting. Cleansing Comes has invited us to take food and a time of rest. We will continue the telling when the sky orb brings light tomorrow."

The Likeness kin moved silently away to the dwellings of their brothers. I walked to the flat stone and considered the reaction of the Likeness kin to the telling from Home Valley. My heart was heavy and my mind tired. I went deep into the grove and fell to the ground to think about my Likeness brothers.

First light brought the Likeness kin back to the meeting place. After thanking Giver for His goodness and provision, He-Follows, True Heart, and Javelin were asked to tell of their adventures. True Heart did the telling.

"We traveled east from Likeness-Image City toward the cities and villages of Possessor's clans. The smaller cities and villages are much like the outer reaches of Likeness-Image City.

"We did not expect the intense way that both males and females are preoccupied with satisfying their carnal appetites. We saw this in the ways they tried to convince us to join them in their lewd gatherings. It was good that Javelin traveled with us. It was much easier for three of us to maintain our integrity.

"You helped by showing us how to act as if we were under the control of the fiery beverage they drink. By remaining together and acting as if we were under its control, we were frequently saved from moral compromise. They laughed at us, and we learned to play the fool.

"The acting also helped us escape the seductive efforts of the females. There seems to be no memory of Giver's design for the two-one relationship among them. They have abandoned themselves to what they call love. It is a horrible, perverted lust that drives them to use their bodies for unbelievably wicked acts. Terrible wasting diseases ravage their bodies. This only seems to push them to greater excesses.

"We searched in every city for evidence of Giver among them. We found none. They continue to practice what they call religion. It does not resemble anything we recognize as honoring to Giver. Most of it is done in the name of some local worship object. They place statues in their meeting areas. We saw them dancing around these objects, cutting their own bodies until blood flowed freely. They use chants that are repeated mindlessly throughout the ceremonies. When numbers of them are involved, the dance grows to a frenzied pitch and the noise unbearable.

"They have started new religions that require giving of young offspring to the worship object. We saw one such ceremony. Ten females brought their youngest offspring. The leader of the ceremony plunged a sword through their bodies. They were then thrown through an opening in the image and into a fire.

"We were told that great numbers of Possessor's kin feel the sting by their own hand. Their thoughts become deluded and twisted until they no longer think that living is worthwhile. We were told stories of them gathering to drink something deadly and waiting for the sting together. Life seems to no longer have value.

"The availability of fire sticks and other weapons make it easy to take the life of another. In most of the cities, it is unsafe to be alone outside a dwelling after the sky orb sinks in the west. Those who are attacked receive no help. Passersby fear that they too will become victims, so they are unwilling to help others.

"Even with this moral decline, they make incredible discoveries. They continually produce new inventions to make life easier. It seems that when they determine to do something, there is nothing that prevents them from carrying it out.

"One evening during our time in Branded City, we witnessed an incredible event. We were passing the sleep time in a wooded area of the city. Far to the north, we heard a loud roar. For a time, we could not tell what was causing it. Then a faint glow appeared in the sky, followed by a trail of fire moving steadily upward into the darkness. It went up, up, higher into the sky, and then the noise and fire abruptly stopped. We had no idea what it could be.

"Two days later, while purchasing food, we overheard a merchant ask another Likeness kin if he had seen the fire flyer. He had not. The merchant said that it had gone far into the heavens. We listened intently. He continued by saying that if there was a Giver living somewhere up there, he had his sleep disturbed. The Likeness kin in the fire flyers will find him and that will be the end of it. They both laughed. The merchant said that Giver is a myth. We quickly left the shop and found out nothing more about the strange object going into the sky.

"While in Branded City, our talk betrayed us. Our use of the old language of creation caught the attention of a large group of young Likeness males. They quickly determined to take our lives. Only our valiant Javelin helped us escape. He was seriously wounded, but we evaded them with the help of Giver.

"Noumaso helped us find the safe places that Naados told about. We traveled only in the darkness. After many cycles of the night sky orb, we safely arrived back in Likeness-Image City. We found no one among the Possessor kin who seek to honor Giver."

Everyone sat quietly. Cleansing Comes cleared his voice and said, "It is evident that our world is in great peril. Likeness kin are beyond restoring. We bow to the desire of Giver and weep for what our kin have become. Rest Giver, we look to you. You are chosen by Giver to preserve life for a new beginning. We will do what you ask to help make this possible. I fear that we can do nothing to convince Possessor's kin to change their thinking."

I wept as I thought of the fate of these my Likeness friends.

Rest Giver's Offspring

We said our goodbyes and headed to Between's village. The sky orb was low in the west when we arrived. My Likeness brothers turned toward the village.

I chose to walk alone and graze before seeking a place to rest in the forest. My mind was whirling with all the telling. *How could Likeness's kin have gone so far from Giver? Will Rest Giver have the help that he needs to build a vessel? Is living vanity?* These and more thoughts occupied my mind until I realized that I had come to the dwelling in the forest. *From this simple shelter, deliverance is to come?* I walked a few steps, located some soft moss, and settled down to rest.

As the sky orb peered over the eastern hills, I heard shouts from the village. I cropped some dew-covered herbs, rushed from my resting place, and trotted down and across the valley. I was relieved as I neared the village to recognize that the sounds were cries of joy. Females were laughing and weeping. Young offspring were dancing and chanting, "They have come! They have come!"

Rest Giver saw me and ran to my side. "Naados, old friend, come see our occasion for joy."

He hurried along beside me to his dwelling. Older females were making sure that those doing loud celebration were directed to other parts of the village. Rest Giver's mata was resting in the dwelling after approaching the sting.

Seated at the entrance to the dwelling were three mature females. Each was gently holding a tiny bundle.

"These are my three new male offspring, Naados. Meet Renown, Persuader, and Swarthy."

I kept my distance but peered intently at each of them. *So these are to be Rest Giver's helpers,* I thought. "May the presence of Giver go with them," I said and then turned away and made room for those crowding in behind me.

Are There
Enough Trees?

I returned to the forest, cropped some of my favorite tender leaves, and started walking north. Rest Giver said that he had marked trees that might be useful for building the escape vessel. I was curious about the size of this forest. *If the vessel is to be built in the valley below, are there enough trees nearby?* I wondered. I need not have been concerned about the availability of trees. I walked north for most of the passage of sky orb and never reached the end of the forest.

All along the way, trees had been marked. The

tall, straight trees had two cuts. One was up and down, and one from side to side crossing over the other. The mark reminded me of how the lanes met in old Likeness Village. The other kind of tree was short with a slick outer covering. These trees were marked by two small cuts separated at the top, but joining a short distance below. A liquid from inside these trees had come out of the cuts and run down to the ground below. I touched it with my tongue. It was sweet and sticky but had become hard near the ground.

My sleep time was refreshing. The sky orb peered over the low hills to the east. I decided to travel west and continue exploring the forest. I was surprised that there were few large Nouma. I later remembered that my kin had moved far away from the cities and the Likeness kin.

After my shadow started pointing east, I found no more marked trees. I had not come out of dense forest when the sky orb disappeared in the west. For the following two Likeness days, I traveled south and then back to the east. All the area was covered by heavy forest. It was full of the two kinds of trees that Rest Giver had marked. Surely there would be no shortage of trees for the escape vessel.

I took my rest on the south side of a small hill in the forest. The western part of Likeness-Image City spread east to west in the distance. Light from the city made a warm glow, but it kept me from seeing the twinkling heavenly lights clearly. My rest was filled with dreams.

GIVER'S PLAN
FOR THE VESSEL

I was grazing as Rest Giver came up the side of the hill. He whistled a happy tune and fairly skipped along. *Not bad,* I thought, *for a Likeness kin who has lived about five hundred years.*

I stood quietly until he was nearby and then said, "Hey, old Likeness kin, why are you so happy?"

He stopped, saw me, and then laughed. "Who are you to call me old, you relic from creation. Compared to you, I was born yesterday."

I snorted and said, "You must know something good in a world gone bad."

"Naados, my friend," he said, "I have three offspring who will help me build the escape vessel. Giver spoke in my head and told me to come here for His instructions. I have decided that life is good, even with the sting."

"Who am I to argue with that?" I said and went back to grazing.

Rest Giver found a comfortable place to sit and look out over the valley. "Do I need to move away and leave you alone?" I asked.

"No, Naados," he replied. "I know that you will be welcome when Giver comes. You may even have some role to play. Fill your belly, and wait with me for his arrival."

We did not have long to wait. The feathered Noumaso fell silent. A strong breeze rippled the tops of the trees overhead. Rest Giver looked up and then stood. I did not move. Giver appeared out of the treetops and descended toward Rest Giver. I remembered and quickly started offering praise and thanks up to him. Rest Giver raised his hands and slipped quickly to his knees. He fell on his face on the ground. Giver let him remain there for a time and then lifted him to his feet.

"Creature of dust," said Giver, "you must now prepare the vessel. Likeness-Image kin all over the earth are corrupted beyond repair. They always choose the evil way. Beaufang's spawn dominate their every thought. You, your mata, and your three offspring with their matas will fill a new cleansed earth with Likeness-Image kin.

"I will melt the atmosphere above and send water to

fill the valleys and plains. I will break open the store-houses of water beneath the earth. All of dry land will be covered. There will be no escape for any creature that requires air to breath. Every living being will feel the sting as the waters cover the earth.

"You, your kin, and the Noumaso will be saved within the vessel.

Two by two they will come to you
Some I will send by seven
Those who walk and those who crawl
Those who fly the heavens
To your good care I send them all
For safety in the vessel
Food you will take and provision make
For every living creature
From my plan
By your strong hand
Life has new beginning
Listen now
I will show you how
To build deliverance vessel

Giver then gave the plans for how the deliverance vessel was to be built.

These things were too difficult for a simple Nouma, so I will tell what I understood. The vessel would fill the valley between the forest and the village on the other side. It would be built so that when rain, as Giver called it, began to fall, the vessel could easily be picked up by the rising waters.

There would be three levels inside the vessel. Larger

Nouma would live on the lower level along with food and water. Each level would have places to meet the needs of individual Nouma. The only openings to let in light would be along the top edge. Only one door would be made to enter the vessel. It would be wide and high and give access to each level for loading supplies and Noumaso. Giver himself would close the door when the time came to seal the vessel.

The earth would be dark and dreary during the time the water fell from the heavens and came up from the earth. The vessel would have light orbs inside. Giver explained how this would be possible. I did not understand.

The journey would be difficult, but Giver would make sure that we had everything necessary to make it successful. Giver himself would send my Nouma kin who were chosen to enter. Rest Giver would hire workers from his kin to help build the vessel. It would take one hundred of what Likeness kin call years to build the vessel and gather supplies for the time inside.

Giver answered all of Rest Giver's questions. They then moved some distance away and continued their talk. I could not hear what they said, so I dozed while Giver finished his instructions. Rest Giver nudged me awake and said, "Giver has something to say to you."

I wished I had not fallen asleep.

"Naados," Giver said, "you are unique among all Noumaso. You will be one of the seven of your Nouma to escape the cleansing. You will keep the results of eating from the life tree. For as long as there are Likeness kin in this world, you will live.

"There is nothing you or any Likeness kin can do to

prevent the coming judgment. Rest Giver has his task and will complete it. You are unable to help him until the time is near to enter the vessel. Return to Home Valley. There is one more event you must witness at Mystery Grove. Until then, live as a normal Nouma of your kin."

Giver then swirled his presence of light around us as he slowly rose up and over the treetops.

Feathered Noumaso resumed their songs. From across the valley, the sound of young Likeness offspring laughing mixed with the barking of their canine friends.

Rest Giver stared into the sky. Breathing deeply, he ran his fingers through his hair, rubbed his beard, and said, "It has arrived. It has finally come." I stood silently until he turned and said, "Naados, we have a job to do. Think of me as you return to Home Valley."

I accepted his words as my permission to travel north and west one last time in Giver's good world. My mind was divided as I turned to walk away. *Can I be of any help to Rest Giver? That question had an easy answer. My body was not designed to do Likeness work. What about the Likeness kin in the area who were trying to follow Giver? What could I do for them? I could think of nothing a simple Nouma could do to help.* I called a goodbye back to Rest Giver and then ran as fast as I could until I was out of sight of Between's village. I would never see many of my Likeness friends again.

GOODBYE TO
PARADISE

My mind was divided as I traveled northwest toward Home Valley. My Nouma brothers filled the hills and valleys where there were no Possessor kin. I stopped often and spent time with them but did not have the heart to tell them of the coming disaster. What could they do? It was not their fault that cleansing was to come. I talked often to Giver about how little I understood about it and why the Noumaso would perish. He reminded me that the Nouma were doing what he had made them to do.

This gave me comfort but did not take away the sorrow at what was to be.

Giver reminded me of his order to live as an ordinary Nouma during my final visit to Home Valley. My Nouma kin knew nothing of the coming disaster. They lived from day to day, enjoying Giver's good world. I determined to make every effort to do just that myself.

My pace was unhurried as I made my way toward Home Valley. I chose the same route my two friends and I had taken to the pass. The city nearest the entrance into the valley had grown even more. I stayed far to the south of it to avoid unwanted encounters. My plan was to arrive at the pass near the middle of the sky orb's passage. I wanted to see what had happened in the valley of the sting.

I approached the pass from the south. A low ridge made it impossible to see the valley until I was halfway up to the pass. I reached a place to look east into the valley below. From the bottom of the hill and out across the valley where the soldiers had been, nothing was growing. No herbs, no trees, nothing. I looked carefully from one side of the valley to the other. I only saw uneven mounds of bare earth.

When I was sure there were no Likeness kin in the valley, I made my way to the old trail and down toward the valley floor. From my new position, I saw the valley clearly. The uneven mounds were heaps of bodies from the slaughter. They had been covered with dirt, some better covered than others. Here and there, bones from the bodies stuck up through the dirt. The slaughter had been so great that the bodies were covered where they fell.

I saw no further evidence that Possessor kin tried to

climb up to the pass. I turned back up the old trail and soon reached the guardians. They watched me climb, stop at the pass, and then descend the other side. I was well on my way down into Home Valley when I realized something strange. Even though the guardians were always looking at me no matter where I was, I never remembered seeing them turn their heads. Did they have more than one face? The thought made the hair stand up on my back. I quickly dropped it from my mind.

Home Valley was beautiful, as always. The sky orb, descending toward the western horizon, created a golden, transparent haze across the valley. This was perfection, Giver's world, my home. I determined to put all thoughts of the outside world from my mind and live as a normal Nouma just as Giver told me to do.

A group of my own Nouma kin was feeding where the trail entered the valley. I greeted them and accepted their offer to share the bounty of Giver. They were talking of Giver and the becoming. How long had it been since I was with Nouma, who spoke so freely? I passed a completely satisfying sleep time with this family. I had no dreams.

Two of these kin had gone east across the pass. They wanted to see if the story about Possessor kin's effort to come into the valley was true. They saw the bodies and stayed to watch those covering them with dirt. This was the only time they had seen Likeness kin living or dead. After they returned, they were called on to do the telling all through Home Valley. Later, when I was asked about my journeys, I pretended to be timid. These young broth-

NAADOS AND HIS KIN: THE BEGINNING

ers deserved their time of glory. They need not know that I had enjoyed centuries of them.

My Nouma kin were grazing toward the west in the valley, so I drifted along with them. After three passages of the sky orb, we arrived near the vast forest surrounding Mystery Grove. I did not plan to enter there. When the elders did the telling and spoke of Giver, I listened quietly. Being with my own kin stirred memories and feelings long forgotten. I often ran with the young of the group and realized that to them I was young.

There were several unattached females among my kin. Since my Nouma instinct was becoming strong again, this did not go unnoticed by me. Three of the young females always pushed near to graze with me. After several days, one of the young beauties chased the other two from my side and became a constant companion. I tried to act uninterested but did not succeed. Little Lubah won my heart. My kin were not surprised when we joined. The delight of being a two-one creature again surpasses the telling.

Years flowed by more swiftly than the rushing waters from the mountain cavern. Lubah and I remained with our kin for several Likeness years and then set out on our own. I wanted to travel through the valley and perhaps a bit beyond. Lubah sought to get away from the shame of not bearing offspring. If only my sweet Lubah had known how merciful Giver was to her. I never told her of the coming cleansing. I never told anyone in Home Valley. I had no desire to spoil the joy they experienced in this little world untouched by Possessor kin.

Lubah and I traveled through the deep gorge where

Northwest River flowed from the valley. Her young spirit bubbled with enthusiasm. When we went out of the valley on the wide plains of Southwest River, she marveled at the vastness of creation. Up to that time, she knew only the confines of the valley. The wide plains and abundance of the Noumaso kept her beautiful eyes sparkling.

We often climbed to the high hills on the north side of Home Valley and spent long periods of time. She loved to explore what were to me old secret places. Lubah never tired of meeting new Nouma kin. What a traveling companion she would have made for some of my long river journeys. No need to think those thoughts. We must live to the full now, doing Giver's good pleasure. I talked to Giver each new day and asked for his help to please him in everything. Life is beautiful, even with the sting.

All too soon, the normal span of living for my wonderful Lubah came to an end. During one of our journeys, she slipped and fell. Until I saw her in distress, I had not realized that she was no longer my young, bright-eyed beauty. I led her to a comfortable place and stayed by her side. She slipped away to return to the dust several days later. Just as the sky orb peered into her face, I wept.

I traveled alone after Lubah felt the sting. Something about Southwest River kept calling me back. I followed the river for three passages of the sky orb out of the valley and made a terrible discovery. A large group of Possessor kin was camped along the river. They had Nouma mounts and one vessel on the river. They were headed for Home Valley. I felt that they were probably unaware of where they were headed, but that did not give me any comfort.

I headed quickly back toward the valley, my mind troubled about what to do. Should I try to warn the guardians? I remembered the wise words of a Likeness brother. Giver is not unaware of what Likeness kin do. This thought helped but did not lessen my need to hurry back to the valley.

Three Likeness days after I was in the valley, I climbed up one of the high southern hills to see if the Likeness kin were in sight. I spotted smoke from their river craft in the distance. They were using it to explore the river before bringing in the mounted group. I hurried eastward along the high ridge until the night sky orb rose.

My sleep time was troubled. Dreams of the battle east of the pass jarred me awake several times. I was far from rested when the sky orb again appeared. I rushed eastward and had just caught a glimpse of the forest around Mystery Grove in the far distance when a loud noise reached my ears.

I turned in every direction trying to find where it originated. Far to the east, I saw light reflecting off something rising into the heavens. It was too distant to see what it was. I dropped to the ground and stared in that direction. I then realized that it was also the source of the loud noise.

Whatever it was moved quickly upward and then stopped high in the sky. In just an instant, it began moving west, high over the valley. Because of the distance, it was hard to determine how fast it traveled. It was much faster than anything I had seen before. As it moved closer toward me, I recognized that it was the guardians from the pass. They were flying quickly through the air, headed toward Mystery Grove.

As I continued to watch them, I saw another movement, this one toward the west. I turned to look and was astonished to see the malevolent presence moving up from the river valley toward the guardians.

By now, the guardians had stopped high over Mystery Grove. Their appearance was fearful. I saw wings with flashing lights on them and round, shining, spinning objects under them. The spectacle was too astounding for a simple Nouma to understand. I do not know how to describe it.

Just as the guardians started to descend toward the grove, the malevolent presence swept in from the west. It swirled around the guardians, and they stopped their descent.

The guardians started whirling rapidly, and their flashing lights became bright like the sky orb. It looked as if the guardians and the presence were doing battle. Horrible rumbling sounds and spectacular flashes of light came from their strange dance high over Mystery Grove. This went on for what seemed to be a long time.

Finally, the whirling of the guardians threw the presence up and above them. They descended again, and I thought that they would disappear into the heart of the forest. Instead, the presence darkened and swept down after the guardians. Almost immediately, brighter, flashing lights appeared over them, and the noise started again. Just as they dropped directly into the grove, the malevolent presence caught them.

Before I could realize what was happening, a blinding flash of light caused me to close my eyes and bury my head in the herbs. It was followed by a loud, rolling sound unlike anything I ever heard before. I looked up and saw a huge glowing ball of fire billowing toward the heavens. Just after the fire, I heard the roar of wind and was hit by a hot blast that bent the small trees nearby to the ground. This was followed by total silence.

I thought that the guardians surely were destroyed by the noise and fire in the valley. Smoke covered the ground and rose quickly heavenward. As the smoke started to clear, I saw another glow near the ground. It was bright and flashing as it rose through the smoke.

When it was above the smoke, I recognized the guardians. They spun faster and faster and in an instant shot toward the sky at such speed that I could not follow with my eyes. I quickly looked all around for the presence, but it was nowhere to be seen. I was unable to rise. I remained on the ground and measured my breathing to quiet my pounding heart. What had I seen?

The smoke slowly cleared from the area around Mystery Grove. I no longer saw the forest. I blinked my eyes quickly to clear them and then looked again. The forest was gone, but a small cluster of trees in the center was standing. The sky orb was sinking toward the western horizon. I found herbs and fresh water, took my fill, and went into a grove of trees to sleep. My mind replayed the fire spectacle through most of my rest time. I did not rise early but lay in a stupor until the sky orb was directly overhead.

When I finally stood and walked to the edge of the grove, the scene below was incredible. The entire huge forest was missing. I hurried down the hill and ran as fast as possible toward where the forest had been. When I reached what had been the outer edges, I saw that the trees were not missing. They were flat on the ground with their tops pointing outward from the grove. I sought a nearby low hill to get a better look at the trees. I went high enough to see the center of where the forest had been. Far inside, I saw the small circle of trees that was Mystery Grove. All around it, the trees were flat on the ground, pointing outward. Since the sky orb was now darkening in the west, I decided to sleep and then try to go into the center.

I went to the south side of the hill and found water and herbs. There were no Nouma sounds as the night sky orb passed. The silence was intense. When first light struck my eyes, I was eager to go. I grazed quickly and prepared to go to the center of the grove.

It was difficult making my way over the fallen trees. Knowing the direction to go was no problem. I followed the direction the bottom of the trees pointed. Sky orb was nearly overhead when I climbed over the final trees and clearly saw the center of the grove.

The trees of Mystery Grove were standing. Those on the outer edge were dry but alive. The flat stone was where it had always been. I rushed forward and found that the trees and ground had not been touched. It was as if something had been placed over and around them to protect the stone and everything around it. I reached the flat stone and immediately noticed that the two special trees were missing. I moved to where they had been. Two round holes in the ground remained where they had been removed.

I stood on the stone and turned to look in every direction. All the trees outside the grove were on the ground pointing outward. The entire vast forest had been flattened.

The life tree and the knowing tree had been removed. The guardians must have taken them.

My first thought was that the cleansing must now be near. I also realized that if Possessor kin came into Home Valley, my Nouma kin would need to move to safety. There was no danger of them eating from the two special trees. They were gone.

Oh, Giver, help me understand all I need to follow you. Your ways are beyond my knowing.

As I finished speaking, Giver descended through the trees and hovered over the stone. I fell to the ground and offered thanks to him. He lifted me to my feet and gently spoke. "Naados, the time for cleansing all my creation is near. Your world will be washed of all corruption and repopulated by the offspring of Rest Giver. I will send Noumaso two-by-two to the escape vessel. Rest Giver will tell you your role.

"You will never again see Home Valley. The cleansing will remake the world you know. Do not be afraid." Just as Giver said *afraid*, the ground shook under my feet; and I cried out.

"This is the beginning of deep distress for all I made," said Giver. "Return to Between's village and help prepare for the departure. The ground will not swallow you up but will tremble in anticipation of the cleansing. Go quickly now. The vessel is almost ready."

Giver swirled his presence around me and then rose up through the trees, sending leaves flying in every direction. I dropped to the ground and tried to breathe deeply. It took me some time to feel steady enough to rise and start out over the fallen trees. Darkness covered everything when I stepped out of the fallen forest and found a place to rest.

I headed east as sky orb peered over the hills. Giver had said to go quickly. With no guardians at the pass and everything changing behind me, I trotted as fast as possible toward Between's village.

THE VESSEL

My return to Between's village was a blur of light and dark. As I journeyed, the ground often trembled beneath my feet. It soon became so ordinary that I only noticed the severe shocks that caused me to fall to the ground. Travel, rest, and travel again was my routine until late on the day that I reached the familiar forests to the west of Between's village. The forest looked different, but descending darkness prevented me from seeing why. I quickly grazed and settled in a sheltered grove. Light from the sky orb arrived to greet me much too quickly. I refreshed myself and stepped out to see my surroundings.

Huge gaps were missing from the forest. Between the gaps were trails cut into the ground. When I looked closely, it appeared that trees had been dragged over the trails. More gaps appeared in the forest as I moved southward. The trails became the wide paths like those leading into Likeness cities. I remembered the flat things with what Likeness kin called wheels I saw on a long ago journey. Marks on the ground made it appear as if they had been on these paths.

The nearer I came to Between's village, the bigger the gaps were in the forest. I remembered the marks I had seen on the trees all through the forest. Those that had the crossing marks were missing. The smaller trees that produced the sticky, sweet juice remained standing. Some of them had containers fastened below the cuts. Juice filled many of the containers. *Naados, old Nouma*, I thought, *you are so slow to understand Likeness ways. Rest Giver has taken the trees to make the escape vessel.* This realization pushed me to run more quickly toward the village.

The sky orb had dropped below the trees in the west when I reached the place where Dedicated had been taken away by Giver. It looked as if the trees had not been touched in that area, although it was already too dark to know for sure. To the east, where the small valley separated the forest from the village, I faintly saw an object nearly filling the valley. Straining my eyes, I realized that it was the escape vessel.

My excitement was not enough to overcome the realization that I must wait for the light from the sky orb to clearly see the vessel. I walked into the forest near the Likeness dwelling and rested on a bed of soft moss.

Whirling lights and large, dark shapes filled my dreams until the sky orb and sounds made by Likeness's kin nudged me awake.

After refreshing myself, I hurried toward the edge of the forest. The sky orb blinded me as I walked out of the shadows, but my eyes quickly adjusted. On the valley floor stood a remarkable sight. What had been a large, obscure shape in the darkness was now boldly visible. It almost filled the entire length of the valley and stood high over the surrounding fields. Where fleecy Nouma had grazed and young Likeness kin had played now stood the huge vessel.

My mouth fell open from astonishment. The question Rest Giver asked so long ago rang in my ears. *I wonder if the vessel will fill the valley.*

It does. It does, my mind repeated over and over. I found it difficult to believe my eyes.

The vessel filled the length of the valley. The shape at the bottom was the same as the valley. Up about as high as a normal Likeness dwelling, from the valley floor the vessel became wide. From there, it curved gently up, all the way to the top. The front is narrow and shaped like a pointed tree. Most of the vessel is wide. Toward the back, it is narrow but not pointed. There is a wide, flat surface all across the back. On both sides of the vessel, where it becomes wide, both front and back, are objects that look like thick wings of flying Noumaso. They stick out about the length of my shadow when the sky orb is halfway to the middle of the sky. I have no idea what they are for.

The missing trees from the forests had been changed into long, wide, thick pieces. These were fastened together in ways that we Nouma cannot understand. When I viewed it from a distance, it looked like one large tree shaped to resemble a giant river vessel. It was far too big for any river I had seen. A vast opening was in the side that faced the forest. Inside the opening, I saw three layers. One at the bottom of the vessel was tall enough to put a Likeness dwelling there. Another was up halfway to the top and was not so tall. A third, not as high as the other two, was near the top of the vessel.

Numbers of Likeness's kin were busily working around the vessel. Some carried pieces of trees inside the vessel. Others, working outside, were changing the trees into usable pieces. Devices that made a noise that hurt my ears were in use by the workers. They had round, spinning parts that screamed when a tree was pushed into them. The trees were flat pieces when they came out the end of the device.

Long lines of the wheeled conveyances stacked with trees were being unloaded and prepared for the noisy changing tools. Many different things that Likeness's kin called tools were in use. They all seemed to know what to do. I looked at the massive vessel with wonder.

I tried to count the Likeness kin working on the vessel but quickly gave up. There were too many, and they constantly moved from place to place. Stepping into the shadows, I concentrated instead on the vessel itself.

My focus on the vessel was so intent that I did not hear approaching footsteps. A familiar voice called out, "Well, old Nouma, what are you doing back in this part of Giver's world?" Rest Giver grabbed me around my neck and laughed loudly. "You don't look another hundred years older, my friend," he said. "Come see the vessel, and let's catch up on the news."

Rest Giver's
Handiwork

Rest Giver led me to the wide opening in the side of the vessel. I tried to look up the side as we approached but realized that I could not see the top. Rest Giver urged me along and up an incline through the opening. I prepared my eyes for darkness, but it was not necessary. Just inside the opening, I saw light orbs like those used in Likeness cities. The small vines that fed them were neatly attached everywhere.

Sensing my amazement, Rest Giver chuckled and

said, "Did you think that Giver would make us live in darkness? His kindness is great. He knows our needs and has made provision for our comfort and wellbeing. Come. See where the largest of your Nouma kin will be cared for."

Rest Giver showed me through the passage and toward the center of the vessel's first level. The smell of the wooden interior reminded me of refreshing forest glades. Wide passages separated compartments different in size. The enclosures were not covered on top, but three sides were high enough to give security to the Nouma inside.

Front openings were large so that occupants would not feel confined and could talk with other Nouma nearby. The smaller enclosures were along the sides of the vessel, the largest ones grouped in the central space. Containers for food and water were attached to the sides of each compartment. They could be easily reached from the front openings.

Light orbs were placed everywhere except in the compartments that were for our night-feeding Nouma kin. "You may wonder about the light orbs, Naados. Giver's design makes it possible to have bright lights during what would be the passage of the sky orb and very dim light for sleep time. Even though we will not see the outside world for almost a year, our life cycle will remain as normal as possible. The wide passages between the compartments will permit the Noumaso to move about during the long confinement.

"You, Naados, will have an important task to do for your kin during our journey. We all speak the ancient language of creation, so communication will not be a problem. However, my family and I will be busy taking care of food and water needs for all the travelers. You must help by encouraging and comforting the Noumaso. This will give you time to tell about Giver and the becoming. During the cleansing, everything will change on earth. All air-breathing land life will feel the sting. Much knowledge about our world will be forgotten. The voyage will be difficult, but Giver is with us."

Rest Giver then led me through all the levels of the vessel. I was surprised by the compartment that made it possible to travel between the levels. It was large enough for all eight of the Likeness kin. I could not see what made it go from one level to another. Rest Giver only had to touch something near the entrance and it moved. I was told that there were three more in other parts of the vessel. There were also several inclines that made it possible to go between levels. I knew at once that I would walk up and down the inclines. I was uncomfortable in the Likeness up-down compartment.

Areas on each level already contained food for the coming journey. I saw many containers the Likeness kin used to keep food for numerous cycles of the sky orb. Rest Giver reached into a large container and held out some round, smelly objects to me. "Eat, Naados," he said.

I sniffed and resisted.

He insisted.

Closing my eyes, I carefully took some from his hand and started chewing. To my surprise, it was tasty but dry in my mouth.

"This is made from the same grain that we Likeness kin eat, Naados. It is very nutritious and will not spoil during our entire journey. We also have supplies of herbs that you and your kin enjoy. They are dried by the sky orb and will sustain you until you graze on the cleansed earth."

"Giver is so good," I said, "to show you how to provide for all our needs."

He also showed me large containers for water, already filled and placed throughout the vessel. The time for the cleansing must be near.

The sky orb had nearly completed her journey when Rest Giver took me to the top of the vessel. In the center was the area where he and his kin would stay during the journey. It was divided into several large compartments resembling the inside of Likeness dwellings. Things their kin needed were already in place.

"Living is very complicated for Likeness-Image creatures," I said. "You seem to need so much. We Noumaso enjoy what Giver made and do not try to change it. Your kin seem to never be content with what is. You turn it into other things. I'm thankful to Giver to be Nouma."

Rest Giver chuckled and patted me on the flank. "When the vessel is completed and the cover is on, there will not be an entrance in the top," Rest Giver said. "There will be small openings around the top edge covered with something that we Likeness kin use to let light enter. These will also serve as observation points for me during the cleansing. They cannot be opened but will permit me to see some of what is happening during the cleansing. When Giver closes the opening we call the door, we will have no access to the world outside. We are in your hands, Giver."

As Rest Giver and I walked down the ramp out of the vessel, a strong shaking started and lasted long enough to knock me off my feet. Rest Giver told me that this happened often.

"Giver also told me it would happen," I said and explained what He said about the coming judgment.

"We must talk about all that soon," Rest Giver said as we reached the ground.

He invited me to the village, but I asked permission to stay in the forest. Rest Giver headed for the village. It was good to have my four feet back on solid ground. The darkening shadows were a welcome friend. I needed time to reflect on all the wonders I had seen in the escape vessel.

Sharing News

After sleeping, Rest Giver and I met to speak of the events since my final trip to Home Valley. He told me of the Likeness kin who had felt the sting.

"Cleansing Comes and Between felt the sting not long before your return, Naados," he said. "They lived a long time in Giver's world and honored Him all their days. During their last years, they tried to convince their kin to follow Giver but were not successful. Possessor's kin have corrupted the entire earth. Even those who don't follow all their evil ways do not take time to honor Giver. They believe in Him, yet they are blinded by the ease of living and act as if there is no coming cleansing.

"Giver comes often to encourage me and give instructions. His visits help me maintain my trust and belief. It is hard, Naados, to see my own kin harden their hearts.

"Even those you see here faithfully working to complete the escape vessel do so only for what they gain. I continually try to convince them to flee the judgment to come. They laugh and make jokes about Giver and judgment. Most of their kin consider me mentally deranged.

"To them, the escape vessel is a worthless venture by a foolish old man. The stories they tell about me are laughable. Some make my heart hurt. They think I am an old man who does not know that water is necessary to float a vessel. I'm afraid, Naados, that there is no way to convince anyone. They live as if time will go on forever. 'Today is just another day,' they like to say."

With a long sigh, Rest Giver sadly shook his head and nodded for me to speak.

"My sorrow, Rest Giver, comes in a different way. The Noumaso are innocent of Likeness's wicked rejection of Giver. Yes, we are hurt by Likeness's bending, but we do not share the gift of choice. I travel and see my kin living in ignorance of the great cleansing to come. I dare not tell them. Even if I told them, they could not understand. A world full of innocent Noumaso are about to be taken away, and I am one of the few who will be spared. This is heaviness to my heart, dear friend.

"But I must be brief as I tell of my visit to Home Valley. The valley where we saw the army feel the sting is now a barren place. Nothing grows but the bones of the soldiers. They stick up everywhere through the sand. Someone covered them where they fell. My hair stood up on my back when I remembered the slaughter that occurred there.

"The guardians were in their places when I arrived, but they are no longer there. I will explain later. I met a group of my own Nouma kin and before a year passed again had a mata. Lubah was my sweet companion for most of my time in Home Valley. She could not bring offspring, so together we traveled Home Valley and the two rivers to the west. I had great sorrow when she felt the sting.

"Not long before I was told to return here, Possessor's kin came to the valley from the southwest. They traveled by river and mounted on Nouma. Before they entered the valley, a striking event occurred.

"The guardians left their place in the pass and flew through the skies toward Mystery Grove in a remarkable manner. There was a great roar, and they came the distance more quickly than I could easily follow with my eyes. When they were high over Mystery Grove, they stopped and descended. From the west, I saw the malevolent presence separate from Possessor kin and rush through the sky toward the guardians.

"There was a whirling battle over Mystery Grove. The guardians threw the malevolent presence high into the heavens and descended toward the grove, but the presence returned immediately and again fell on the guardians. In an instant, there was a horrible flash of light and an ear-splitting noise. When I was able to see clearly, the guardians flew up through the smoke and in a flash of light disappeared into the heavens.

"The malevolent presence was nowhere to be seen when the smoke cleared. The huge forest all around Mystery Grove was flat on the ground. The trees all pointed outward from the grove. Later, when I finally reached the grove, I saw that the trees around the flat stone were standing. The two special trees were missing. Only round holes in the ground remained to show that they had ever been there.

"While I pondered this sight, Giver came down. He told me that the cleansing was coming soon and that I had something to do to help you. He reminded me that I would not feel the sting.

"Even as Giver spoke, the ground shook under my feet. He told me to expect the shaking often before he melted the heavens and opened the rivers under the earth. He then told me to return here and prepare for the cleansing. I want to please Giver, but I am torn with feelings about living while the sting is coming to all other life. Giver told me again that he will be with us in this difficult time. My hope is in him. Life is good, even with the sting."

We sat quietly until Rest Giver's three male offspring arrived. They brought news of work on the vessel. Renown spoke.

"In two days, we will finish placing the covering on the vessel. The interior work is complete. Water containers are full, and the refill channels from the top of the vessel have been tested. When what Giver calls rain falls from the skies, we will replenish emptied containers and have adequate water for the journey. Final food supplies are being loaded, and we have more than enough for the entire year. Today, we are doing final testing on the waste disposal system. We will be ready to enter when Giver tells us it is time."

As Renown finished speaking, a severe tremor shook the forest. Small openings appeared in the ground near the front of the vessel. What looked like mist rose through the openings and sent a sharp, foul smell into the air. While we talked about this latest shaking, Giver's shining presence swirled down toward us through the canopy of trees.

"It is time, Rest Giver. In seven days, I will melt the heavens and bring rain upon earth. Gather your family, and prepare for the Noumaso I will send to you. Take them into the vessel as I instructed you. You must be ready for the day when I will close the door. Your coming deliverance will also be the destruction of all life on dry ground." With this, Giver rose rapidly through the trees and disappeared into the sky.

The Noumaso Are Coming!

Excitement was high as Giver disappeared from sight. Rest Giver stood to his feet, trembling as he shouted, "It is time! It is time!"

His offspring, Renown, Persuader, and Swarthy, jumped to their feet, stunned expressions on their faces as they hurried toward the village. I remained calm but was shaking inside as Giver's news spread through the Likeness kin still working around the vessel. I was surprised as I heard some of the workers' comments.

"I guess we will have to find another job," said one.

"I needed some extra time to attend a joining ceremony," said another. "They are great parties."

"Maybe we won't have to listen to Rest Giver's ranting about Giver anymore. I don't enjoy those fables."

One lone worker remarked to his fellows, "I hope there is nothing to the tale. I'm looking forward to living many more years. I'm afraid of the sting."

Rest Giver regained his composure and turned to me. "Naados," he said, "the next days will be busy ones for you. Even now, the Noumaso must be on their way here. Giver told me long ago where he would send them for us to bring to the vessel." With that, he turned and said, "Come with me, old friend. I will take you to the gathering place."

We walked quickly to the north and west. Ground tremors were frequent as we moved through the patches of trees. Away from the trails I had often traveled, we entered a thick area of forest. A worn path led us deep into the shadowy quiet of ancient trees. After traveling well beyond the vessel, we started down a long incline. Trees different from those used by Rest Giver to build the vessel grew here.

The path emerged into a vast clearing. On the north was an area of remarkable beauty. It was evident that no Likeness kin had been here. To the south lay a lake surrounded by the kinds of marsh that many behemoth kin enjoy. Several were floating on the still waters, grazing on tender leaves and water plants. Noumaso were scattered across the clearing. The gathering was already under way.

Rest Giver explained my task and told me to remain here for one more day before leading the Noumaso to the vessel. "Giver has spoken in the heads and hearts of the Nouma who have been chosen for deliverance. They will come to you for instructions about what to do. Their kin who are with them will not follow when you take them to the vessel. Be strong, Naados. Giver has entrusted you with a heavy task.

"Giver has called the Noumaso to come two-by-two in order to preserve all kinds of life on earth. In addition, numerous Nouma kin will come by sevens. There will be three of each with his mata, and one extra male. I'm not sure about the full meaning. I think it will be made clear after the cleansing is complete.

"Naados, all creatures must be brought aboard the vessel. This will include Beaufang's kin. They will not be influenced by the malevolent presence, so please treat them well. Giver wants all Noumaso represented on the cleansed earth. Many of the smaller Nouma who are unable to travel great distances are gathering near the dwelling in the forest. They will be taken aboard the vessel when you arrive. Winged Nouma are already nearby in the forests and streams. Tiny winged and crawling creatures are in special containers and will be placed in compartments when your kin are aboard."

"I do not fully understand why Beaufang's spawn are to be included," I said, "but I do want to please Giver. I bow to his desire and will do as he has instructed you."

Rest Giver started back toward the vessel but turned for one last word to me. "Remember, Naados. One more day after today and then you must lead the Noumaso to the vessel." He then started back up the trail at a quick pace.

Not bad for a six-hundred-year-old Likeness kin, I thought. I set out at once to meet the gathered Noumaso and plan how to lead them to the vessel.

Even though I had met almost every Nouma kin on earth, I did not know any of the individuals gathered here. I did know the general temperament and abilities of most Nouma, so I began to select helpers for the trek. By now, Nouma were arriving in great numbers. I chose seventy capable helpers and gave each one specific instruction about the Nouma kin they were to guide.

The night sky orb was shining brightly overhead when I cropped a few leaves and settled down to rest. My mind whirled with faces and places from the past hundreds of years. Most of the faces had long been dust. All places were soon to be so devastated that they would never be recognized again. I slept fitfully until jarred awake by a pair of early rising simians grooming the hair on my neck. I laughed at them even though I did not feel ready for today.

By the time the sky orb reached the middle of the sky, no more Nouma were arriving in the clearing. My helpers took their tasks seriously and worked hard to get their groups of Noumaso ready for the walk. It was only after seeing the orderly way the groups were forming that I realized all those chosen to go were young.

I saw many mature Noumaso from most Nouma kin, but they were not being arranged in the groups for travel. Instead, their young offspring were the ones going to the vessel. Those who gave life were standing quietly beside their young offspring, sometimes gently touching them. Mostly, they were speaking quietly and lovingly to their kin.

I was strongly moved by the realization that this was their goodbye. I could not tell them what was going to happen.

You are good, Giver. All your ways are perfect. I, a simple Nouma, do not have the ability to understand your ways. Innocence, separation, and the sting all look back at me as I prepare to take these young ones to deliverance. The remainder awaits their destruction. Yet I must say that life is good, even with the sting.

Morning came too quickly. Last touches and gentle words were exchanged as each group moved to follow their leader up the long path and out of the clearing. I stayed to watch each group leave, not wanting any to be left behind. The final group walked up the trail, and I turned to face those left behind.

Silent acceptance of Giver's decision said it all. Through my own tears, I saw theirs flowing down and dropping on the ground. *Oh, Giver, accept their tears as a measure of their sacrifice to your will.* The scene was overwhelming, so I shouted as loudly as I could, "Giver go with you," and then turned and ran up the path. In times of sadness, my mind will recall that gathering, a reminder that the family of Noumaso never suffers alone.

SAFE IN THE VESSEL

We arrived at the vessel when the sky orb was halfway down toward the western horizon. Orderly groups of Noumaso of every kind and kin were in the fields and forest around the vessel. The gathering was silent except for grazing and subdued conversation.

As the sky orb was about to disappear in the west, Rest Giver spoke to us from the open door of the vessel.

"Giver has brought us together by His mercy to preserve life on earth. Tomorrow, we enter the deliverance vessel. Eat; drink the pure water of this place, and think of Giver as we wait for the sky orb's arrival tomorrow."

The Noumaso needed no further urging. Group leaders selected places where all their needs could be met. I snatched a mouthful of fresh herbs and headed for the vessel to talk with Rest Giver. I enjoyed the sweetness of the herbs and thought of what the cleansed earth would offer.

Rest Giver saw me coming and moved to meet me on the ground at the end of the entrance to the vessel. He wrapped his arms around my neck and hugged me close. "Naados, what can I say? Giver is our only hope. I trust because he is Giver but also because he has been faithful to me. Be strong and courageous, my friend. Go pass sleep time in your favorite place in the forest near my old dwelling. Eat the sweet herbs and leaves. Smell the richness of Giver's good earth. It will soon change.

"Watch the sky tonight, Naados. Likeness's kin in the nearby city will send fire flyers high into the heavens. To be so wicked and so smart is a paradox of Likeness-Image creation. They stir the heavens and help prepare the great melting that will destroy what we know and turn it into that which we cannot imagine. Rest with Giver, my friend."

I ate in my favorite place in the forest and then drank deeply of the sweet waters from the brook. I lay on a bed of soft moss and looked through the overhead leaves toward the city to the south. It was not long before I saw the fire flyers burn their way into the heavens. I counted six, one after another reaching toward the sky. One went only a short distance and then made a huge fireball of light. Were there really Likeness kin inside the fire flyers?

I knew that a loud noise would follow, so I prepared myself for it. The sound was not as loud as that from

Mystery Grove when the guardians and the malevolent presence fought, but it was disturbing. The other five slipped through the thickness of the upper sky and left only thin lines of light that soon disappeared.

I had no idea what Likeness kin wanted to do in the heavens. They had no use for Giver in this world. I fell asleep with the comforting sounds of the tiny night creatures in the forest chirping in my ears. The sky orb nudged me awake for one more day in this world. Rest Giver met me at the edge of the forest and asked that I join him at the entrance to the vessel. He wanted me available if any of the Nouma feared to enter. Fear was not a normal part of the world of Noumaso. Likeness's kin had introduced it to all creation.

I was amazed at how orderly the Noumaso came into the vessel. My seventy helpers did their work well. Rest Giver's family directed the pairs of Nouma to their compartments. Because of the light orbs, they could see their surroundings, so they settled in quickly.

I was only needed three times to speak encouragement and comfort to members of the Nouma kin. One was when Beaufang's offspring came aboard. There was an outcry from some of the smaller Nouma. I assured them that Giver was in control and that there was no need to be upset.

Another incident came when a large Nouma was told that there would be no trees from which to strip the bark. Tree bark was among his favorite foods. Finally, two young behemoths were unsure that there was enough water for them to be well-soaked every day. Swarthy showed them the special water containers, and they asked no further questions.

Last to enter were the winged Noumaso. They had

waited in the trees and along the nearby waterways. Rest Giver spoke to each group as they flew through the entrance and directed them to the upper level. Some of them would be permitted to leave before those of us who needed dry ground.

Rest Giver had not shown me my compartment during my visit to the vessel. After the Noumaso were safely on board, he indicated places on all three levels for me. Since I would be involved in helping his kin with the Noumaso, he thought that I should have places on each level.

I was especially pleased that my place on the third level was next to Rest Giver's own compartment. I was honored and for an instant tempted to puff out my chest. The thought passed quickly, and I moved through the lower level, speaking with my Nouma kin. Dry, sweet-smelling herbs covered the bottom of the compartments, helping give comfort for the journey.

Rest Giver invited me to go outside the vessel with him and wait for Giver to return. The shaking from the ground was now almost constant but not severe enough to cause me to fall. The early evening sky had a strange, troubled look. Over the city, where I saw the fire flyers go heavenward, the normally smooth patterns and colors of the sky were twisting and swirling. I heard rumbling and saw flashes like light orbs in the distance in every direction. Breezes blew first from one direction and then another and carried the smell of a rushing river. I'm happy that Giver selected me for deliverance.

"Very soon, Naados," said Rest Giver, "the door to our vessel will be closed by Giver Himself. When he closes the door, it will never again be opened. It can only be opened from the outside. After the cleansing, when we are permitted to return to dry ground, we will remove the covering and open the door in the back of the vessel. It opens from the inside."

The light orbs were dimmed inside the vessel. Rest Giver and I settled down outside the large door to wait. I was surprised that no Likeness kin from the city were around the vessel. Even those from the nearby village did not seem interested in recent happenings. *Am I simple-minded to believe Giver?* I wondered under my breath. A strong shaking from the ground sent a shiver through my body in answer. Cleansing was coming.

The early morning light had an eerie quality as the sky orb made her appearance. Rest Giver remarked that the sky looked ripped like a worn Likeness covering. It reminded me of the water on Northwest River that became hard like stone and then shattered under the weight of a large Nouma. The sky looked broken to me. Rumbling sounds came nearer. Even sky orb was not sending all her light through the gathering darkness above.

Several Likeness kin from the city came down the path toward the vessel. Rest Giver greeted them and invited them to join us in the vessel to escape the cleansing. They made it clear that that was not the purpose for their coming.

"Since you are going away," they said laughing, "we thought you would not mind if we take your tools for changing trees into planks. It seems a shame to let them rust away while you turn to dust inside your big box."

Rest Giver said, "Take whatever you wish. It will be of little use to you or anyone else."

As they moved away toward their new possessions, a strong, damp breeze swept across the field and nearly knocked them off their feet.

Just as suddenly, Giver swirled out of the darkening sky and hovered in front of the vessel. "It is time, Rest Giver, to enter the vessel. The rain from above and the waters from below are coming. Be brave. Trust me. I am with you. Comfort your kin. Care for the Noumaso. A new world awaits you after I complete the cleansing."

Giver then wrapped us in his presence and moved us toward the open door and up the ramp. As we entered, Giver began lifting the door up and into the opening. Rest Giver quickly made the light orbs shine as the door slipped into the opening. I heard several noises that I did not recognize and then silence. I looked around the closed door and could see no light or opening. It looked like part of the solid side of the vessel.

I moved from compartment to compartment to calm my Noumaso kin. With the opening firmly closed, we could hear no noise from outside the vessel. Our own Nouma sounds were the only disturbance to break the strange silence surrounding us. Occasionally, the shaking of the ground was strong enough for us to feel it.

I wondered what was happening in Home Valley and other areas I had visited over the years. Using the inclines between levels, I quickly trotted to the top of the vessel. Light diffused through the covered openings reminded me that I was still on the earth. Rest Giver peered intently through one of the openings on the front of the vessel.

Rain

Rest Giver nodded me toward the transparent opening beside him. My head and face are not shaped like that of Likeness's kin, so it was difficult for me to see clearly through what Rest Giver called a window. I found it easier to turn my head and use only one eye near the window to see. I later learned how to stand away from the window and see through it.

The darkening sky shattered with flashes of light. It looked as if the sky had descended close to the ground and was spinning in every direction. Strong wind caused trees to wave wildly. Likeness's kin who had laughed at us earlier were running along the path toward the city. I had never seen such wind.

Rest Giver pushed closer to the window and started breathing deeply. He spoke without turning toward me. "Naados, look there in the distance. See what looks like a wall of black? I think that is what Giver has called rain. We will know soon."

The blackness reached the vessel and almost hid the front from view. In an instant, it struck the windows where we were watching. There would not have been more water if I had dived into a river and opened my eyes. The rain beat against the windows so hard that I was afraid and jumped away. Rest Giver also appeared concerned. He motioned me back to the window and reached around my neck to comfort me. We stood and watched but saw nothing except the driving water and the constant flashes of light.

Is this happening all around our world? I wondered.

Rest Giver called his offspring and sent them through the vessel to check for water coming through windows or other places. "Giver showed me the trees from which we made the material to keep water out," said Rest Giver. "We know it works. We tried it for many years while building the vessel. The vessel is covered inside and out. This is the final test to make sure that all openings have been completely sealed."

Noise from the pounding rain caused a loud rumble through the upper level of the vessel. I left the window and walked down the lanes between the compartments to speak with the Noumaso. It was good that I did. Some were agitated because of the strange, loud noise.

I took time to locate my seventy group leaders and tell them what was happening. I then went to each Nouma who was disturbed. Rest Giver had wisely ordered the light orbs be at full strength throughout the vessel. The Noumaso could see clearly inside their compartments even though none could see what was happening outside the vessel. I told what I saw to those who asked but admitted to them that it was unlike anything that had ever been on earth.

Up to this time, rain had never fallen from the sky. Dew was on the herbs and leaves every new day, but water did not fall from the skies. Springs, brooks, streams, and rivers flowed throughout our world. Rain was new and frightening to the Noumaso. I reminded myself and then reminded the Nouma that Giver was well-prepared for this day. It too was part of the change he was bringing to our world with the cleansing.

Rest Giver's offspring moved throughout the vessel, making sure the Noumaso had food and water. The round, prepared grain food became a favorite of the Noumaso. Combined with the fragrant dried herbs, the large Nouma were satisfied. I was told that the winged Nouma were fully satisfied with dried grains. The vessel had been well-stocked by Rest Giver and his kin to meet our needs. Water from the driving rain was carried through what looked like huge, round vines to holding containers on the two lower levels of the vessel. All during the rains, fresh water was added to our supply.

A Likeness male was constantly at one of the windows during the days the rain fell. They could do nothing to direct the vessel, but it was felt that they should be on watch. They moved between the windows at the front and back of the vessel. Rest Giver, his offspring, and their matas all worked to be sure that everything necessary was done.

During the time the vessel remained in the small valley, Rest Giver told me what our routine would be for the Likeness year we would be inside. I passed his instructions to my seventy leaders. We shared the information with any Nouma who asked. Most asked no questions so long as they had adequate food and water.

Dark periods of heavy rain were broken occasionally by lighter skies. The rain fell for forty Likeness days. From time to time, it would clear enough for us to see through the falling rain. This first happened during our third day in the vessel. The passing of days was confusing to me since I could not see the sky orb or the night sky orb. Rest Giver had a way to know the difference. He kept the light orbs in a cycle that let us rest as we had before the rain started.

On the third day, Rest Giver called me to his small compartment by the front windows. We looked out over the rain-filled world. The sky was light enough for us to see well into the distance. I was surprised by how much water was on the ground. It rushed around the front of the vessel and flowed swiftly down the valley. The path leading toward the city was covered. Large trees were blown flat on the ground by strong winds. A small spring on a nearby hillside was now a gushing stream. Unused pieces of the trees left in the field floated in the deepening water, as did small trees and branches from larger ones.

I looked toward the forest and saw small groups of

Nouma huddled under the rain-soaked trees. My glance at Rest Giver told me that he had already seen them. I wondered about my friends in Home Valley and those along the rivers and streams of our world.

"What will this do to the rivers?" I asked.

"Naados," said Rest Giver, "wherever the rivers flow, they will overflow the fields and forests alongside. How can I explain, old friend? Giver said that the waters will cover the entire earth so that no life can remain except that which lives in the water."

I caught my breath as I thought of the countless members of my Nouma kin throughout our world. I tried to picture Home Valley covered with water. My mind was not big enough to see it all. The valleys—yes, that I can see filled up. The low hills—maybe. The peaks surrounding the valley—how can that be?

"I know this is hard, Naados." Rest Giver said. "It is difficult for me. No one has ever seen what is about to be. No one can fully understand. We must cling to Giver, who alone knows best."

Two days later, Rest Giver called me to follow him to the back of the vessel. He indicated a window and said that I should look outside. He peered through the one alongside. I could not believe my eyes. Through the heavy rain, I saw a vast lake of water behind the vessel.

"What is it, Rest Giver?" I asked.

He shook his head and replied, "Naados, the water has filled the valley below the vessel. The vessel will soon be riding on the rising water."

I saw terrible things when I looked at the water.

Noumaso who had felt the sting were floating on the surface. Large trees, small Likeness dwellings, and objects I could not identify swirled on the rising waters.

"Now, Naados, come quickly to the front of the vessel," said Rest Giver. We returned to the front windows, and he pointed toward the city. A group of Likeness kin struggled through the driving rain and deep water toward the vessel. Young offspring were floating on wooden objects being pushed through the water toward us.

I looked at Rest Giver, who wept as he said, "We can do nothing, Naados. This is only the beginning of the end of all life on earth. We alone will survive."

I watched as the group of Likeness's kin struggled toward the vessel. Two who were leading raised their arms like tiny Likeness offspring pleading to be picked up. The sky darkened and the rain became heavier, hiding the group from our view. We never saw them again.

Floating Free

I awoke with a start three days after seeing the Likeness kin trying to reach the vessel. I stood and then fell back into the dried herbs. I stood again and leaned against the side of the compartment. The floor was moving beneath my feet! I walked slowly to the opening and started toward the front of the vessel. I again slipped and went down.

As I stood, Rest Giver rushed toward me headed for the back of the vessel. "Naados, old friend, come with me. I think the back of the vessel is rising on the waters."

He steadied me as we moved to the back of the

vessel to look out the windows. Everything behind the vessel was covered with water! The water was moving swiftly and swirling in the valley behind the vessel. We slowly rocked from side to side as the back of the vessel floated free.

The water was full of floating objects. Noumaso large and small, those living and those who had felt the sting were swept along by the rushing waters. A small group of my own kin tried to fight the raging waters. They held their noses high as they kicked and tried to swim toward a safety that did not exist.

"Get the word to the Noumaso, Naados that they should not try to stand while the waters are lifting us up."

I found most of my seventy helpers and gave them the news. They too had felt the motion and were unsteady on their feet. They hurried off to give the word to remain reclined until told that it was safe to move about.

Rest Giver decided to darken the light orbs even though it was early in the day. He feared for the safety of the Noumaso until the vessel floated completely free. Rest Giver hoped that the large motion wings low on each side of the vessel would make it steady in the water.

Light sticks were given to all the Likeness kin, and the light orbs were completely darkened. I stayed by Rest Giver's side. We watched the rising waters together. Water covered everything we could see from the front of the vessel. Trees in the forest to the west were more than half covered. Water also covered everything we could see looking toward the city except the tops of tall trees.

During the next sleep cycle, while I was in my compartment, the vessel was lifted free from her valley resting place by the rising waters. Until then, the motion of the vessel had been in only one direction. It now moved from side to side and from front to back. I think that the Noumaso were happy to stay reclined until that passed.

I woke, sensing that the vessel was moving. The light orbs were set for sleep. I stood to my feet and found that I could walk without falling. Voices from the front of the vessel caught my attention, so I headed that direction.

Rest Giver and his three offspring were peering through the windows. The vessel had turned around and was being pushed forward down the valley by the swiftly moving waters. I spoke quick greetings, and then a nod from Rest Giver sent me to my window. The rain was hard, but light from the sky orb made it possible to see clearly for some distance.

We were not alone in the waters. Parts of Likeness kin dwellings kept pace with the vessel. Huge trees and other floating objects also moved alongside. From time to time, I saw soaked Nouma perched on the floating objects. More often than not, the Nouma I saw had felt the sting and were carried along with their stiff legs pointed skyward. I saw Likeness kin perched on parts of their dwellings. Those who saw the vessel and had the strength to do so waved and motioned us to come to them. We could do nothing. There was no hope for Likeness kin nor Noumaso.

Rain poured from the heavens for forty days. Our living cycle was well established in the vessel. Light orbs shined brightly during the passage of the sky orb and then were darkened for sleep time. I spoke with some of the Nouma every day. My helpers were reliable and kept their groups satisfied. Rest Giver and his kin filled the food and water containers each day. The vessel was our small world. It took on a life of its own.

On each new day, I visited the windows to look out on the cleansing. The waters continued to move, but not as swiftly as in the early days of the rain. It was not unusual to see the floating remains of forests, villages, and even the large cities. The early violence of the rushing waters had battered and shattered most of the things the Likeness kin had made. Forces of the rushing currents were far too strong for the small Likeness river vessels. Huge structures reduced to piles of floating wood mingled with the remains of Likeness kin and Noumaso.

Currents in the water sometimes brought us near high hills or mountains. Almost every such place we passed was packed with pitiful creatures, some living and others dead. On more than one occasion, I saw Likeness kin leap into the rushing water and try to swim to the vessel. The force of the moving water always dragged them down. Rest Giver reminded me that we had no way to rescue the poor ones caught in the cleansing.

During my dreams, I often saw rivers from my past travels. I saw the rushing waters of the cleansing sweep through the broad valleys and plains alive with behemoth kin and other huge Nouma. Lifeless bodies were rolled along by the water and piled into high hills and then mountains of my kin. Wide valleys filled with life were covered and stacked deep with those who felt the sting. When I woke from these dreams, my heart hurt and felt empty from seeing the destruction and the loss. *Oh, Giver, hear my cry. Life is good, even with the sting.*

The heavy rains finally stopped. Skies that had been clear since Giver made them remained filled with what Rest Giver calls clouds. The rains, he said, came from the clouds. The sky was covered for a great number of days after the rain stopped. From time to time, light from the sky orb peeked between the clouds and smiled down on the now water-covered earth.

On each new day, Rest Giver went from window to window, scanning the horizon for sight of dry land. Not one hill or mountain was visible. Just as Giver said it would be, all dry land was covered. For nearly fifty days after the rain stopped, great floating heaps of what had been life on earth rode the waves of the vast water world. Then, bit by bit, it soaked through and sank to whatever was solid far beneath. After a hundred days, endless open water was our constant companion.

Rest Giver had no idea where we were. He only knew that we floated above wherever it was. Sometimes, the water was smooth and calm. I woke many days, felt no movement, and thought I was back on dry land. One look from a window ended the illusion. Water followed by more water was our only view.

After water covered the entire earth, we sometimes had visitors from the deep waters. Early one day, as the sky orb rose in the east, great creatures from the salty waters of earth surrounded the vessel. Some of them were so huge that if three of them were to swim end to end, they would be as long as our vessel. They came and inspected us on every side. They rubbed their huge bodies against the side of the vessel and made beautiful water creature sounds.

This group put on a special display for us. They swam alongside slowly and then turned and swam swiftly away from the vessel. As they moved away, they dived beneath the water. It must have been a great distance, for after a time they appeared and leaped into the air the full length of their bodies. When they splashed down flat, it made a huge spray of sparkling water drops. Evidently, this was something they loved to do, for they continued most of the day. We never saw them again after that day.

Riding the Waves

For well over a hundred days after the rain stopped falling, we drifted on the waters. The gentle motion of rising and falling on the waves became an expected and comforting pattern. Many of the smaller Nouma added new life to our numbers. When this word passed though the vessel, the Noumaso were filled with hope. Giver's promise for a new world after the cleansing seemed more possible each time a tiny new voice was heard.

Rain fell from time to time, but nothing like the deluge of the forty days. I enjoyed watching from the windows as clouds appeared in the distance and emptied sparkling droplets toward the watery surface of our planet. Shafts of light from the sky orb passed through the clouds and sent dancing patterns across the watery world. We drifted peacefully for many days.

When enough time had passed to cleanse the earth of all life on dry ground, Giver sent wind. The familiar gentle motions of the vessel were replaced by stronger movement from side to side. Rest Giver said that the winds were to dry the waters from off the earth. They blew strongly and moved the vessel first in one direction and then another. Most activity in the vessel stopped during the strong winds. I used the time to visit the Nouma and encourage them. Rest Giver and his kin faithfully gave food and water to the Noumaso. Sleep times were often extended due to the motion of the vessel.

I did not spend much time looking out the windows when the strong wind blew. The motion of the vessel on the water caused me to feel uncomfortable, and I had no desire to eat. Rest Giver reminded us all that this too would soon pass. His words were of no great comfort to the Nouma who wished for dry ground for their feet and fresh herbs for their unhappy stomachs.

I was pleased beyond telling when Rest Giver called to me one morning. "Naados, come quickly. I think the waters are leaving the surface of the earth."

I ran to a window beside him and looked in the direction he pointed.

"Look," he said. "See the dark shadows in the water?"

I could see dark scattered across the area he indicated.

"I think those are the tops of mountains. The water is leaving the earth. Stay and watch with me, old friend."

For the next few days, we saw shadows in the water. Then, early one morning, the vessel shuddered and then steadied and glided on across the water. This happened several times during the next two days.

"There is no doubt, Naados," said Rest Giver, "that the waters are being taken from the earth."

Excitement ran high in the vessel at this news. My seventy helpers had to remind the Noumaso that it was not time to leave the vessel. My heart beat fast at the thought of leaving the confinement of our rescue vessel. We were all ready to step out on the cleansed earth.

TOPS OF THE
MOUNTAINS

Clouds had covered the sky for several days and now hovered low over the water. Early in the morning, the vessel shuddered and then made a long, grinding sound. I was thrown off my feet and could feel the vessel slowly coming to a stop in the water. I ran to the third level and found Rest Giver peering out a window.

"Look, Naados," he said. "The mountains are standing out of the water."

I looked in the direction he indicated and saw

the tops of several peaks outlined against the sky. We looked in several directions and saw more peaks.

"While the clouds were low over the earth, Naados, the waters went farther down. We are somewhere in a mountainous area. I think that we are lodged near the top of a peak. All we can do is wait and watch what happens."

The winds continued to blow, and each day we saw more dry land. The vessel had settled into a nearly flat area on the side of a mountain, for we were no longer moving. As the days passed and the water receded, the vessel became more firmly fixed to the land. Rest Giver said that the weight of the vessel caused it to be held by the water-covered soft earth on the mountain. Giver is good. He caused us to settle into a place where the vessel would remain fully upright. Each day that passed fixed us more firmly to the land beneath the water.

Every day was a new adventure as we watched the water recede. Every new distant mountaintop or nearby hill we spotted brought excitement. The vessel sank lower between the sides of the mountain. It finally became impossible to see beyond the peaks where the vessel rested.

After forty more days, the vessel was no longer moving. Rest Giver, with the help of his offspring, opened a large window in the top. Giver had told him how to make certain that the waters were gone from off the earth. When the window was open, a large, black-winged Nouma flew to Rest Giver, who then released him through the opening. He never returned.

Rest Giver also released a much smaller, dainty-winged Nouma. She returned a short time later and was brought back into the vessel. He sent her out again after seven days. When she returned, she held the leaf of a special tree in her beak. After another seven days, Rest Giver released her again. She never returned.

Rest Giver and his offspring knew that it was time to leave the vessel. The following day, they began to remove the covering. They started by removing the windows over the back of the vessel. This gave them access to the panels that covered most of the top. A large section over the back of the vessel was then uncovered. Light coming from the sky orb streamed into the interior of the vessel, causing a great cry from the Noumaso. The cleansing was finally over.

The Likeness kin opened the large door in the back of the vessel. From the inside, it could be lowered like the one Giver had closed from the outside. It became a long ramp for the Noumaso to descend to the ground.

When the door was opened, Giver descended through the cloudy sky and hovered over the opening.

It is time, Rest Giver, to go forth from your deliverance vessel. Take your mata, your offspring, and their matas. The world is vast and must be filled with your kind. Take all creatures from the vessel. They also must fill the earth with their kind. I am with you.

Joy and Sorrow in a Cleansed World

Algiv Naados was among the first Nouma to descend the ramp from the interior of the deliverance vessel. The months of confinement had only intensified his desire to stretch in the warmth of sky orb; smell the clear, fresh air of home; and run the hillsides as he had done when he was very young.

Devastated beauty greeted all our amazed eyes. Was this the world we had left behind only months before? Evidence of a catastrophe of incomprehensible dimension scarred the mountainside and broad valleys falling away before us.

Confusion replaced anticipation as Algiv stepped lightly onto the water-stained ground and tentatively sniffed the air. Smells of decay and death were heavy and nearly overwhelmed his senses. He apparently shared the unbelief of his fellow Noumaso upon seeing their devastated home.

Rest Giver carefully watched him descend. Before Algiv could move to join the others scurrying away, a hand fell gently on his head. Rest Giver, kin of Likeness, looked him full in the eye, sorrow and pity on his face. Algiv Naados shuddered slightly, and then began to follow the son of Likeness. The path was not long. The other sons and daughters of Likeness were standing quietly around a heap of water stained stones. Other selected Nouma were also standing by, eyes darting in questioning glances at one another and then at the offspring of Likeness.

Algiv Naados was the first led to the pile of rough stones. Rest Giver gently cradled his head, hugging him to his bosom. He then lifted Algiv onto the flat stone that topped the pile.

Rest Giver's tear-stained eyes looked briefly heavenward. Algiv, neck extended, head thrust backward; briefly saw an upside-down world.

Algiv never saw the sharp blade that slipped quickly across his throat. Out of the corner of his eye, he saw the red bubbly flow coursing down the stone altar. Algiv, in that instant, remembered the stories of the becoming and Naados's willing submission to the desires of Giver. Those were his last thoughts as he drifted into unconsciousness.

EPILOGUE

I watched silently from the shadowy interior of the vessel as Algiv felt the sting. He was only one of scores of Nouma who offered up their blood that day. This was a painful day of new beginning in our cleansed home. The scores of innocent Nouma who passed under the blade that day as did Algiv brought profound sorrow to me.

I would gladly have taken the place of any one of them. That was, of course, impossible. I must forever bear the consequences of my actions so long ago in Mystery Grove. It is as fresh in my memory as though it had happened yesterday. I can never forget how I snatched a mouthful of leaves and ate from the life tree. As a result, I am not permitted to feel the sting.

Another weight is on me today. Just as strongly as I experienced the foul smell of hate when Beaufang instigated the bending, today, I sense a great fear among the Noumaso. Scores of those already debarked are hurrying away in all directions from the new sadness descending on us. They grieve the untimely death of their fellows but also the word that our relationship with the seed of Likeness has drastically changed.

I'm trying to grasp the implications of Noumaso becoming part of the food source for Likeness's seed.

What will become of us and our world? Only time will tell, I suppose; and I apparently have enough of that to find out. I often wonder what would have happened if I had also eaten from the knowing tree. The load is heavy, but Giver still smiles on me. I often see evidence of that in the colorful sky arc he has given to promise his mercy and care. Life is beautiful, even with the sting.

Bible passages which inspired
Naados and His Kin: The Beginning

Genesis chapters 1:1–9:17
Isaiah 14: 12–15
Ezekiel chapters 1 and 10
Matthew 24:36–39
Hebrews 11:1–7
Revelation 12: 1–9
Revelation 22:1–3